THE PEONY SUTRA

The Peony Sutra

Nicholas Hochstedler

Nicholas Hochstedler Books

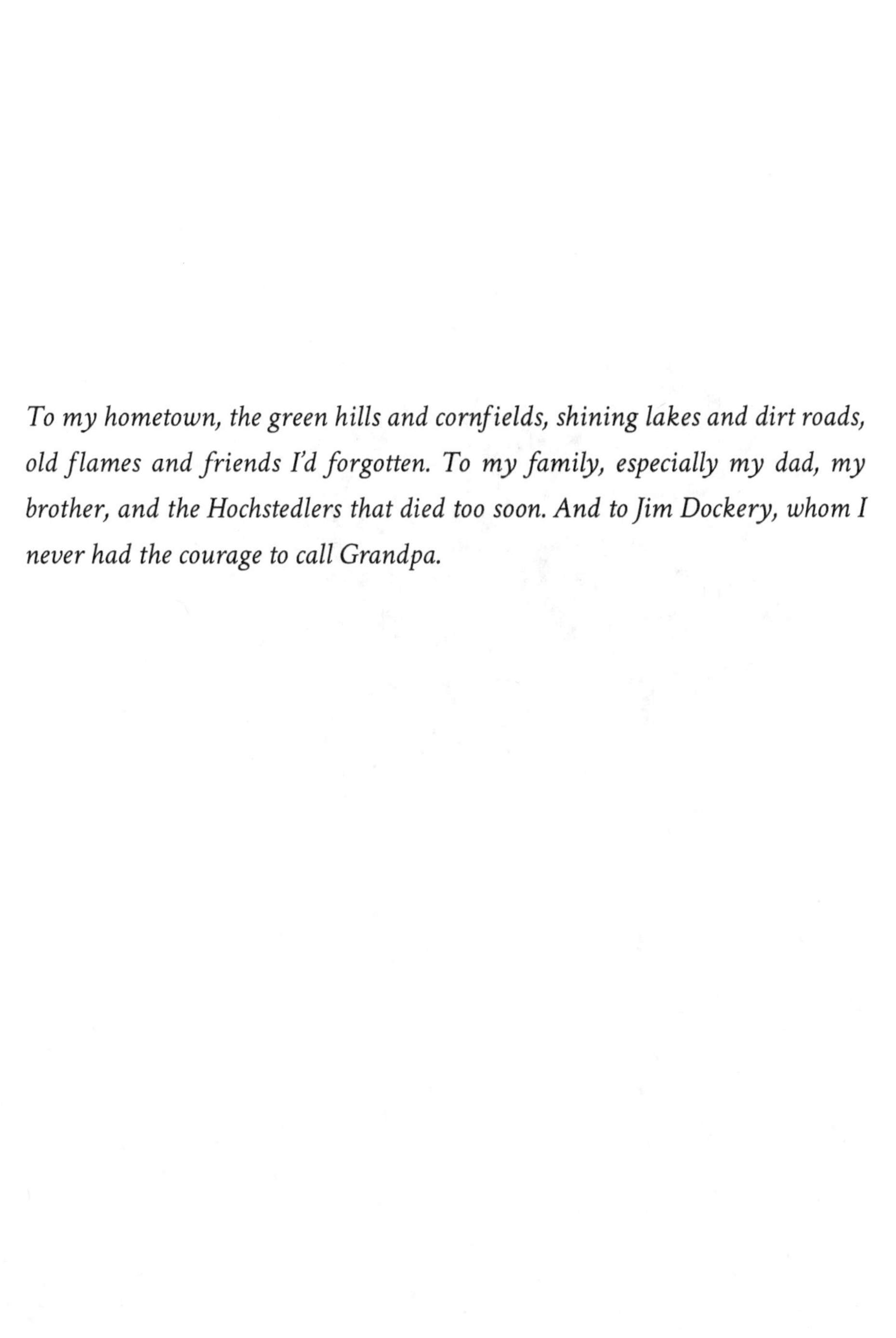

To my hometown, the green hills and cornfields, shining lakes and dirt roads, old flames and friends I'd forgotten. To my family, especially my dad, my brother, and the Hochstedlers that died too soon. And to Jim Dockery, whom I never had the courage to call Grandpa.

PREFACE

There is a remarkable group of people in the Buddhist tradition. They discover how to end the cycle of pain and reach Nirvana, but they leave the process undone so that they may die and reincarnate in near-perfect form. They spend an infinite number of lives teaching others the path to Nirvana, vowing to save every living being before allowing themselves the same reward.

They are the Bodhisattvas, and he was sure he was one of them.

I

The wheel turns. It never stops. I have lived through infinity—through the darkness of forever, the fabric of time that came from nothing. I was there when the light came, a cosmic burst shooting in every direction. I remember when the stars formed, and the planets around them.

I have lived a forever of lives on billions of worlds. I have been bugs atop leaves, trudging up sweaty stems a million miles long. I have been animals of land, both the hunter and the hunted, across the vast fields of a trillion earths. I have been creatures of the sea, cutting through boundless dimensions of underwater beaches, caves, and mysteries; beasts of air, flying through the folds of reality with the sting of wind in my eyes and a tickle in my belly.

I belong to no one, to nothing. I have been an infinity of people, beings, and energies in a limitless reality of nameless dimensions.

But here, walking home on the crack-toothed sidewalks, a timeless bead of sweat rolling down my forehead underneath the choking blanket of another humid summer, beat-up trucks pushing dark clouds into my lungs, I grow tired.

The bead of sweat passed over the monk's forehead and down his nose, clinging to the tip before falling to the dusty sidewalk with a soft splat. He watched his dirty toes shuffle past where it landed, staring at his bare feet for a few seconds before looking up. The sun was bright. He shook his head, closing his eyes and blinking from time to time to adjust to the light. Purple circles, stars, and more sweat gave way to the sidewalk's end, its last square of cement bleeding into a grainy side ditch. He followed it as it twisted past the lush green lawns of Pleasant Lake, Indiana.

I see a family man in sunglasses with a sunburn on his belly, pushing an old mower over green grass. He laughs and yells at his wily son and daughter as they run and trample flowers and catch bugs. The hot afternoon fades into soft twilight over a beautiful family and their happy little yard. I grow tired.

I see an older couple in the cool shadow of the porch. A loving woman holds her hands in her lap as she sits near a side table with her open book turned face-down upon it. A man in a mesh hat sits next to her, leaning back in his chair with a glass of tea in his bony hand. I feel the weight of infinity.

I gaze upon the lake, its glimmering ripples expanding across an omnipresent surface that, like the void, is everywhere at once. I just don't care.

I have lived a billion lives and I will live a countless number more before my work is done. I know how to reach Nirvana but I don't. I stay here. I stay here and help the others.

The monk trudged along the side of the road, gnats and mosquitoes making little swarms in the light of the coming dusk. He sighed.

Forever makes me tired. Indiana kills me slowly.

II

Voices call over the lake, reminding me of people I used to know. I shake my head. I die and I am reborn—that is all.

It was late June, and the days were long. The monk spent most mornings in the old wicker chair on his screened-in porch, sweating in his brown robes and contemplating the universe over small cups of water. The rest of his time he spent tending to his garden and collecting daily alms.

He reached for his cup. Condensation coated the outside, droplets sliding down the cup toward a small pool where it sat. He picked it up, took a sip, swished the water around in his mouth, then swallowed. He gazed out of his mesh window screen, seeing a happy, middle-aged woman with a leash in hand as her dog sniffed through his tiny yard. The woman smiled back at him. He raised his eyes beyond them, toward the grassy hill overlooking Pleasant Lake.

He could see the glimmer of the lake through the bending limbs and dense leaves of Indiana trees. Some grew atop the hillside, bowing slightly down the grassy incline and motioning toward the water; others grew just before the sand, their tall crowns and outstretched branches casting shadows on the beach. He inhaled slowly, his lungs expanding to their limit with hot, humid air and fresh lake vapor. He lifted his bare feet from the spongy, turf floor and folded his legs underneath him, ankles burning from the wicker as he rested his upturned palms on his knees. He closed his eyes. The sounds of distant lawn mowers, children laughing, and chirping birds swept across the lake, reaching his ears and fading into one harmonious buzz. He took a deep breath, exhaling slowly and counting his first breath.

One.

He sat still, focusing on the dark red of his eyelids. He inhaled, holding it in for a few seconds. He let it out slow, the sounds of the lake drowning in his quiet concentration. A gentle sensation crept from his stomach and down his arms, softly tugging his upturned palms. The sensation washed over him then rose from the crown of his head, dissolving in the void and leaving all parts of him relaxed. The lake disappeared, his shabby home and uncut grass with it, and he was left alone in the dark plane of his mind's eye. His neighbors walked by and thought he was asleep. He didn't notice them. He sat suspended in time, floating in the dark of the universe, knowing nothing but the black. The words of the Bodhisattva Blessing for Humanity came to mind:

May I be a lamp in the darkness...

A small flame appeared in the center of the black, flickering in the deep of the cosmos. He floated over to it, legs still crossed in his ghostly wicker chair. He bent over his lap and toward the flame. He could feel its heat on his face. The flame danced in the dark, its orange and red wisps quivering in silence. Its edges were tinged with emerald. He studied it for a while, watching its translucent threads weave and crackle to make vague impressions.

He recognized something in the fire and felt a strong urge to touch it. He extended his hand toward the flame, forgetting the heat on his face.

RRERF!

A peculiar bark shattered the silence of the cosmos, and the fire was consumed by its green edges. The blaze doubled in size, roaring hot and angry. The green engulfed his yearning hand and seared his skin. His eyes were overwhelmed with it.

RRERF!

He gasped, jolting upright in his wicker chair. He held his right hand in the sunlight and spread his fingers. He turned his hand over a few times, eyes wide and searching for blisters.

RRERF!

He looked toward the sound and reality flooded back to him. His meditation ended and he was on his porch, gazing across the yard. The smiling woman and her dog were still in front of his home. The dog huddled over, hopping as she tugged at the leash with mock surprise while he finished taking a hot, stinking shit.

She held her hand up apologetically as her dog pinched off its last turd on the sidewalk. She made a face like she was helpless and her dog scampered away, tugging her down the winding road. He watched them disappear around the bend, remembering that he was attached to nothing—neither his anger, nor his sidewalk.

I die and I am reborn—that is all.

He sighed and closed his eyes.

One.

III

The monk didn't like to listen to music when he worked. In fact, he didn't like to listen to music at all. The wind was enough for him.

Today, he could hear it well as its warm current rippled across the water and up the gentle curve of the grassy hill surrounding Pleasant Lake. He stood and wiped the sweat off his brow with his dirt-stained forearm, careful not to touch his head with his even dirtier hand. He gazed across the narrow road and onto the lake. He smiled.

It was a rare treat, hearing the wind in summer. Most days were hot and still. Even so, when the wind did blow, the sounds of June—the distant drone of a lawn mower, the gruff bark of a dog, the happy shrieks of kids swimming at the public beach, playing whiffle ball, chasing down the ice cream truck—created a much louder song. He listened to the wind dance across the lake and through the trees, savoring its score for a bit longer before bending over the garden.

He worked in his flower garden every day after his morning meditation. It sat at the northwest corner of his house, and if not for his wild and untamed lawn running up against it, would have been the jewel of the neighborhood.

The butterfly weed was in full bloom, their sunset-orange and yellow petals pushing up from slender green stalks to beckon the monarchs, bees, and hummingbirds. Nearby was the soft violet of the coneflower, their "she loves me, she loves me not" petals spiraling around molasses-colored blooms. The wild iris's deep blues and purples with yellow streaks swam through the garden too. He didn't have to do much with those—they'd grown free since he could remember. Then there was the sedum, its beautiful magenta buds and bushy green stalks checkered throughout. In three or four weeks the deep purple of the balloon flower would be in full bloom, and a few weeks after that, the bright yellow of the black-eyed Susan would stand next to it. He reached for his watering can and gave each a little extra water. They would hold the garden together from the time the midsummer flowers faded until the white asters, pink lilies, and big buds of the hibiscus carried it to frost.

He worked hard on his garden. It was his sanctuary—the closest thing he had to the monastery since he'd left. Every flower had beauty; every flower had purpose. But the prize of his garden was the peony.

The peonies grew in the middle of the garden. Each was a different pink—the lighter ones colored rose, blush, and bubblegum; the darker ones colored punch, fuchsia, and a deep hot pink that was almost red. They flowered in layers, their petals a series of intricate folds radiating from their giant blooms. He put his watering can down and walked over to them. He chose one of the darker ones and bent down, putting his nose against the blossom. He inhaled deeply and the layers of the flower rippled toward him, tickling his cheeks and covering the whole of his face. The smell of earth and citrus filled his nostrils.

He hadn't seen the lotus in this life, but the peony was close enough.

…..….…

Tat, tat, tat.

Mrs. Baker placed the casserole dish on the stove top, its handles burning hot from the oven. Floral oven mitts on her hands, she removed the glass lid and set it down on one of the burners, steam rushing up toward her smiling face.

Tat, tat, tat.

She grabbed the thick plastic serving spoon and slid it into her famous chicken casserole. Then, turning slightly over her left shoulder she asked, "Honey, could you get that?"

Mr. Baker looked up from his old red recliner in the living room, crinkling his newspaper as he scowled incredulously at the door. "It's that GOTDAMN Mormon again!" he growled.

Mrs. Baker tore her gloves off and threw them on the counter, moving quickly toward the door. Mr. Baker slapped his paper on his lap, lumbering to his feet over a belly made big from beer and casserole. "Don't answer it!" he yelled.

Mrs. Baker turned toward her husband in the twilight of the doorway. He stood firm on the hardwood between kitchen and living room, right hand raised in objection, the television playing sounds of the baseball game at his back. He wore a burgundy dress shirt tucked into faded brown slacks, his gut spilling over a tight black belt. No matter how fat he got, how hot it was, or how informal the occasion, Jim Baker always wore a belt. He was a man of conviction, if nothing else.

Angela Baker sometimes found his convictions disagreeable, especially when it came to charity. Her strong Christian sensibility wouldn't allow her to turn anyone away, let alone her poor young neighbor in those dirty brown robes. Not that Jim Baker wasn't a God-fearing Hoosier—they both went to church every Sunday. She was just better at seeing the connection between the sermon and her routine. She was always the first to volunteer at the Methodist Church, be it for keeping up the garden, doing dishes after the fellowship potluck, or cooking meals for funeral receptions in the basement hall. She had kind eyes, a warm smile, and thick, shoulder-length hair, cut like a 1970s housewife, fading slightly but still a healthy brown. Both Bakers were somewhere in their sixties, getting older and bickering more, but still happily married after thirty-nine years.

Tat, tat, tat.

The monk pulled his clenched hand from the flimsy screen door, able to hear the Bakers' hushed argument from where he stood on their porch. His gaze fell to the empty clay bowl cupped in his right arm. Each day he'd rise in the early morning, gather the alms bowl, and wander barefoot around Pleasant Lake, asking neighbors from house to house to "drop a lump." According to the Buddhist tradition, he couldn't keep food beyond midday: a reminder that each day starts anew, and nothing is ever certain. It was the only way he ever ate. He looked down at his dirty feet, blackened from a long, fruitless walk, drops of sweat falling on their tops from his sweat-drenched robes. It was dusk.

His stomach growled, empty as his bowl. He raised his left hand to knock once more. He could always count on the saintly Mrs. Baker.

Angela gave one last pleading look to her husband and turned toward the door.

"No more of my casserole's goin' to that GOTDAMN MORMON!" Jim bellowed as she turned the knob.

She spun back around, hand still on the knob with the door cracked open. "He's a monk!" she whispered tersely, now visible to her hungry neighbor. "And this is my casserole, not yours." She turned back to face the porch, pulling the door the rest of the way open. "Well hello there," she said, smiling from behind the screen.

"Many blessings, Mrs. Baker," the monk said with a slight bow, lifting his bowl gently with eyes to the porch.

"He's a bum is what he is, a gotdamn beggar," Jim grumbled over his wife's shoulder, marching back to his chair and snapping his paper open.

Angela rolled her eyes and huffed through her nose, shaking her head. "I'm sorry," she pleaded, "don't mind him."

"The root of suffering is attachment, Mrs. Baker," the monk said to the porch.

She furrowed her brow, tilting her head with a quizzical smile. "Care to come in?" she asked.

"No thank you, Mrs. Baker," he said.

She knew he wouldn't—he never did. Still smiling, she suppressed her Midwestern urge to insist three or four more times and said, "Alright dear, let's get you some supper." She hurried off to the kitchen, leaving the large wooden door open and her neighbor visible through the screen.

Jim Baker peered over his paper at the young man on his porch, head lowered and arms still raised for food. Jim chuckled to himself, settling deeper into his chair with a self-righteous grin. "Don't you people usually wear ties?"

....

The grass felt good on the monk's weathered feet as he crossed through his yard to his door. Mrs. Baker's chicken casserole had cooled some on the walk home, but he could still smell its savory aroma rising from his bowl. He always asked her for one lump, in line with tradition. She always filled the bowl to the brim. The sky had darkened into a soft blanket of gray and blue by the time he got home, and he was famished. He'd make sure to say a blessing for Mrs. Baker during meditation tonight.

The faded white screen door opened with a long, painful creak. His feet bounced slightly on the spongy green turf of his enclosed front porch. His wandering hand found the old metal knob of the oaken main door, turning it softly as he pushed it into the dark of the front room. He stood there for a second, hand clutched around his bowl of casserole, letting his eyes adjust. He pushed into his simple living room, banging his shin on the coffee table with an annoyed grimace before setting his alms bowl on its rough surface. He disappeared into the kitchen, returning with a silver Tibetan spoon—the only kitchen utensil he had—and a small cup of water. He set both on the table and pulled a weathered mahogany chair over to sit down.

The house was mostly empty. The table at which he sat was the only in its three rooms, its chair also without companion. He had his wicker chair on the porch, but that was strictly for meditation. His kitchen had a plain laminate countertop, no stove, and no refrigerator. Aside from one tiny bathroom, the bedroom was the only other room in the house.

He stared at the casserole for a while, trying to suppress his craving before reaching for his spoon. He closed his eyes tight, clutching the spoon and hoping to meditate his desire away. Pleasure wasn't a part of his diet; food was intended to remove hunger, and nothing more. It was especially bad that Mrs. Baker's casserole had so much chicken. He was supposed to be a vegetarian.

He remembered the first time he stumbled upon Mrs. Baker, seeking alms with his simple bowl. Jim Baker answered the door with arms crossed, Midwestern masculinity dominating the frame. After a brief altercation which the monk still didn't understand, Mrs. Baker rushed to the door with her bacon-covered macaroni. He longed to resist, remembering the words of the Buddha:

"To avoid causing terror to living beings, let the disciple refrain from eating meat. The eating of meat extinguishes the seed of Great Kindness."

He wanted to ask for rice, but he couldn't. Somehow he knew it would be more unholy to refuse the offering than to swallow its sacrilege. She wore the face of a saint. He left it at that.

He dug the spoon into Mrs. Baker's chicken casserole. He brought it up to his mouth, pausing for a second.

First, let us reflect on our own work and the effort of those who brought us this food.

He thought of Angela Baker as he took his first bite. No matter how hard he tried to detach himself from its flavor, its delicious and simple Hoosier charm brought him great joy. He'd d have to say two blessings for her tonight.

· · ·· ·· ···

The old wicker poked his ankles as he sat with legs crossed in the chair. The night was thick and balmy, and a gentle breeze blew from the lake and rustled the leaves. The crickets chirped from their grassy hiding places, and the cicadas cackled softly in the trees. To him, it all blended into the great symphony of the *om.*

He drew a deep breath and exhaled. He meditated every night on the porch, even in winter. Tonight he'd been at it for a few hours. He was thankful for the weather.

He took his last meditative breath and let it out with a great sigh. He opened his eyes and nodded to himself, satisfied. He rose from the wicker chair and headed inside, crossing through the main room without banging his shin this time.

His bedroom was small and simple. There was a little window that let in the sun in the morning and the breeze at night. His bed was a small twin mattress on a box spring that rested directly on the floor. He knelt beside it and closed his eyes, reciting the Four Bodhisattva Vows:

Sentient beings are numberless. We vow to save them all.
Delusions are endless. We vow to cut through them all.
The teachings are infinite. We vow to learn them all.
The Way is inconceivable. We vow to attain it.
He rolled onto his bed and fell asleep.

IV

BYYUMMMM.

The smell of cut grass filled the room, and a loud, boring drone came to his ear. He rolled over in bed. The window was open. He was between sleep and wakefulness—had been for some time—but the cool morning breeze brought summer sounds through the window, dancing around his sleepy brain. He rolled over again. His eye opened halfway, taking in white bed sheets and the limited view of his tiny room. Pale morning sunrays cut through the window and onto the wooden floor. Little pieces of floating dust swirled in the soft glow of each beam. His eyes grew heavy again, lids falling over them as the room faded away.

BYUMMMM.

He gasped and woke up, choking on his breath for a second. He scanned the room in confusion until he could place the sound. He let out an annoyed, although relieved, sigh. It was a lawnmower, and it was in his yard.

He sat up, staring at the wall with his mouth partway open. He considered lying back down, pressing the pillow over his face, and going to sleep. The drone of the mower dug into his ears. He looked down at the mattress, resting his face on his palm, his nose and lips pressed against it and his bony fingers falling across his cheek. He sighed again and raised his head. He gazed up at the ceiling momentarily before shaking his head and pushing himself up out of bed.

He rubbed the sleep from his eyes, walking from his room to the porch. The old oaken door whined in baritone as he pulled it open. He took a step onto the spongy green floor of his porch, sunlight making him squint. He blinked his eyes again and again until finally holding them shut for about three seconds and forcing them open. The morning light rushed back to his eyeballs, white heat blinding him as he

17

staggered to the edge of the screen and braced himself on the window-sill. The annoying drone of the lawnmower grinded his ears as he tried to survey the yard.

BYUMMMMMM.

The yard was white like the sun, and then big, bold images drifted into view. First it was the tree, dark and brown, shimmering over his eyeballs and then sharpening into its rough bark and green leaves. Then came the flower garden and the messy grass surrounding it, dandelions, crabgrass, and weeds spilling into his pupils. And finally, the screen came into focus, and he found himself staring through each individual square with complete clarity, eyes narrowed through the black mesh and zooming in on the sweaty leggings of a woman pushing her Lawn-Boy mower through the tall, impenetrable grass. The mower blade started, stopped, and started again as she struggled through the thick. She had mowed a strip, surrounded by jungle on either side, and the last patch of it was wild and wet with dew. Her sporty hat was pulled low over her determined eyes, her thick mom build set in a stance best for pushing a car up the street or driving a football sled across the practice field. He watched her toil for a while then shook his head and went toward the screen door. He wrapped his fingers around the handle and put his thumb on the worn plastic button. He paused, dreading the interaction. He shook his head and pushed the door open. It banged shut behind him, leaving him on the tiny square of dirt that once was a section of cement walkway.

She looked up and smiled, giving him a quick, pitying wave before her grasp returned to the handle and her eyes to her work. He opened his mouth to say something, decided against it, and settled for an awkward head nod. Sweat poured from her brow and onto the grass as she pushed. After a few seconds he raised his hand in a tentative wave, lowering it again when she ignored him. She let out a powerful grunt, exerting her strength to finish the patch. He took three steps toward her and extended his arm, then gave up and let it swing by his side. She pushed hard, as if against a wall, and for a moment the blade slowed and the grass coiled around it, time suspending as she strained in one final standoff with the thick. The coil snapped and the mower lurched forward, its front tires slamming down over the patch and devouring the grass. She slid over the last few blades and turned from him, speeding away to start a new strip. He rolled his eyes to the sky and shook his head. "Peace comes from within," he said to himself as he walked across his yard and toward his neighbor.

She was near the sidewalk by the time he reached her, her back turned to him. He raised his hand to poke her sweaty shoulder. He realized how uncomfortable that would be and lowered his arm.

"Excuse me," he said softly.

She pushed further away, unable to hear over the buzz of the mower.

He shook his head in disbelief and took a few steps toward her. "EXCUSE ME."

She finished the strip and turned around, startled by her exasperated neighbor standing in her path. He took a small step back in fear of losing his toes, feeling foolish now for starting the confrontation.

She smiled. "Hey neighbor!" she hollered over the mower, keeping it running.

"Greetings Ms., uh."

"Stone!" she yelled. "And you are?"

He furrowed his brow at the question. "I'm not sure how to answer that."

"What?" she yelled.

"I said I'm not sure how to answer that!" he shouted over the mower.

"Oh," she said, giving a quizzical smile. She waited for him to elaborate. He waited for her to shut the mower off. The two looked at each other for a few seconds, neither sure what to say.

"Well, pleased to meet you," she finally offered, keeping a grip on the handle while talking. "I would shake your hand but mine's a little sweaty." She grinned. He half smiled, feeling awkward.

He didn't own a mower. He didn't believe in it. His grass would grow wild and long, dandelions, white clover, and even little shrubs ruling the yard. His stomach turned at the thought of how many bugs could be uprooted or even killed—let alone a baby rabbit or infant starling getting caught in the blade. But in small-town Indiana, an unruly yard is a blight to the block. Your neighbors will make sure it's mowed whether they call the county or do it themselves.

"I uh, really wish you wouldn't do that," he said.

"Do what?" she yelled.

"Mow the grass!"

"Oh!" she cried, waving off his concern with her left hand. "It's no trouble. No trouble at all."

He frowned. "No, it's just that..." He looked into her kind eyes, not knowing where to begin. He didn't understand his neighbors, and they didn't understand him. He thought himself to be a cosmic being, reincarnated over a billion lifetimes—maybe he was once a caterpillar inching along the grass, cut down in his prime by just another well-intentioned neighbor.

Her smile shone bright like the sun. To her, she was doing him a tremendous favor, and in so doing, beautifying the neighborhood.

"It's just that..." he tried again, but he couldn't beat her pitying eyes. They stared at each other for a while, two forces in the universe. "Just watch out for the flower garden," he muttered.

Her charitable cheeks flushed with pride and her eyes glowed wide and pretty. "Okie dokie neighbor." She flashed a quick thumbs-up with her left hand and returned her grip to the mower, pushing past him. He watched her go, happy ponytail swishing from shoulder to shoulder through the back of her hat. He shook his head.

I will never understand these people.

V

Joe drummed on his steering wheel to the country piano and twang of guitar, his beat-up gray truck barreling south down Old 27. Wind rushed through the open windows and tousled the longer strands of graying hair sticking from underneath his Old Milwaukee hat. He wore a faded blue work shirt with his name patched underneath the factory logo.

He reached toward the fold-down cup holder that extended from the lower part of the dash. There was a warm beer there, his third or fourth Old Milwaukee that morning. He grabbed it with his right hand and held it near his stomach for a while, looking out the windshield at the fields of green rushing past. He raised it up and tilted his head back for a drink, then placed the cheap beer back into the cup holder. He smiled at the faded paint of the farmhouse sitting on the old country road to his left, '88 Chevy S10 speeding through the humid Indiana June. It was another easy Sunday morning.

Joe worked a nine-to-five at a factory, Monday through Friday. It was a moderate size and employed a good number of people in town. They made all kinds of products: tables, ladders, chairs, dollies, and other tools, but most of their profits came from docks and boating equipment for all the lakes in the area. A few men like him worked there—gruff, blue-collar country boys—but it took all kinds, including college kids, working women, and a few urbanites who, for some reason or another, found themselves moving to small-town Indiana. The factory was in Angola, "the big city" just north of where he lived in Pleasant Lake. Joe would work all week, have a few drinks on Friday, get drunk on Saturday, and stagger home underneath the streetlights sometime around midnight. He'd wake up in the late morning and head to the liquor store for a case of beer and a happy Sunday, then start it all again on Monday morning.

He drummed some more on the steering wheel as he zipped past the trailer park to his right. He reached for his beer, humming the chorus through the can just before the beer hit his mouth. He placed it out of sight, saving it for after the fork in the road and its impending speed trap. The road bent but his truck kept straight, breaking slightly as he took the fork past the small, crumbling brick building to his right. Slowing more, he passed Old Man Crowley's somber, half-finished house, the town cemetery his own backyard. He stopped at the stop sign and signaled right.

The monk was in his flower garden pulling weeds. He didn't like doing it at first for the same reasons he didn't like his yard being mowed, but he realized that sometimes he had to make sacrifices to maintain his sanctuary. When he did pull them, he did so with great intention, taking extra care not to disturb the bugs taking refuge near the plants.

He knelt beside the flowers and pinched the low stem of a thistle with his thumb and forefinger. His forearm bulged as he tried to rip it out, but the top broke off the stem, leaving the root. Chuckling to himself, he set it atop a small pile by his foot and turned back to the root, using his fingers to dig deeper around it.

Joe turned down Main Street. He passed a few houses and the elementary school came into view. It was an old brick building with high stone archways and tall dark doors. The navy and gold of the state flag and the red, white, and blue of Old Glory waved atop two shiny flag poles overlooking the long cement pathway that led to the entry. The front yard was full of lush green grass, and there was a marquee sign in the middle that usually read "Doughnuts with Dad February 17th" or "School Book Fair May 20th," but now read "Have a Great Summer!" in thick black font. It was a proud old school with a rich history. It used to be a high school before the fifties, small and quaint, the graduating classes no more than fifteen. Now it was the rural elementary school of the district, and though filled with kids of the county's blue-collar families, had a reputation among middle schoolers as the "place where the smart kids come from." There was even a small green sign by the fork in the road saying so. "Home of Pleasant Lake Elementary, a 4-Star School," it declared. No one really knew what that meant, but they were damn sure proud. Joe passed the school and turned left just before the fire station. The twang of his favorite guitar solo blared from his open window.

The monk had dug a tiny circle around the weed to expose the thicker part of the stem just above the root. He put his thumb on one side and his index and middle fingers on the other, right up against the dirt. He pulled with less strain this time and the root came out with ease. He said a quick blessing for the bugs and placed the rest of the thistle on the pile. His bent knees cracked as he stood up to survey the beauty of his garden.

Joe's truck rolled down the small incline at the start of the lake road, the decaying two-story brick of the Lion's Club Lodge to his right. Next to the lodge was Crazy Craig's garage. It was a giant, run-down shack that looked more like a small warehouse than a garage, its insides packed with knickknacks, drum kits, car parts, and Lord knew what else. Its exterior was half stone and half gristly wood, the façade just below the roof covered with rotting deer skulls. The yard next to the garage boasted a small, perfectly manicured patch of soybeans, an odd juxtaposition to anyone driving down County Road 150 West for the first time. A shirtless Crazy Craig stood out in the yard, a watering hose in one hand and a friendly wave in the other. Joe waved back as he gave it a little more gas to get up the small hill toward the next row of houses.

The monk waded through the rainbow of his garden, stopping to inspect each flower. He stooped over a coneflower and cupped its purple blossom. Its radiant petals spiraled around his fingertips. He noticed some movement at the corner of his eye and turned toward it, catching the graceful landing of a monarch atop the butterfly weed. He gently released the coneflower and edged closer. The monarch spread its wings, its royal gold and black covering the blossom. It flapped a few times and flew away, the orange glow of the butterfly weed beckoning after it. He smiled in awe at the beauty of his sanctuary.

Joe was down the road, drumming hard on the steering wheel as the guitar solo finished. The chorus came and he bellowed along with it, feeling a little drunk now. He reached for the Old Milwaukee can and tilted his head back.

The monk finished admiring all the other flowers before coming upon the peony. He caressed the soft velvet edge of one of the blossoms before gently using his thumb to count each of its many folds. It reminded him of the Lotus Sutra, perhaps the most important lesson of the Buddha. He gazed into the deep pink of the peony and recounted the teaching. A mass of people had formed around the Buddha to hear him speak. They had come from miles around to seek enlightenment. They waited many hours in the hot sun, but the Buddha sat with hands cupped and legs folded, saying nothing. Anticipation grew and the throng became restless, but they were met with silence. Finally, the Buddha raised a quiet hand and unfolded his fingers, revealing the simple beauty of the lotus flower. Those who understood were immediately enlightened; more were left puzzled.

VRRRRREEHHH!

An awful sound from down the street shattered the monk's contemplation. He looked up from the peony and down the road, seeing a beat-up truck barreling around the bend. The howls of what sounded like a man flew from its windows.

Joe slugged some more beer, leaving about a quarter of the can. The monk grew uneasy as the truck drew nearer. Still holding his beer, Joe wiped his mouth with his shirt sleeve, preparing to down the can before the song's big finish. The monk could see him now, red-eyed and drunk and grinning through the windshield. Joe threw his head back and slammed the rest of his beer. He bellowed the last bit of song lyrics, eyes closed and head back like an old dog baying at the moon. He passed by the garden and the monk watched with horror as his calloused hand flung the beer can out the window. It sailed through the sky, end over end, then crashed at the monk's feet like a meteorite. The raucous sound of the engine filled his ears and the truck sped off, leaving a trail of black exhaust. The monk stared at the thing in the dirt.

VI

For a long time the monk stood there, not knowing what to do. The can sat just beyond his toes. He continued staring, afraid to touch it. He presumed the can burned a hole in the dirt.

He extended his right foot, pointing his big toe at the can like a kid afraid to swim. The pad of his toe came within a hair of the thing and he snapped it back to where he stood. He raised his foot from the dirt and inched his pointed toe toward the can a second time. His toe came to the silvery base of the can and he imagined the horror of touching it. He gave it a frightful kick and jerked his foot back again, watching the can as if it was a snake that might be alive. The aluminum made a hollowed *doot* sound and the can rolled a foot or so away, stopping at the stalk of a sedum.

He hung back for a moment, afraid the thing would strike. Then, he slowly dropped his guarded hands and leaned forward, taking a hesitant step toward the can. He took another, extending his right hand and bending lower as he crept. He stopped short of the thing and crouched down. His face hovered over it and his bent fingers lay just beneath its curved body, palm open and knuckles in the dirt. He flinched his fingers so their pads might touch the side of the can. He was glad when they missed. He flinched them a few more times, missing once or twice before finally tapping the side of the thing with his middle and ring fingers. It moved an inch and rolled back into place. He tapped it again. He was afraid to rest any part of his hand on it—that it'd burn him if he held it too long—but he knew he had to move it. He took a deep breath, opening his hand wide in anticipation of grabbing it. He closed his eyes. His palm itched and he prepared for the aluminum's sacrilegious burn.

He snatched the can with a loud yelp, imagining it seared his skin. He tightened his grip like a man electrocuted; his hand shook and sweat covered his face, but nothing happened. He cautiously opened his eyes and noticed he'd brought the can toward his face, close enough to read. He loosened his grip and read the label, mouthing the words, "*Old Milwaukee.*"

He rose from the dirt, straightening above the row of flowers. His eyes stayed on the can. He noticed something to his left and shifted his gaze. One of his neighbors stood on the edge of the sidewalk, staring at him with concern. He must've yelped louder than he'd thought. He gave an awkward smile and a quick wave to signal that he was okay. His neighbor responded with a slight nod, wearing an uneasy look. He smiled again and looked down at the can. He studied it for a while then decided to head inside, continuing to inspect the can as he walked through the garden. Below the logo was the word *BEER* in a simple font; an inch down from that were the words *SINCE 1849.* The whole thing was silver and crimson, almost the color of blood. He crossed through the last row of flowers and stopped at the front of his house. He turned the can over in his hand to read the tiny lettering on the back. Down the side of the can were a few nutrition facts and some kind of warning. Below those were the small words *Joseph Schlitz Brewing Company* and *Union Made* separated by a silver bullet point. He opened the weary screen door and walked across the spongy green turf, finding his wicker chair and sitting down. He turned the can over in his hand again, noticing the long-legged pinup girl next to the logo for the first time. Her heels were the same color as the red of the can. She wore a blouse with red and white stripes and her Daisy Dukes were a deep navy blue. Her hair was dark brown with a matching red bow, and her delicate fingers twirled about the ends of her hair at her shoulder. She wore a playful smile made more beautiful by her dark red lipstick and her mysterious brown eyes. She was gorgeous, but he tried not to notice such things.

He got up from the chair and set the can on the windowsill, hoping to ignore her beauty. He sat back down and pondered for a moment, the fragments of the song rattling in his brain, the horrible sound of the old truck in his ears.

VII

Joe eased the S10 into his gravel driveway. He shut off the engine and opened the door, stepping down onto the rocks. There was a small pile of crinkled beer cans at his feet that he'd been meaning to recycle. He closed the door and walked around the truck to grab the open case of Old Milwaukee from the passenger side. He reached for the handle then stopped, hearing the sound of a 2017 Buick pulling into his neighbor's driveway. It was Jim and Angela Baker, home from their after-church breakfast. Joe turned and waved to them, but they didn't see. Jim was arguing with her about tipping at the diner: "Ten percent is enough, by God!" He lumbered out of the car and shut the door, then walked over to open hers for chivalry's sake. She opened the door herself before he and his belly got there, standing up with purse in hand and turning to see Joe in his driveway.

"Oh Joe," she declared with a warm smile, "how are you today?"

Mr. Baker quit grumbling and stopped short of his wife, also turning toward his neighbor. "Hey there Joe," he called with a slight wave of two fingers and a thumb, "whaddya say?"

"Oh, I don't know," Joe grinned. "Say alotta things, believe about half." The Bakers laughed. They liked Joe.

"You watchin' the game today?" Joe asked.

"I'll have it on this afternoon," Jim said. "Cubs gotta chance this year."

"That they do, hate to admit," Joe said. He turned toward Angela. "How was church?"

"Wonderful, Joe," she said, smiling sweetly. "Pastor Bill gave such a lovely sermon." Her eyes twinkled, and Joe saw The Spirit in them. "I really wish you'd come with us some time."

Joe grinned sheepishly and looked at the ground. He thought of his own church—the shimmer of the streetlights when he stumbled out of the bar, seeing his calloused hands after a hard day's work, his sunlit porch and a can of beer on a Sunday afternoon. He returned his gaze to Mrs. Baker's kind, pleading eyes. "One of these days," he said, feeling guilty for lying.

"We'd really love it if you came," she said. "Maybe Jim could let you borrow a shirt."

Jim shot a quick scowl to his wife, then put his hand on her shoulder. "Well Joe," he said, "game'll be on at one if you wanna stop over."

Joe tipped two fingers from his temple and toward the Bakers to say goodbye. "Always a pleasure," he said. The Bakers smiled and turned to go, walking up their porch stairs and shutting the door behind them.

Joe turned back to his truck and opened the passenger door, grabbing the case of Old Milwaukee with both hands. He pulled it out of the truck and shifted it to his left arm, cradling it against his chest to keep the beers from rolling out. He shut the door with his right hand and faced his house. It was painted white with black shutters, the roof gray and shingled at a slant. Underneath an overhang of roof was a small stone porch with white wooden columns and faded brown steps. An old black rocking chair sat on the porch next to a wicker chair of the same color. He walked across his small, tidy yard, pulling a warm beer from the case and tossing it on the wicker before going inside.

He wiped his work boots on the entryway rug. They echoed deep and hollow as he walked across the wooden floor and into his kitchen. He made his way to the fridge and grabbed the handle, stopping for a second to admire some old pictures on the door, then opened it and put the case next to a carton of eggs and a pack of tortillas in the bottom left corner. He grabbed three more beers from the box then shut the fridge door, hot sauce bottles and other glass jars rattling inside. He opened the overhead freezer and put the cans next to a sleeve of burgers and a fish filet he had frozen after catching and cleaning it at the lake. He shut the freezer and walked to the screen door at the back of the kitchen, pulling it open and stepping down the stone stairs into his backyard.

The backyard was small and square with a brown wooden fence around it. On the right half of the yard was a set of chairs next to a small firepit and a gas grill pushed into the corner where the fence met the house. The left half of the yard was dedicated to his vegetable garden. He grew two types of peppers as well as tomatoes, onions, squash, and zucchini. He walked over to the hose on the backside of the house near the corner where he kept the grill. He picked it up in one hand and turned the rusty metal spigot with the other, putting his mouth to the open end to get a cold, hose-flavored drink. He wiped his lips then pulled the hose over to the garden.

A few small jalapeños were beginning to sprout, and the tomatoes were getting big. The onions were starting to swell, and the squash was all but ready. He sprayed a nice, even mist on them until the soil grew dark with moisture. He dropped the hose and it imprinted itself into the grass, then he walked to the screen door and pulled it open.

He passed through the kitchen, making a mental note to grab the three beers from the freezer in about twenty minutes. Sometimes he'd forget, the beer would freeze, and he'd have an Old Milwaukee slushy. It was still beer, and he still drank it, but he didn't like it much.

He grabbed the warm beer from the wicker chair when he reached the front porch, cracked it open, and plopped down into the rocker with a loud, contented grunt. The chair rocked back and forth under his weight. He took a big drink and lowered his hand, still clutching the beer with his wrist resting on his knee. He thought for a moment about his garden. The tomatoes would be red and ripe a week or so after the squash, then the onions and jalapeños. The green peppers would come next, and hopefully the zucchinis would do better this year than last. He took another slug of beer and let his wrist fall back to his knee, rocking a few seconds before hocking some spit and shooting it over the porch rail. He watched it sail midway across his yard and into the grass, then lifted his eyes across the street. There were a few small houses with paved driveways and yard signs; one of them had red and blue wind spinners in the front lawn. Behind the houses was a thin row of trees. They blocked the lake from where he sat, but he knew it was there.

Two kids came around the bend on their bikes, laughing, shrieking, happy it was summer. In the lead was big sister, hair blowing carefree in the wind just beyond her shirtless brother's handlebars.

"Hey Mr. Joe!" they cried in unison, zooming by the house. He smiled warmly and waved with his free hand, but they'd already turned their attention back to the street, standing up from their seats to pedal faster up a small hill.

Joe shook his head. "Damn kids," he chuckled as he took another drink. He rocked back and forth in his chair, staring at the porch ceiling and thinking.

After a few minutes he sensed some movement in the yard. He shifted his gaze toward it, seeing a small gray tabby cat trotting up the lawn. Her soft, striped paws made gentle bumps against the porch steps as she climbed them. She pattered across the floor to where Joe sat, stopping to rub her furry side against his shin. She stuck her tail high in the air, contented and purring loudly.

"Sadie, old girl," Joe cried, running his hand over her back. She rubbed up against his left leg then turned around, brushing hard against both legs with her other side as she raised her back to better feel his hand. She walked past his right leg until her striped tail ran through his palm, then sat down by his shoe.

Joe hadn't always liked cats. Until Sadie came around, he was a dog man entirely. He used to have a bluetick coonhound—Old Blue he called him—with gray spotted fur, loving eyes, barrel chest, and a snout that treed racoons from here to Hamilton. Joe took him everywhere: parties, restaurants, even church, when he used to go. Old Blue would sit up straight in the pew with his head slightly cocked and his ears at attention, listening to the gospel. It got so the congregation joked that he was taking Joe to be saved, and the preacher would laugh and urge his church to "be like Old Blue." When the sermon was over, Joe and his dog would hop in the truck and speed down Old 27, Blue's face out the window and his droopy black ears blowing in the wind. Sunday night he'd crawl into bed with Joe, like he did every night, and Monday morning he'd whine when Joe got up for work. He'd whine all the way to the front door, begging his friend to stay.

When Blue got older and stopped running the woods, Joe would carry him places. He'd carry him to the truck and make sure he was comfortable before they went for a ride. He'd carry him up the porch steps when they got home, and he'd carry him to bed when it was time to sleep. But Joe noticed that he didn't stick his face out the window anymore, and that his old bones would crack when he picked him up. He still whined on Monday mornings, but it was a soft whimper from the bed, and he stopped following Joe to the door. When it came time to put Old Blue down, Joe held his friend's paw and looked into his big, loving eyes until the light went out of them.

The cat came around a few years later, lean and stray and looking for a home. Joe got up from his rocker and grabbed a broom, ready to chase her off. She sat still at the top of the stairs, her big glassy eyes looking deep into his own. He remembered Old Blue and how his paw felt in his hand when he died. Joe put the broom down. He didn't want to be alone anymore.

Joe sat his beer next to the rocker and reached over to scratch Sadie's furry head. She closed her eyes and titled her head closer to his fingertips.

"Yep Sadie, it's just you and me." He reached for his beer and sat back in his rocker. "Just you and me." He drained the can then stood up from his chair, heading back inside. She followed him to the door.

"I suppose it's about time for you to eat," he said, reaching down to give her another scratch. "Let's get you inside." He opened the door and followed her into the kitchen. He walked over to the sink and opened the cupboard just above it, grabbing some food to put in her dish. He turned toward the freezer. The beers weren't quite ready yet, but he'd manage.

....

The sky grew dark and the air sweet as night fell on Pleasant Lake. The cicadas cackled and the tomcats left their porches for the hunt. Mothers called for kids to come home, and kids came racing into yards on bikes.

Fathers sat in the blue light of TVs, hoping the kids would mind their mothers so they wouldn't have to get up.

The monk sat in the same place on his porch, staring at the can. He hadn't moved since he put it on the windowsill that morning. His stomach growled, angry and empty against his bones. He'd forgotten to seek his daily alms.

Down the street, a plate of cold casserole sat wrapped on a kitchen countertop, and a worried Mrs. Baker looked out an empty window. Her husband sat in his chair in the den, watching cable news. "Still waiting for the Mormon?" he grumbled.

"I'm just worried dear, that's all."

"Maybe he found a job," he snickered.

Next door, Joe dozed on his porch, a dozen empty cans at his feet. Sadie lay curled in his lap, while a half-empty beer slipped slowly from his right hand. After a while, the beer fell from his sleepy grasp and splattered on the porch. Sadie shot from his lap and Joe sat up, startled and drunk.

The lightning bugs flickered and danced, and you could hear the echo of the old bullfrog by the lake. It was time for bed in Indiana. Tomorrow would bring work.

VIII

The monk was in the darkness near the fire. It burned green, bright, hot. He looked at it for a while, the heat of it on his face, the light of it in his eyes. There was a small tendril of green in the center; it burned brighter than the rest. He reached his right hand toward it, then withdrew. He remembered how the fire had felt last time, how it seared his skin and blistered his hand. He rubbed his left palm over the back of his right hand but kept his gaze on the flame.

A second tendril sprouted near the first, the two flickering back and forth like blades of grass in the wind. He peered closer. A third sprout came, then another, and another. Soon the fiery center gave way to sprouting blades of grass pushing one by one through the cosmic dirt.

A vase of plenty...

Each blade popped next to the last; a billion blades became a giant field. He took a deep breath and let it out slow. At first he welcomed the new life as it pushed outward from the fire—a sense of awe washed over him as it grew. But the sea of green grew bigger, unmanageable. He watched with alarm as it devoured the blackness in front of him, spreading closer and closer until only a few feet remained between the wicker chair and the vast expanse of hungry, growing grass. The last foot it ate quickly, and he closed his eyes as the raging field toppled the chair and forced him on his back. He took another deep breath, hoping his exhale would push the awful, dizzying feeling down and out from the pit of his stomach. Instead it submerged him, and a sudden rumble in the plane beneath shook his queasy gut. Soon, the entire universe rumbled too, and he opened his eyes to the dark sky of the cosmos. There was a loud, rattling boom, as if heaven and earth were moving, and a large shape burst from the section of plane where the fire began. He couldn't see it, but it grew tall, green, and bright, its heat looming over his wincing face as it bloomed upward to infinity. He closed his eyes as sweat broke on his forehead, trying not to throw up from the relentless quake of creation.

Enduring like the earth and sky...

His eyes shot open as he awoke on the porch. His chair had tipped over; his back was on its rest against the ground, his legs were in the air. There was vomit in his mouth.

He looked to his right and his vision slowly cleared, revealing the playful smile of the pinup girl on the fallen beer can. He swallowed the vomit and closed his eyes. He laid on the porch for a while, trying not to puke.

IX

The monk tossed the can away and lumbered to his feet. Dizzy at first, he took a step to regain his balance. It had been two days since he'd left his porch.

He walked up to the window and leaned his hands against the sill. It was midmorning, beautiful and sunny with a pleasant breeze. He needed to go outside to check on the flowers, and to seek alms so he could eat. But he was afraid of the gray truck and its horrible, screaming engine, and even more so the crazy old man in the driver's seat.

The wind rippled across the lake and tousled the cattails on the shore. He wondered how long it had been since he'd bathed in the water, or even washed his clothes in it. He lifted his arms and sniffed his robes, then wrinkled his nose. He turned back to look at the beer can, remembering the words of the Buddha. "Never fear what will become of you," he said to himself, heading for the screen door and pushing it open.

The sun was too bright for his eyes at first. He squinted, blinking a few times to adjust. He took a couple wary steps into his yard, glancing over at his flower garden when his vision finally cleared. They seemed all right. He could inspect them more closely later; right now, he needed a bath.

He walked to the edge of his yard, stopping just before the sidewalk. He looked right down the street toward the Bakers and then left toward Crazy Craig's. Nothing came. He took a deep breath and crossed, tiny rocks from the road clinging to his heels. On the other side was the grassy top of the little hill that rolled down to the lake.

A car turned onto the road by Crazy Craig's and its engine roared down the street. Fearing the truck, he ran the rest of the way across and dove down the hill, sliding partway on his belly before spinning to face the road. He watched from the cover of the grass as a battered Monte Carlo rolled by. He sighed and let his face fall to the ground, lying there for a few moments before sitting up and turning to face the lake. Shaking his head, he stood and brushed himself off, then walked to the water's edge.

There wasn't much beach. The grass ran to the water, and the shore was lined with cattails. He reached his hands into their tall, dry reeds and parted them so he could step through. He took a long, awkward step with his right foot, scratching his leg on the coarse grass as he hopped through the rest and stumbled into the lake. His legs and hands made small splashes until he found his footing in the mucky sand, and then he straightened up and looked around.

The lake was small, tranquil, and the sun gleamed on its gentle waves. The water was mostly clear, reflecting the deep blue of the summer sky. Wooden rafts painted white or gray floated peacefully in the water on blue or black barrels. Some fishermen coasted in the current offshore, their lines cast in the water from their rusty metal boats. Across the lake was the public beach, "the school" as the locals called it, where a sharp hill ran from the backside of the elementary into a big beach of good sand and smooth rocks. He could hear the kids laughing and splashing, playing king of the raft and other such games while their parents watched them from their towels on the shore.

He looked to the center of the lake, pristine and untouched by man or boat. Occasionally, an emboldened child or drunken adult would swim the half mile or so across, but today it belonged to the fish. He admired the depth of the lake in quiet contemplation, feeling one with the water.

After a few minutes he felt the minnows nibbling on his toes. He didn't mind—it tickled more than anything. He shuffled his feet and they receded; a few seconds later they'd drift back, nipping cautiously at his feet. He smiled at them and stuck his fingers in the water, waving a quick farewell as he stepped deeper into the lake. The water came to his waist and he stopped again, turning to scan the shoreline.

The green grass of the hill surrounded the water, dotted with wind-tossed trees and modest lake homes. The shore was a mixture of sandy beach, lily pads, un-mowed yards, and willows. To his right a neighbor's house sat on a smaller section of the hill, their front door only a few hundred feet from the shore. He checked to make sure no one was watching, then took off his robes. He dunked and pulled them from the water, repeating the motion enough times to give them a good rinse. Satisfied, he turned and flung them toward the shore. They fell into the tangles of the cattails.

He turned back to face the lake, naked and content. Unbeknownst to him, his neighbor opened her front door and stepped outside, drinking lukewarm coffee and smoking a Marlboro. She saw him there but didn't think much of it; she couldn't tell he was naked with half his body under water.

He took one last look toward the center of the lake then let his body fall into the water. The low drum of it rushed over his face and filled his ears. He blew lightly from his nose, opening his eyes as the short burst of white bubbles gave way to the fuzzy blue and green of the lake. He reached both arms through the water and pushed against it to propel forward, coasting for a few feet then stopping to let his body float. Rows of green and amber seaweed appeared below him, little bluegill and trout weaving back and forth among the leaves. He swam a little further then stopped to drift again. The seaweed disappeared except for the occasional stalk, stretching up from the bottom and swaying gently in the current. Rays of sun cut through the water all around, shining into the darkness below. He grabbed at them but they stayed out of reach.

He marveled at the void for a bit longer, but then a slight pressure in his chest told him it was time to breach. He turned and swam upward, breaking through the surface and filling his lungs with air. He looked around as he bobbed up and down. The beauty of landscape, water, and sky hung over him like a lotus in bloom. It reminded him of the peony. He still needed to check on his flowers.

He turned and swam toward the shore. The lake floor got closer and closer to his belly and the water got thinner on his back. The sand started to kick up under him, and he reached out his fingers until they were half-buried in it. He dropped to his knees and rose from the water, shaking as it fell off him. He rubbed his eyes and the cattails came into view. He walked over to them.

Ashes formed on the end of the cigarette in his neighbor's mouth, and she dropped her coffee. She watched his naked body come to shore and struggle to put his robes on. He finally clothed himself, then wrestled through the cattails and into the grass, stopping to look around. He saw her standing there, her cigarette entirely turned to ash. He gave her a slight bow and walked up the hill.

………..

He cupped the peony in his hand, then took one of the petals and rubbed it gently between his thumb and forefinger. In full bloom, they lasted a little over a week, and they'd been full for a while.

He stopped and surveyed the rest of the garden. The other flowers were fine, but he was afraid they were dry. He found his watering can next to a patch of balloon flowers, their violet petals folded like pursed lips a few weeks before bloom. He picked up the can and went inside to fill it. The screen door rattled behind him as he came back out. He walked the rows of the garden, watering and inspecting each flower, going inside and back out again as he emptied and refilled the can.

He got to the third from the last row and stopped, putting his can down and wiping his brow. He walked up to the sedum. He blew lightly on its blossom and watched the furry, pink petals ripple under his breath. He smiled to himself, feeling foolish for ever being afraid of a crazy old man and his beat-up gray truck.

Just then, a truck turned down the road. The sound of its rusty old engine reached his ears as it accelerated around the bend and toward his house. He hit the dirt like a soldier under fire. He reached for the flowers in front of him, parting their stems to see the road.

A 1994 Chevy Silverado passed by. It was green. It looked nothing like the other.

He shook his head. He'd have to get over his fear if he was ever to get anything done.

X

"Hey neighbor," a woman's voice called, "what are you doing in those flowers?"

He parted a few stems in front of him, seeing a pair of women's shoes on the edge of his yard. He rose from the flowers and peered over their blossoms. Mrs. Baker stood smiling near the sidewalk, holding a plate of food wrapped in plastic.

"I, uh, oh, I…I…"

"You haven't stopped by in so long," Mrs. Baker said, "I was starting to worry."

He saw empathy in her eyes and felt compelled to comfort her. "Oh, Mrs. Baker," he answered, "all life is temporary—why worry about anything temporary?" Even he knew his words weren't that comforting.

"That may be so," she said, "but as long as I'm alive, you'll have something to eat." He stood there, admiring her simple goodness. "Now come over here," she called, "I brought you some quiche." He hesitated for a moment, then walked toward her. "Don't tell Jim now," she grinned. He got up to her and her warmth turned to concern. "What happened to your clothes?"

He looked down at his robes. They were still wet from the lake, and the front was caked in dirt from when he dove to hide. "I, uh, washed them in the lake," he said.

She frowned. "Oh dear," she said, putting the plate down on the sidewalk. "Come here." She reached out and beat her hands against him to brush him off.

"Mrs. Baker," he protested.

She kept at it, furrowing her brow and swiping forcefully at his robes. She stepped back and licked her fingers, then leaned in to wipe the last bit of mud off his chest. "There we go," she said.

"Thank you, Mrs. Baker," he mumbled.

She smiled and bent down, picking up the plate from the sidewalk. "We missed you the past couple nights," she said, offering it to him.

He took it from her. "Many blessings, Mrs. Baker." He looked down at the plate in his hands. Steam coated the underside of the plastic; she must have just pulled it out of the oven. His stomach rumbled.

"I saved a plate last night and the night before," she went on. "Jim got up and ate them in the middle of the night. Lord knows he didn't need it." She laughed. The smell of the quiche made his mouth water, and he started feeling faint. He tried to listen to what she was saying. It took enormous restraint to not wolf it down in front of her. "So I figured I'd take the day off, do some baking, and bring you something," she added.

"May you be well, Mrs. Baker," he said without looking up from the quiche, "may you be free."

She put her hand over her heart and gave a teary smile. "Please come over tomorrow night," she insisted. "I'll have more for you to eat, and you can use our washer." He looked up at her. Her face was full of kindness; he forgot both fear and hunger for a moment.

"I'll come," he answered.

She clasped her hands together in excitement, then reached out and put a hand on his shoulder. "Take care of yourself," she said. She turned to go, then stopped and faced him. "I'm praying for you," she declared. He didn't know what to say. She turned around and walked down the street toward her house. He watched her disappear around the bend, suddenly remembering how hungry he was.

XI

Joe used his sleeve to wipe the sweat off his forehead, then sighed and shut off his machine. A set of wobbly metal stairs clung to the wall across the shop floor. He walked over to them and headed up, laminated signs on the wall next to him saying things like, "Safety is Our Business," "Think Safety!" and "Where's Your PPE?" He got to the second floor and turned past the door to the plant manager's office, walking down the hallway toward the break room.

The break room was small and square with white tile floors and eggshell-colored walls. Five plastic round tables sat throughout the room, each with three or four chairs pulled up to them. He walked to the center table. There was always a box of doughnuts there, never fresh but hopefully less than two days old. He opened the lid and weighed his choices. There was a jelly doughnut, a glazed apple fritter, and a round frosted doughnut with sprinkles. He grabbed the latter, closed the lid, and took a bite. It was a little stale, but it'd go fine with coffee. He walked over to the machine and poured some in a paper cup, then sat down at a table near the window.

An older coworker came in, a little fat but with broad shoulders and strong arms.

"Hey Don," Joe said.

"Joe," Don grunted, heading for the coffee. Don poured some in a cup and sat at a table of his own. "This kid's gonna kill me," he groaned.

Joe took a sip of coffee. "The Miller boy?" he asked.

"That fuckin' kid," Don grumbled. "Nothin' like his old man."

"Give him some time."

"I'll be dead before I train him, kinda time he needs."

Joe chuckled. "We were young once."

"Shit, when?" Don scoffed. "I sure as hell can't remember."

"You ain't lyin'," Joe laughed, biting into his doughnut.

"Sometimes I think I was born old," Don went on. "Old, fat, grumpy —right here in this fuckin' place." He took a drink of coffee, then set it down on the table. "Probably die here too."

"Least you'll die doin' what you love," Joe smirked.

"Shiiitt," Don answered, shaking his head. He looked down at the table, his old, weathered hands on either side of the cup.

Two more workers walked into the breakroom, a man and woman in their late forties. Don's gaze didn't move. Joe looked up to meet them. Julie and Ray Washington had worked in the factory for twenty-two years; they'd been married just as long. Joe smiled at them.

"Well if it ain't Big Joe," Ray declared with a huge grin. "What's happenin' brother?" He and Julie headed toward him, Ray reaching out for a handshake, Julie close behind wearing a wry smile.

"What's up man?" Joe said, shaking his hand. "Hey Julie," he added as Ray moved left and she took a step closer.

"Hey Joe," she said.

Ray and Julie Washington worked on the first floor along with the other blue-collars. She was in packaging at the end of the plant, making sure all the parts got boxed and shipped to the commercial customers; he was the shop mechanic, spending most of his time in a small cement office until the machines broke down. People used to give him grief— they said he was lazy. The way Ray figured, as long as he was sitting, the factory was running. That, he always said, was when the company made their money.

"How're the kids?" Joe asked.

"Ah, they're okay," Ray answered.

"They're doin' fine," Julie interjected. They had two kids. Their daughter was twenty and a pre-med student in Fort Wayne. Their son was a few years older, living at home and working at Citgo.

Ray shot a quick glance at his wife then turned back to Joe. "Tryin' to get Junior on at the factory, but that boy don't wanna do nothin'," he said, grabbing a chair. "Jen's doing great though." He sat down. Julie pulled up a chair next to him.

"Well, tell 'em I said hi," Joe said with a smile.

"We will, we will," said Ray, ready to change the subject. He looked down at the table and let his words die. After a few seconds he looked back up at Joe. "So listen," he began, taking a quick look around the room before leaning in and lowering his voice, "when're we gettin' the union in here?"

Joe folded his arms and leaned back in his chair with a knowing grin. "I don't know, Ray," he answered, "still recoverin' from last time."

Ray's eyes were wide as he pointed at the table, tapping against it in time with his whisper. "This time," he said, "this time it'll be different."

Joe blew air through his nose, unfolding his arms and leaning in on the table. "Listen man," he said, "I *just* got off third shift." Joe paused, looking Ray in the eye. "You ever been on third shift?"

"You're not alone this time brother," Ray pleaded.

"Shit," Joe went on, with a faraway look, "midnight coffee makes you feel like a bone-dry engine, chuggin' along with no gas—third's full of the loneliest sonsabitches you ever saw."

"Joe—"

"Even made me come in on Saturday."

"*Joe.*" Joe looked back at Ray. Ray's eyes were sincere, and his face was full of purpose. "We need you brother," he said. Joe smiled, admiring his dedication.

"Just think about it, alright?" Ray drummed the table, and he and Julie left to get some coffee.

"Still talkin' about that damn union?" Don grumbled, "my cousin's stepdad's brother-in-law..."

A young man with slacks and a polo shirt walked in. The room fell silent. "Hey, guys," he said with an awkward, mumbling laugh, "ready for the weekend?" Don scoffed, rolling his eyes. No one said anything. The interloper acted like he was looking for something, then turned and walked out of the breakroom.

"Fuckin' punk," Don muttered. "Never worked a day in his life. Straight outta college, gets an exec job."

Joe laughed. "Ahh, lay off the kid," he said. "We had the same choices he did."

"Shiiitt," Don griped. "I didn't choose to be the son of no poor bean farmer from Wauseon fuckin' Ohio." Even Ray and Julie laughed.

"Shoulda married rich," Joe said.

"Shiiitt," Don grumbled.

"Either that, or voted for the union," Joe grinned, winking at Ray.

………

Quitting time came and first shift headed out the door. A few old-timers hung back in the parking lot to smoke one last cigarette before going home. Joe said his goodbyes and climbed into his truck, pulling around the factory and onto Wayne Street.

Wayne Street was the town's main thoroughfare, one long, straight shot through the center of Angola. Though it changed names a few times, you could drive it the whole twelve miles from the edge of Fremont, just north of town, to the edge of Pleasant Lake, due south. In between, you could see all the banks, stores, and restaurants Angola had to offer.

Joe passed the bowling alley and stopped at the light. He used to bowl league on Tuesdays, but it'd been a while. The light turned green and he accelerated, but soon found himself behind a Suburban in a small row of traffic. "Damn lakers," he muttered.

Every summer, Wayne Street got a little busier. The locals cursed the vacationers that came to the big boating lakes on the north side of town, and an eight-minute drive became twelve.

Joe moved into the left lane, cruising through the light outside the Walmart Super Center and passing the Suburban. Ten seconds later, he was behind a family in a Bronco, mom and dad chain-smoking cigarettes while driving five under the speed limit.

"Damnit," he grumbled. He realized there was no music; side one of his tape had ended. He pressed eject on the radio and flipped the tape over, starting side two.

The sun was hot and the old slide guitar mocked his struggle. He switched back to the right lane, passing the Citgo where Ray Jr.

worked. He gave a slight wave then crossed through the next four-way light, the Shell station on one side, Buffalo Wild Wings on the other.

Just past the Shell was an old shopping center with a Hobby Lobby pushed back against a row of small, one-story businesses. A new Mexican restaurant was over there that the locals were excited about. It had nice booths, old-world decor, and good food—they even had a server who made fresh guacamole right in front you. But the locals were always excited about new restaurants, whether a semi-authentic joint with a name like Casa Del Sol, or a run of the mill chain like Moe's Southwestern Grill. They'd call their expat friends and relatives, living in Florida, Denver, or Seattle, and at some point in conversation they'd ask with pride, "You see we're gettin' a Jimmy John's?"

Joe looked at his speedometer, then checked his rearview mirror for cops. Angola had a reputation for speed traps. He looked back to the road and saw the light by Taco Bell turn from green to yellow. He pressed the brake, making a slow, easy stop.

The Angola Taco Bell made more money than any business around. Locals could tell by how often it upgraded—it always seemed like new. The whole town ate there once a week; about half of them once a day. When noon hit Monday through Friday, there'd be welders, teachers, and the occasional kids playing hooky, if they were bold enough. On Saturdays, old coaches would show up, talking to forgotten players and fans from table to table until long after their order was called. Saturday night came around and the parking lot would be full of high schoolers and dropouts in big trucks, eating tacos and looking for fights. Every kid smoking weed for the first time had a drive-thru story, laughing hysterically into the order box and too stoned to say how many gorditas they wanted; most adults could say they risked a DUI to satisfy a late-night craving, or got caught pulling out of the drive.

Joe shook his head and smiled, and the light turned green. He cruised for a bit, the two-lane went to one, and somewhere past Pizza King the traffic slowed into a long, single-file line heading toward The Mound.

The Mound was a four-way roundabout wrapped around a Civil War monument in downtown Angola. It got its name in the 1860s, when the center of town was a small hill of dirt with a line of horse hitches. In 1917 the monument was built; Lady Columbia stood high on top, one hand holding a laurel for peace, the other holding a flag for country. Four of her best Union soldiers stood guard at the base, one at each cardinal direction. The space around the monument was a well-manicured lawn with thoughtfully planted flowers, fixed into a circle to help the flow of traffic. Once every five or ten years a hapless driver jumped the curb and roughed up the landscape, and Angola called on her dedicated Garden Club to restore the floral arrangements to their original splendor.

Circling The Mound were most of Angola's local businesses, many of them housed in historic buildings with high facades. There were some good restaurants, a conspicuous number of defense attorneys, one or two spots that forever changed hands, and a few too many antique stores. But the jewel of The Mound was the movie theater.

The Brokaw Movie Theater had been around forever. Grandmothers told stories of when they were girls, eating candy with their friends and giggling in their seats; grandfathers talked of teenage years as ushers, shining flashlights on rowdy customers as they worked through *Ma and Paw Kettle* for the forty-sixth time. The next generation spent weekends watching *007* and Paul Newman movies, drinking Pepsi from glass bottles with a box full of Now and Laters. Their kids grew up in the theater, meeting middle school dates to watch rom coms one night, sneaking past the ticket counter into R-rated movies the next. Nowadays, it was still the place to see a movie for miles around, and most of its Bogart-era charm was still intact.

Joe idled up to his spot in line, three cars back from the entrance to the roundabout. The car at the head of the line was having trouble figuring out when to go; sometimes, especially in summer, The Mound had a constant stream of cars going round, and it was hard to recognize the cue to go. Finally, a big truck exited northbound, and the car entered the roundabout. Joe inched up past the crosswalk, waiting for the SUV in front of him to go. The driver signaled and Joe laughed, rolling his eyes. Locals could always tell when strangers were in town— they'd hit their right blinker and wait instead of moving casually into the flow of traffic. The SUV found a spot and went for it. Joe followed closely behind, circling The Mound and peeling south toward Pleasant Lake. He passed the Old High School and headed up the small hill near the city limit. Wayne Street turned into Old 27, and soon he was on the open road. He reached underneath his seat and fished out a warm beer, cracking it open and taking a nice, long drink. He set it down in the cup holder and turned up the radio, putting his foot on the gas. Green trees and gentle hills flashed past as he sped down the long, straight road.

His beer was three quarters empty by the time he reached the speed trap. He put it back in the cup holder and pressed gently on the brakes, looking down at his speedometer. He was going slow enough, but while his eyes were on the dash, he noticed his gas gauge read low. For a moment he considered going home and getting gas later, but one of the worst mistakes a working person makes is adding an extra errand in the morning. Joe would wake up just the same, get ready just the same, then jump into his car to rush off to work with an "oh shit!" as soon as he saw the gauge. He slammed his beer and tucked it under his seat, following the fork left to the gas station.

On the other side of the lake, the monk exhaled in his chair, finishing his meditation and opening his eyes. He felt a little better after yesterday's talk with Mrs. Baker. He had straightened out his porch and resumed his routine; he even planned to head to the Bakers' for dinner. He'd walk over soon.

Joe eased his way toward the pump. He shut his car off and walked toward the door. He pulled it open and it fell shut behind him, the bells on the handle jingling to alert the clerk.

Joe looked around. There were newspapers and car mags on his left; just beyond were a few short aisles of wiper fluid, generic medicine, and overpriced snacks. He stepped up to the counter, drumming his fingers on the glass that covered the multicolored Lotto tickets underneath and guarded the array of cheap cigars and blunt wraps behind.

A young country blond came around the corner, walking to the counter with a sweet, disarming smile. "Hey Joe," she said, twang in her voice, "what can I do for ya?"

"Hey there Mandy," Joe said with a smile. "How ya been?"

"I been alright," she answered, "workin' workin'." She grinned, shaking her head. "How 'bout you?"

"Livin' the dream," Joe chuckled, reaching into his pocket and sliding two twenties across the counter.

"Still at the factory?" Mandy asked, slipping her hand over the money and punching open the register. "Thirty on three, right?"

"Yeah, yeah," Joe replied, "put it on three." Mandy slid a ten across the counter. "Yeah I'm still at the factory. You still with Clint?"

Mandy rolled her eyes. "I left him, but he don't listen."

"Goddamnit." Joe shook his head, then decided to change the subject. "Yep, yep, factory's got me five days a week. All that workin', it's hard to get my drinkin' done."

Mandy laughed—a sweet country laugh with slightly crooked teeth. "I'm sure you find the time," she said.

Joe took the change and put it in his pocket. "When you're right, you're right," he said with a shrug. "You take care now," he added with a slight wave, turning toward the door.

"Take it easy," Mandy said. The bells on the door rang again as he pulled it open and it fell shut behind him. He walked to the truck and grabbed the gas pump, then unscrewed his cap and filled the tank.

The monk rose from his chair, then turned and walked to the kitchen. He couldn't remember ever having gone to "dinner" before and wasn't sure what to expect. He grabbed his alms bowl from the sink, tilting it in the light to see if it was clean. It looked fine. He tucked it under his arm and walked back to the porch.

The pump clicked, signaling the tank was full. Joe squeezed the handle a few more times and hung it up, then opened his door and climbed into the truck. He started the engine and pulled away. The blue Marathon sign with its giant red "M" hung in his rearview as he returned to Old 27 South, following the curve of the lake to take the back way home. He turned right on the narrow lake road and eased past the long grass and trees. He looked across the lake, admiring it from a vantage point he seldom saw. He slowed around the twists and turns, winding past the old red barn with the words "Hillbilly Haven" written on the façade, then pulled into his driveway. He shut off the engine and stepped onto the gravel.

Sadie came running from across the road as Joe walked to the house. He stopped to pet her but she trotted past, climbing the porch steps to wait at the door. He glanced over at the neighbor's house, seeing Mrs. Baker through the window. She bustled about the kitchen with an apron over her blouse and a hot dish in her hands. She set it on the counter and went back to the stove. Joe turned toward his house and walked up the porch, opening the door and following the cat inside.

The monk stopped at his screen door, hand wrapped around the handle. He looked out across his yard. There was a gentle breeze running through the trees and tickling the flowers. Some kids raced past on their bikes. A reckless little boy screamed after them, riding a skateboard with no shoes and clutching a leash as his hapless dog pulled him down the road. He could hear a few car engines echoing across the lake from the highway on the other side. He shuddered.

He turned to look around the porch, still clenching the handle. His chair sat empty and upright; everything else was in order. He started to move his head back toward the door when a gleam caught his eye. It was the empty beer can, still on its side a few feet from the chair. A pang hit his chest, and the beginnings of fear welled up inside him. He shook his head and brushed it off, letting out an angry sigh as he yanked the door open and stepped outside. The grass was long and felt good on his bare feet. Soon one of his neighbors would be by to cut it. He crossed the yard and its gentle caress gave way to the scratch of pebbles and dirt on the sidewalk. He enjoyed the roughness against his feet as he walked down the road.

He got to the stop sign and the Bakers' house came into view. He could see Mrs. Baker rushing around the kitchen through the window. He smiled at her sincerity, feeling more excited than nervous. Jim

Baker came into the kitchen, looking cross. The monk stopped at the lawn's edge, watching them through the window and imagining what they were saying.

"Goddamnit Angela, why all this fuss?"

"He's our neighbor!" she snapped over her shoulder, as best as the monk could tell.

"What the hell does that got to do with anything?" Jim probably retorted, throwing his arms up.

"Love thy neighbor, Jim," the monk imagined her saying as she rushed back toward the stove. Jim pushed his arms out, throwing his hands down as if to say, "ahh Christ." The monk shook his head and laughed. Usually Mr. Baker made him anxious; tonight, he was grateful for the company, and even more so for the meal. He walked through their yard and up the porch steps, too excited to see the beat-up gray truck that so haunted him in the driveway next door. He lifted his right hand to the side of the screen and gently balled his fist to knock, cupping the alms bowl in his left with nervous energy. He could hear the muffled footsteps of Mrs. Baker and the garbled reproach of her husband coming from inside. He paused for a second, then rapped his knuckles on the door.

Tat, tat, tat.

"That's him," Mrs. Baker cried from the dinner table, rushing to set the dinnerware.

"Goddamnit," Jim grumbled under his breath from the living room entryway.

The monk heard more footsteps, and the kitchen light around the doorway changed. Angela reached to open the door. Jim stumbled over and grabbed her shoulder. The monk could hear the hushed tones of their argument from the porch, then a brief silence as Angela turned to glare at her husband. He lifted his hand to knock again, but the sudden, rattling slam of the neighbor's screen door turned his head. A small, gray tabby cat came through the door alone, sauntering down the porch steps and into the yard. He watched her little paws cut through the grass toward the driveway, feeling more and more uneasy as she neared the gravel. She crossed the grass line, her feet making little *tik-tik-tik* sounds against the rock, and an unknown fear gripped his chest. He continued to watch the cat, heart racing as she plopped down by some object in the driveway. On the other side of the Baker's door, Angela rolled her eyes one last time and reached to pull the door open.

The monk lifted his gaze from the cat. Just beyond her ears was a black rubber tire. Just above the tire was the familiar side of the gray Chevy S10.

His eyes took in the rest of the truck. The horrid memory of its engine and the raucous voice of its driver filled his ears; he relived the sight of the driver's gnarled hand shooting out the window and throwing the abominable can into the sanctity of his garden. His stomach clenched as if to puke. He shook his head in terror, stepping backward.

"Hey neighbor!" Mrs. Baker cried as she opened the door, her smile quickly turning down. The monk reached his hands out, stuttering as he reeled toward the steps. She stepped from the door and onto the porch, trying to calm him.

"No, no," he stammered, shaking his head. He stumbled backward, tripping down the stairs. Mrs. Baker gasped and came toward him. "No!" he screamed from the dirt, throwing his hands out. She put her hand over her heart and stepped back. He scrambled to his feet, taking one last look at the truck before turning and sprinting down the road. She watched him go, eyes full of worry.

Jim stepped into the frame behind his wife. They stared in silence as the monk disappeared around the bend.

"Well," Jim shrugged, "more for me."

XII

There's no better place to be than Indiana on the Fourth of July. In Pleasant Lake, the locals raise Old Glory over the beach, proud of their waterfront slice of the American Dream. Moms set picnic tables with potato salad, chips, ham-pickle rollups, and paper plates as dads with no shirts and worn out, bent-billed dad hats watch meat sizzle on their grills. Kids run around playing tag, catch, or jumping in the lake between swiping snacks off the table.

Down the street, Crazy Craig wrapped 800 sparklers as tight as he could in a half-roll of electrical tape. He walked back to his deck to down his cocktail, grab a lighter, and say "watch this" to the half-drunk partygoers that stood there. One sparkler was pulled partway from the bundle like a fuse on a stick of dynamite. He walked up next to it and flicked the lighter, but the flame went out. After a few more flicks the flame caught, sparks shooting from the makeshift fuse with a crackling hiss as Craig ran back to the deck screaming, "She's gonna blow!" His friends scampered behind the deck, careful not to spill their drinks. His pal Buck threw him a cold Busch Light when he reached them. Craig cracked open the beer and waited with his friends, the group murmuring in anticipation. Nothing happened. A minute passed and the group's excitement turned to disappointment. Sarcastic chuckles and quiet groans reached Craig's ears.

"Huh," he wondered, "looked a lot cooler on the innernet." He took a few steps toward the sparkler bomb, inspecting it with narrowed eyes.

KABOOOOOM!

The bomb exploded, its force knocking the beer from Craig's hand and throwing his whole body backward. "Holy shit! Holy shit!" he yelled, scrambling to his feet and turning to his friends. The party jumped up and down, hooting and laughing, proud to be Americans on the Fourth. Craig smiled as he watched them, unable to hear a thing over the loud ringing in his ears. They came over and slapped him on the back, putting their arms around his shoulders and leading him to the bomb site. Their jaws dropped when they reached it.

"Holy fuck," Buck said. A crater two feet wide and three feet deep was blown into the yard, smoke billowing from it like a wrecked space-ship in a Martian movie.

Neighbors wandered into the street, a mix of concern and confusion on their faces. The explosion had shaken their picnic tables, knocking snacks into the grass; even a few burgers had slid off the grill. Families hanging inside saw their walls tremble, a few picture frames breaking on the floor as dishes rattled in the kitchen cupboards.

Some people walked toward the sound. Others couldn't place the boom but were intuitively drawn to Crazy Craig's.

"Hey buddy," Buck said, "better go talk to the neighbors."

"What?" Craig yelled, ears still ringing. Buck pointed to the edge of the yard. A big group had gathered there. "Ah shit," Craig said, running over.

Craig's grass line was full of trees and other plants, arranged in such a way that nobody could see in. The neighbors milled about, parting a few bushes here and there, craning their necks and trying to get a look.

Craig burst through the foliage and his neighbors jumped back. "It's okay, it's okay," he yelled with a big, disarming grin, "just a few sparklers!" Most of them chuckled, a few shook their heads, and all the kids in the crowd made a mental note to ask him for instructions later that week.

Down the street, Joe opened his fridge to look for some beer. He and his factory buddies were going to a party in Angola, and he didn't want to come empty-handed. "Shit," he muttered, seeing a single beer on the shelf. He grabbed it and cracked it open, heading to his truck. He'd have to go around the lake for some overpriced Miller Lite at the gas station.

He put his opened beer in the cup holder as he pulled into the Marathon and parked by the entrance. The bell chimed as he pulled the door open and again as it fell shut behind him. Mandy came around the corner, looking tired but wearing her bright, country smile. Joe felt a little guilty when he saw her.

"You ever stop workin'?" he asked, pausing to greet her on his way to the beer aisle.

"Take my birthday off, work four hours each on Christmas and Christmas Eve," she said. "Other than that, I'm either here or the BP."

"Bet the overtime's nice," Joe said, trying to find a silver lining.

"Nah, forty hours at each place," Mandy answered. "Same owner, different company, so he gets away with it." Joe shook his head in disbelief. "I don't mind though," Mandy added, "really, I like workin'."

Joe grabbed two cases and put them on the counter. "I like workin' too, but shit," he said, paying for the beer. "You take care now Mandy, and for Chrissake, take a day off."

"Take it easy Joe," she said with a smile.

Joe stepped outside, put the cases in his truck bed, and headed out to Ray and Julie's.

....

In Angola, there was a parade at eleven. The city lined the streets near The Mound, waving little flags from lawn chairs and picnic blankets. People smiled from floats and classic cars, passing out fliers and throwing candy. Kids in the audience scrambled to the curbs and back to their families with handfuls of Jolly Ranchers and Tootsie Pops.

The parade ended five blocks south from The Mound, right by the public library. The Parker family sat there every year. Grandma Parker got there early in the morning to set up chairs and blankets to claim their spot. Grandpa Parker was known about the town—he'd been on City Council since '96. They watched the parade, beaming with pride as the Chamber of Commerce, Angola Marching Band, and the local little league teams passed by.

Grandma and Grandpa Parker had three girls, all happily married and raising kids of their own. The two oldest had two boys each; the youngest had a girl. Their kids were playing around the curb, waving at floats and dashing to the street for candy.

The trouble started when Angola Heating and Plumbing passed by. Every kid knew their float had the best candy. A pretty lady from the top of a papier-mâché air conditioner threw a big handful of Skittles, Snickers, and Laffy Taffy—all full-sized bags and bars—and the kids broke into chaos. Two of the grandkids ended up rolling around on the street, wrestling for the last bar; finally, the younger cousin wrenched it away from the older and ran giggling back to the curb.

The older cousin didn't say anything at first. He picked himself up, dusted himself off, and went back to the group. Earlier in the parade, many of the floats had thrown out Dubble Bubble gum; knowing they lost their flavor after fifteen seconds, the older cousin had shrewdly refused them. Now, however, he went to work trading his best candy for them. His brother and three cousins were happy to trade, thinking him crazy for choosing tasteless gum over primo candy. When he was done, he put at least ten pieces in his mouth, chewed until his jaw was sore, then sat by his little cousin. When no one was looking, he spit the wad into his hand and slapped it into his cousin's golden bowl cut. The older cousin pointed and laughed, the parents started yelling, and all the kids were sent home before they could further embarrass their well-respected grandparents.

A couple blocks west from the Dubble Bubble fiasco was the college part of town where the Esposito family lived. Fi and Frank Esposito were good, Christian folk: their house, fridge, and couch were always open to anyone who respected the rules, and their doors were always swinging back and forth from their sons and their friends running in and out. They threw a big pool party every Fourth. It started around the parade—sometimes, one of the boys would be so bold to pour a few Schlitz into a thirty-two-ounce Colt's cup and walk over to see the floats—and went well into the night. Fi was cool as long as she didn't find a joint on the floor or some liquor on the table, and Frank was cool as long as he got to sneak a few shots and play some ping pong.

Down the street was the Stackfelders' house. The old coaches from Angola High went there, eating hot dogs and drinking beer until their wives drove them home. Today, the old baseball coach was getting drunk. "Remember when Deeko thought he was somethin'?" he laughed, taking a swig of beer. "That sonnofabitch had the ball caught, then jumped into the fence, trying to look like Griffey," he said, flailing his arms. "Bobbled the goddamn thing right over. Home run for the Eagles!" The old timers laughed and reached for their beers.

"I got one for ya," the basketball coach said. "Regionals, '99, down by five in the fourth quarter..." Over his shoulder, the neighborhood kids were playing an intense game of lightning in the driveway. Four of them had been knocked out already and had taken to playing freeze tag in the grass. There were three left—two cocky boys and an unassuming little girl. The first boy was lined up on a crack in the cement which was a little too far for a free throw, the little girl right behind him. He shot and missed, and she let it fly.

Swish.

"And they didn't know what hit 'em," laughed the basketball coach. "Scrappiest buncha hicks you ever saw!"

The old timers smiled and grabbed their beers. "To the '99 Hornets!" exclaimed the football coach, holding up his bottle for a toast.

"To the '99 Hornets!" they echoed, holding up their own.

Swish.

Joe parked his truck and came through the driveway with the Washingtons, passing two pissed-off little boys and a grinning little girl. "Looks like Coach's tellin' stories again," he called. The old timers turned their heads.

"Ahh, Joe," the baseball coach yelled, "who invited you, ya lame bastard?" Everyone laughed.

"Thought I'd class up the place," Joe chuckled, raising the two cases of Miller Lite. He walked over to the garage and started unloading the beer into the cooler.

"Ray, Julie," said the football coach, shaking their hands as they stepped up to the table.

"Hey Coach," said the Washingtons. "How we lookin' this year?" Ray added.

"Gotta tough schedule," he replied, "but this Dillinger kid can throw it over the goddamn Second Basin. It's gonna be—hey, you two wanna sit down?"

A plastic chair slid against the concrete as the baseball coach stumbled to his feet. "Take mine," he said.

"That's okay," Ray said, holding his hand up.

"No, really, take mine."

"No, we couldn't," Julie said.

"No, really, I want you to have it."

"No, we'll just, uh," Ray said.

"No, really, I'm tired of sittin'," said the baseball coach, stepping back from his chair, "I hate sitting." The Washingtons walked over, feeling awkward but trying not to break Midwestern decorum. The baseball coach realized he'd only offered one chair and turned and slapped the basketball coach on the shoulder.

"What the hell ya do that for?" the basketball coach hollered. The baseball coach motioned and whispered, trying to rope the basketball coach into his act of generosity. Luckily, Stackfelder, the host of the party, came around the corner with a plate of burgers.

"Who wants some b—Ray! Julie! Let me get some more chairs." He set the plate down and headed to the garage, seeing Joe at the cooler. "Joe! Ya lame bastard," he said before coming back outside with three folding chairs. "Saturday, in the park—hey, turn up the radio!"

Back in Pleasant Lake, the monk sat sweating in his robes. Three days ago, he ran all the way back from the Bakers', ripped open his screen door, and dove onto the porch floor. The spongy turf pricked his cheek and the tops of his outstretched feet. His heart beat on the floor as he lay.

After a few hours he noticed the can out of the side of his eyelid. The brunette pinup girl slowly came into focus against his squished cheek—her deep red heels and her long, thick legs; her navy-blue daisy dukes; her red and white striped blouse; her thick, red lips.

He pushed himself up from the floor and crawled over to the can. He picked it up and turned it around in his hand, examining it from his knees. Her beauty scared him, and its presence in his sanctuary made him angry. He went back to his chair, staring at the can the whole way. He was still there on the Fourth, feeling hungry and slowly losing his mind.

……..…

I think it was the Fourth of Julyy.

The song drifted over the pool in the Espositos' backyard. Two kids were splashing at each other in the water while their beer-belly stepdad floated by in an inflatable chair with a drink in his hand. The other parents sat around in lawn chairs or at umbrellaed tables eating Doritos and pasta salad. One of the Esposito boys' elusive crushes had her toes hanging over the diving board, standing on the precipice and ready to jump. The rest of her classmates were either packed ten deep in the pool house bathroom smoking joints or in the Esposito basement listening to their rocker friends jam on guitar, bass, and drums. Frank was in the basement too, trying to convince his sons' friends to play him in ping pong.

Fi pulled a tray of mini hotdogs from the kitchen stove and walked toward the pool with a big smile on her face. She stopped near the pool house bathroom and flared her nostrils.

"Sorry dude, gotta go see my dad," Coach's kid said. He took a step toward the door, then paused. "Let me hit that one more time though." He grabbed the knob and opened the bathroom door, then closed it immediately. "Shh, shh! Dude, she's outside," he whispered to the group.

Fi looked over at the door. Everybody got quiet. The kid hitting the joint held his breath, scared to let the smoke out. One of the bigger kids sucked in his gut for some reason. The rest looked toward the crack in the door, waiting for Fi's shadow to move.

After a few seconds she wrinkled her nose and walked away. They let out a collective sigh. Some smoke came out too.

"Alright dudes, seriously," Coach's kid said, grabbing the knob, "I'll see ya'll later." He stepped outside, found a Solo cup and poured some beer in it, then put on a pair of sunglasses and headed down the street.

He could see his dad from the sidewalk. He shook his head and smiled, then tilted his head back and finished his cup before throwing it in a random neighbor's trashcan. He blinked five or six times and gave himself a couple of light slaps on the cheek to make sure he wasn't too high. When he got close enough, he cut into the grass and toward the round table where his dad sat with his friends. A few of them were drunk. His dad's buddy Joe was pounding a Miller Lite and already had two empty cans in front of him.

"Hey Coach, tellin' stories again?" he said, patting his dad on the back. The old timers looked up, laughing when they saw Coach's kid.

The baseball coach turned around and grinned. "Hey bud, glad to see ya."

"Thought I'd stop by before the fireworks," he said.

"You want us to pick you up from the Espositos'?" the baseball coach asked.

"Wouldn't miss it," Coach's kid said.

"Say, how's college treatin' ya?" asked the basketball coach.
"Hey coach, treatin' me great," Coach's kid answered, shaking his hand. "Hey coach," he said, reaching out to shake the football coach's hand. "Ray, Julie, Joe," he added with a slight wave.

"They teach you how to shotgun a beer yet?" Joe asked with a grin.

"I, uh," he stuttered, glancing down at his dad. "Uh, no."

"Shit, first time for everything," Joe laughed, draining his beer and standing up. "Not that I believe ya, though," he muttered to himself as he headed for the cooler. He came back with two Millers.

"One for you," he said, tossing it to the kid, "and one for me. Now, the first thing you do is—"

"Joe," the baseball coach said sternly. Joe stopped and turned toward Coach, his face a mixture of protest and guilt. Coach's kid looked down at the ground. Everyone else looked up at his dad.

"Grab me one," the baseball coach grinned. Everybody smiled, rumblings of "alright," and "hell yeah," in the air.

Joe came back with another beer. "And one for your old man," he laughed, tossing it over. "God I love the Fourth."

. . . .

There's an energy in Angola when dusk fades to night on the Fourth of July. The air hangs low and balmy sweet with possibility. The smell of it fills the noses of old timers—they can't quite name it, but they're reminded of long forgotten games of capture the flag, of night swims in the dark of the lake, of sleepovers and kick the can and midnight kisses. It gets harder to name as they get older.

The monk sat gripping the pinup girl in his lonely wicker chair. He was oblivious to everything—he hadn't noticed his proud little neighbors and their raised American flags, Crazy Craig and his sparkler sonic boom, Joe and his cases of beer, small towns and their parades and dreams and farfetched romances. All he knew was his sanctuary had been invaded. He glared at the can, anger in his heart.

The streets of Angola were lined with kids throwing firecrackers in the gutters and shooting bottle rockets in the air. Cars rumbled and footsteps echoed as everyone hurried to the park for the annual town fireworks.

Joe killed his beer and threw it on the ground. "Everybody get in!" he yelled. He jumped in his truck and revved up the engine. The Washingtons headed toward the truck.

"Hey man," Julie said, putting her hand on the ledge of the open passenger window, "you sure?"

"Just had a few beers, Julie," he smirked, "no liquor." He wasn't going to mention the secret flask in his pocket. The Washingtons climbed into the truck.

"Hop in back Coach," Joe hollered. "Air feels great." Most everyone had left already. It was just the baseball coach and Stackfelder standing in the front yard.

"Appreciate it, Joe," Coach said, "but I gotta get home and grab the '66. My wife and son go with me every year."

Joe turned toward Stackfelder. "Stack, you comin'?"

"Joe, ya bastard," he said, red-faced and drunk. He turned and stumbled back to the house, knees wobbling and arms searching for balance.

"Lightweight," Joe chuckled. He put the truck in drive and cruised east, night air blowing through the open windows.

The fireworks were at Commons Park. Spectators drifted away from the hot dog stands and carnival lights sometime around nine o'clock, finding nice grassy spots in the dark. Thousands of them came with their blankets and folding chairs, and the city prided itself on giving them a good show. But for the best view, and to avoid the crowd, Joe and some of the other townies would go two or three blocks west to the ball field by Hendry Park Elementary School. He pulled in and parked, then shut off the engine. The Washingtons got out and grabbed some folding chairs from the truck bed.

"Right behind ya," Joe said, "gotta check on somethin'." Ray and Julie shrugged and walked toward the ball diamond. Joe waited until they were a few yards away then fished around in his pocket. His fingers closed around the flask and he pulled it from his jeans. He unscrewed the top and took a big swig of whiskey. His mouth puckered and his exhale was hot; his eyes burned from the liquor's strength.

He reached for the cap to cover the flask and put it away, then paused. "Eh, I'll be fine," he muttered. He took another swig then put the flask down on his thigh. He knew he should stop. He looked down at the flask, hand still wrapped around it. He shrugged and took another shot. "Wooo," he said, wiping his lips with his wrist. He screwed the cap back on and put the flask away, then climbed out of the truck and shut the door. He saw Ray and Julie waiting by the bleachers and walked toward them. He didn't stumble, but the ground felt strange to his feet, and the world seemed long and wonky through his eyes. He reached the Washingtons faster than he thought he would. "Guys ready?" he said, a little too loud.

"Been waitin' on *you*, Big Joe," answered Ray. "Hey, what's that in your pocket?"

"It's uh—"

"Pass it over here," Ray grinned.

"Christ," Julie muttered. Joe smiled sheepishly and handed his keys to Julie, then pulled the flask from his pocket and gave it to Ray.

Ray took a long drink behind the bleachers. "Damn," he shuddered, passing it back. Joe took another quick shot and the three of them walked around the bleachers, through the gate, and into centerfield.

The monk placed the beer can on the sill and turned his mind to the truck. How long had it been there? Why hadn't he noticed it before? He could feel his anger swelling. He took a deep breath and exhaled, trying to suppress it. He closed his eyes and prepared for meditation.

A low murmur hung over the crowd in Angola, their excitement building as the sky grew darker. Coach and his family looked upward from their spot in the grass, his kid high but clinging to a childhood lost. "Remember when…?" he asked his parents.

Joe and Ray laughed as they traded stories, passing the flask back and forth until it was gone. Julie thought about her kids. One was too busy to come home. The other was off at a party somewhere.

FFFT!

The sound of the first launch echoed over the crowd. There was a mixture of excited gasps and "ooh!" as they watched its red tail rocket into the night. It climbed to its zenith then burst into a giant web of twinkling red stars. The whole town cheered.

Firework after firework shot into the dark, each exploding into a multicolor beauty of willow trees, American flags, and flower blossoms. By halftime Joe was drunk, lying on his back in the grass. The glow of each burst rained over the crowd and lit his face.

"Sit up man, you're missin' it," Ray whispered, slapping him on the shoulder.

The monk was on his back in the dark, in deep meditation with the phantasmal grass all around him, green heat rising higher and casting its glow on his wincing face. He fought against the sickness in his gut and the spinning in his head and propped himself up on his elbows to look at the light.

Joe lifted his head in time to see the green tail of a firework soaring in the sky. He smiled as it exploded into a giant weeping willow, streaks sinking to the ground. He imagined the embers falling on him like dandelion dust.

The light was blinding at first, and the monk closed his eyes. He reopened them slowly, and what looked like a giant, fiery tree came to form through his squint. He opened his eyes the rest of the way and beheld its frightening beauty.

A tree of miracles...

"Get up, man."

The Washingtons helped Joe to his feet. He stumbled but they caught him, straining to pull him up again. The fireworks had ended and everyone was rushing to their cars to beat the traffic. Joe leaned hard on his friends as the townies, their cars, and nearby orange street-lights came to him through blurry eyes and a spinning head.

The monk struggled to his feet. He staggered backwards for a second, overcome by dizziness. He closed his eyes until he found his balance, then reopened them and looked up at the tree. It burned tall and bright, with a multitude of leafy branches starting about six feet from its base and continuing all the way up to its leaf-covered crown. He studied it in silent awe.

Ray, Julie, and Joe got to the truck. Julie went around to the driver's seat while Ray opened the passenger door and helped Joe inside.

"Thanks brother," Joe mumbled as he squeezed in next to Julie. Julie rolled her eyes and started the engine. Ray shut the door and she put it in drive, heading home.

"I ain't goin' all the way to Pleasant Lake," she grumbled. "He can sleep on the couch."

The monk traced the lowest branch from its base to its spindly fingertips and back again. His eyes stopped on a gentle sag near the middle of the bough. He looked beneath and noticed what seemed like a tire swing hanging from it, glowing bright and spinning softly in the void.

The Washingtons lived just east of the small hill that separated the Angola city limits from the open road of Old 27. Julie signaled left and turned past the cop at the speed trap. She drove a quarter mile in the country breeze then pulled into their long gravel driveway. She got out and shut her door, ready to leave the others behind.

Ray got out and turned to Joe. "You comin'?" he asked.

"Be right there," Joe answered, slumped in his seat. Ray looked over the truck at his wife. She rolled her eyes and went into the house. He shut the door and followed her.

The monk walked over to the tire swing. It looked familiar and he wanted to feel it in his hands. He reached for the rope, his fingers suspended around it. He slid them up and down without touching the fire, trying to imagine the hard knots and loose frays in his grasp. After a few seconds he stopped and reached for the tire. He flattened his hand and brushed his open palm just above it, remembering the cracked rubber against his skin. He thought about what it'd feel like to climb on it. He imagined himself swinging back and forth like a child. He could hear himself laughing from the joy of it. It was a happy, boyish laugh—excitable and a little high-pitched. He felt a warm rush of nostalgia that he couldn't quite name, but he longed to embrace.

A voice called to him from the far reaches of the void, and the laughter stopped. He looked past the swing, trying to pinpoint the sound. In the distance was a shining gray light. The sound was coming from there.

The voice cried out again, and he heard a name he didn't recognize. He said it softly to himself, and it echoed in his ears. He stepped back from the tree.

He kept his eyes on the light. It got bigger, brighter: he realized it was traveling toward him. He took another step back, feeling curious. It appeared to be some kind of train or vehicle, shooting through the night like a silver bullet. There were more sounds coming from it now—a far-off din, like music from an open car window. He stood still, half-mesmerized as the light got closer and the noise grew louder. He started feeling nervous at how quickly it approached.

The voice called to him a third time. For a moment he knew what it meant, but its words were drowned in the rest of the noise, breaking down and reforming as a howl over rock music and a ratty engine. Dread filled his stomach as the bright light split into headlights. The truck was coming for him.

He turned to run but his legs were heavy, and for every five steps, he could only take one. The truck got faster and faster, its horrid chorus filling his ears, its headlights burning his neck. He turned his head; the truck was a block away. He looked down at his feet, cursing them for their slow motion. He turned back to the truck and it was inches away, its grill open like teeth to devour him, its nightmarish driver leaning out the window with a lurid grin.

"Hey buddy."

He gasped and woke up on his porch. His heart pounded and he was covered in sweat. He looked outside. The sun was pale yellow and there was a cool morning breeze. He should be out there, he thought.

He looked over at the can on the windowsill. Whatever remaining fear turned to anger, red-hot and smoldering. He stood up and snatched the can, crushing it in his hand. He sat back down in his chair. He'd be ready this time.

XIII

"Hey buddy."

Joe didn't move. Ray tapped him again.

"Hey buddy," he said, "time to go."

Joe scrunched his face against the sunlight. He strained to lift his head a few inches before falling back to the metal with a heavy groan. After a few seconds he opened his eyes, and the morning sky came into focus through his squint. He was on his back in the bed of his truck. He scrunched his face again, hungover. "How the fuck did I get here?" he groaned.

"Don't know man," Ray answered, "Julie's pretty pissed." Joe chuckled, raising his hand and dragging it down his tired face.

"I'm serious," Ray said. "Gotta bucket of cold water on the porch. She about threw it on ya."

"Jesus," Joe said, still rubbing his face. "Better get goin'." He sat up and put his head in his hands.

"Probably won't see you for a while, outside the factory," Ray said. He patted Joe on the shoulder.

Joe reached out for a lame, nauseated handshake. "Take it easy brother," he said. Ray turned and went inside. Joe sat on the edge of the tailgate with his head down. He slipped his hand over his temples and ran his fingers through his hair. "Holy shit," he grunted.

He shook his head and put his hands down, pushing off the tailgate and onto his feet. He stumbled to the door and climbed in.

He saw his keys in the middle seat. Julie had put them there an hour or so ago. He picked them up and turned the ignition, leaning over the wheel. The truck started up and the radio kicked on. He shot up and turned it down. He backed out of the driveway, put the truck in drive, and headed home. He held his head and slouched most of the way.

He got to the fork and signaled right, passing the old town cemetery on his way to Main Street. He turned right at the stop sign. The last song on his cassette was wrapping up as he drove by the elementary school and prepared to turn left down 150 West.

The monk sat in his wicker chair, clutching the beer can and waiting for the truck.

Joe passed Crazy Craig's and the garish sneers of its deer skull trophies. He headed up the small incline toward the bend, engine rattling hard as he accelerated.

VRRRRREEHHH!

The monk cocked his head. It was the sound he was waiting for. Heart racing, he jumped from his chair and ripped open the screen door, dashing through the yard and into the street.

The song ended and the player spat out the tape. Joe reached over to flip it but fumbled it onto the floor. "Damnit," he grumbled, fishing around for it. He traded glances between the road and the truck carpet, fingers searching for the tape.

The truck came into view around the bend. The monk's heart skipped a beat, but he held his ground. He raised the can in the air in defiance, ready to confront the beast.

Joe's finger closed around the cassette. "Gotcha bastard," he huffed, sitting up in his seat. He looked up to see a disheveled young man in dirty brown robes in the middle of the road. Their eyes locked for one terrifying second.

"Holy fuck!" Joe yelled, slamming the brakes and yanking the wheel to the right. The monk closed his eyes. There was a terrible sound as Joe skidded into the yard, missing the monk by inches and coming to a screeching halt just shy of the garden.

The monk touched his face and then his chest to see if he was still alive. He opened his eyes. The road was clear. He sighed in relief and turned toward his yard. Smoke poured from the truck next to his flowers, ratty engine still running. He dropped his arms and stared in horror.

Joe released his grip from the wheel and fell back into his seat. He took a deep breath and leaned forward to put the truck in park, then turned to look out his window. The man he almost killed hadn't moved from the road. He stared at Joe, and Joe stared back. He looked too skinny and like he needed a shower. He seemed lost and afraid.

Joe cut the engine and leaned toward the window. "You alright bud?" The man didn't answer. Joe stepped from the truck and onto the grass. "Hey buddy, you alright?" The man stared back in silence.

Joe shrugged and turned back to the truck, walking around and craning his neck to inspect it. He got to the tailgate and looked up, noticing the flowers. "Holy shit," he said to himself, "would you look at that." He took a few steps toward the garden. "These yours?" he called over his shoulder.

"Well yes, I uh," the monk stuttered from the road.

"Fuckin' beautiful, man," Joe answered, taking a step into the garden. "I always wondered."

"Hey, no, hey, don't touch it," the monk stammered, scurrying over.

"Got a little vegetable garden myself," Joe went on, stopping by a petal and running it through his fingers, "but nothing like this." The monk followed him anxiously, stumbling over words and reaching for his shoulder.

"A'course," Joe continued, "can't eat no flowers." He took a step toward the coneflower and plucked one of its petals, then turned toward the monk. "You growin' peppers out here?"

"No," replied the monk, mortified at the petal in Joe's fingers.

"Tomaters?"

"No."

"Zucchini?"

"No."

"Onions?"

"No."

"Lettuce, strawberry, watermelon—anything you can eat for Chrissake?"

"No," answered the monk, getting annoyed.

"Jesus man, anything you can use?" Joe asked incredulously.

"I, uh—"

"Tell me you're growin' weed, at the very least," Joe pleaded.

"Weeds?" asked the monk, a little confused. "They grow every-where. I can't pick them fast enough."

Joe laughed, deep and genuine in his belly with a twinkle in his eye. He slapped the monk on the back. "I like you," he said.

The monk choked, taking a second to recover from the backslap. "Well, uh, thank you, but I, uh, must ask that you—"

"What's your name anyhow?" Joe asked.

The monk stopped, surprised by the question. He furrowed his brow. "I'm not sure how to answer that," he said.

Joe gave a quizzical smile and shook his head. "The fuck you talkin' about?" he laughed.

The monk frowned, taking a step back. "I mean I don't have a name," he answered.

"Sure ya do," Joe scoffed. "Everyone's gotta name."

"Well, I do not," the monk declared.

"What do people call you then?"

"I, I don't know," the monk said. "Mr. Baker calls me a 'Mormon', everybody else–"

"Fuck him," Joe laughed. "What does your mamma call you?"

"My mamma?" the monk asked, confused.

"Yeah, you know, your family?"

The monk felt a sudden pain in his stomach. "I...I don't know," he said, looking at the ground.

Joe sensed his pain and moved on. "Well what should I call you?" he asked. The monk looked up at him. Joe could see he was lost. "What do you call yourself?"

"Nothing," he said.

"No, I mean—who are you?"

The monk thought about it for a second. "I am a Bodhisattva," he answered. "I stay here and help the others."

"The others?"

"Sentient beings are numberless. We vow to save them all," the monk recited on impulse.

"Okay," Joe chuckled, "so that means, what exactly?"

"I am a Bodhisattva," he repeated. "I stay here and help the others."

Joe sighed, shaking his head. "So what does that mean?" he asked again, exasperated.

"It means I have no name," he said. Joe stared at him, unamused. The monk stared back, wanting the conversation to end. He didn't like this man. He had violated his sanctuary twice, and his dreams even more. But he thought of his great tradition, and his sacred vow—the vow to help *all* sentient beings, no matter how distasteful they seemed.

"It means feelings, time, earth," the monk went on, "all of these are transient, all pass in an endless cycle of conflict and desire. It means I have been here for an eternity, an eternity that only ends with Nirvana, a Nirvana I delay until I can help the others reach it first."

"So, reincarnation?" Joe asked.

"I suppose."

"So you're reincarnated?"

"Well yes, I—"

"So you started as a fuckin' cockroach or something, became a rabbit, maybe a cat, worked your way up?"

"In a sense."

"And every other being in the universe, they're gonna move right past ya, and you're gonna help them do it?"

"Yes, that's my—"

"So you're enlightened, then."

"For the most part."

"And you're a Bodhisattva?"

"Yes."

"Well riddle me this then, Bodhi," Joe smirked. "If you're so goddamn enlightened, what the fuck were you doin' in the middle of the road?"

The monk frowned, taken aback. He felt the crinkled can in his hand and looked down. "You threw this in my garden," he said, lifting it up to Joe.

Joe looked at the can, then glanced up at the monk. "So let me get this straight," he said, with an incredulous face. "You went from bug to rat to cat, from shit to man to monk; you reincarnated across an infinite fabric of reality where time, feeling, and the very ground we walk on mean nothin'. And then you stood out in the middle of the fuckin' road and almost got us both killed in broad fuckin' daylight—for a, for an empty beer can?"

"Yes, I suppose I did."

"Jesus," Joe said, "doesn't that seem a tad bit insignificant to you?"

The monk could feel his anger returning. He glared at Joe. "Insignificant as it may be," he said, "it has no place in my garden."

Joe nodded his head and squinted his eyes, then broke into a sly grin. "I knew I liked you," he said. "Here, give me the can."

The monk hesitated for a second.

"Give it here."

The monk handed it to him. Joe looked at the crinkled image of the pinup girl and smiled. He turned and threw the can toward the truck. The monk watched as it sailed end over end, landing in the truck bed.

"That takes care of that," Joe said, wiping his hands. The monk looked at him, not knowing how to feel.

"Alright then Bodhi." Joe stuck out his hand for a shake. The monk looked at it, then back up at Joe. Joe waited for him to take his hand. "Alright then, *Bodhi*," Joe repeated, hand in the wind.

The monk stared at him. He wasn't sure what he wanted. He put his hands together and bowed. "Many blessings, sir," he said. Joe gave a slight shake of the head and a quizzical grin.

"Now if you'll excuse me," said the monk.

"Uh, sure man," Joe said, still puzzled. The monk bent down and started working in the garden. Joe took a couple steps toward his truck, then stopped and turned around. "You want some help?" he asked.

"No," the monk said without looking up.

"Alrighty," said Joe, waving to the flowers. He took another step then stopped and turned again. "My name's Joe, by the way."

"Goodbye Mr. Joe," the monk said to the dirt.

Joe chuckled and shook his head. He walked to his truck and climbed in. As soon as he sat down, his hangover came back. He started up the engine and drove home to sleep it off.

XIV

The sound of the truck receded, and the monk felt a great sense of relief. He continued pulling weeds to rid his mind of Joe. He thought of other work that might help him forget and realized he couldn't remember the last time he'd watered the flowers.

He shot up to grab his can but noticed something wrong from the corner of his eye. The garden was less dense in the middle, and much less colorful. "Oh no," he gasped, dread in his chest, trickling into his stomach. He scrambled to the center of the garden and fell to his knees.

The peonies had wilted, their multitudes of pink fading into one, flesh-colored death.

Tears came to his eyes as he lamented in the dirt. *Mr. Joe took this from me,* he thought. He held his face in his hands and pitied himself.

At least an hour passed before he wiped his face and prepared to stand. He opened his eyes, tear-stained and blurry, and witnessed his first miracle.

Two perfect blooms sat in the center of the peony graveyard. They were a little short, initially hidden by the dying stems and petals of the others. They were a beautiful pink, deeper than he'd ever seen. He crawled through the dirt and beheld them.

They were real, and they were here, but he didn't know how. They were well past their bloom period and should have died with the others. He cleared space for them to get more sunlight, then ran for his watering can. As he watered them, he thought of the events that had led to the miracle.

It was Mr. Joe and his beer can that had brought him outside today. Could that have been a blessing? He cringed at the thought. Besides, it was Mr. Joe and his beer can that had forced him inside in the first place, causing him to miss the last days of all the other peonies.

No, he thought, *my fear did that.* Even so, he couldn't help but dislike the old man and his ratty gray truck.

He emptied the watering can then went inside to meditate. It was dark when he finished, and his stomach roared with hunger. His thoughts were so many that he'd forgotten another meal.

XV

At work the next day, Joe thought about the monk. He stood next to his machine, watching things go by on the belt without seeing them, pressing the buttons he needed to press without thinking, preoccupied with what the monk had said about eternity. The bell rang for lunch and he didn't hear it; he just shut off his machine and headed for the stairs, wondering about Nirvana. He sat down in the break room, not hearing Don's cynical grumbles nor noticing Ray and Julie's quiet rejection. The monk and his loneliness weighed too heavily on his mind.

Work ended without Joe counting down the clock for the first time in twenty years. He walked past the old timers and their cigarettes without saying goodbye. He climbed into his truck and started the engine, pulling onto Wayne Street and wondering about the monk, his name, his family.

He got to the Taco Bell light before he knew he was driving. The smell of fried cheese and cheap meat wafted through the window and he realized he was hungry. It reminded him of the monk and how skinny he was.

"That boy hasn't ate in three, maybe four days," he said to himself. He frowned, scrunching his brow with worried eyes. He wanted to help but didn't know what to do.

The truck crossed the city limits up the hill when he had his epiphany. "The squash and onions are ready—little bastard can eat those." He smiled and turned up the radio, cruising down the road and excited to share his food with the monk.

He pulled in the driveway and parked his truck. Sadie came trotting through the yard and met him at the door. He reached down and scratched her head. "We're gonna do somethin' nice, old girl," he told her. She grinned her little cat grin, eyes closed while his fingers ran over her furry head.

He opened the door and Sadie ran to her dish. He went to the kitchen cupboard and got her food out, opening the tin and plopping the food in her bowl before heading to the back door and pushing it open. He walked to the garden and bent down to inspect the vegetables. He wanted the best for his new friend.

He ran his fingers through the onion's green blades. He stopped at the base and gently rubbed its ivory bulb. He wrapped his fingers around the bottom and pulled it out, roots tearing gently from the dirt. He looked at the onion in his calloused hand and turned it over a few times. He smiled and tossed it in the grass beside him, pulling out more onions to go with it.

After pulling five or six of them, he turned to the squash. They were pale yellow on a dark green vine, not perfect but good enough. He picked three big squash and tossed them next to the onions. He wiped the sweat from his forehead then gathered the vegetables in his arms, heading through his house and into the front yard toward his truck.

Mrs. Baker looked out her window and noticed Joe. She watched as he cradled the produce in one arm and tried opening the passenger door of his truck with the other. She turned into the kitchen and bent down near the counter, opening a cabinet drawer and fishing for a plastic grocery bag among the collection she'd saved. She pulled one out and shut the drawer with her leg, then went back to the front of the house and opened the door.

"You need some help?" she called from her porch, lifting the bag for Joe to see. Joe turned, grinning wide when he saw her.

"I think I got it, Mrs. Baker," he said. She cocked her head with a playful, disbelieving look before coming down the porch stairs and striding across the lawn. "I guess it couldn't hurt," Joe said. "Thank you," he added when she got closer.

"You're welcome," she answered as she stopped in front of him and opened the bag. "Can't have such nice veggies jostling all over the place." Joe shifted his arm and let them drop awkwardly into the bag as she held it. An onion slid against the plastic and fell to the ground; he picked it up, dusted it against his shirt, and dropped it in.

"Thank you Mrs. Baker," he said, taking the bag from her. "I really appreciate it."

"No trouble at all," she said. "Where are you going with them?"

"You know the guy down the street?" Joe asked, shrugging his shoulders toward the bend. "Kinda funny, with the flower garden?"

Mrs. Baker opened her mouth in surprise and her eyes grew wide with compassion. "That poor boy," she said in a loud, piteous whisper. "I've been worried about him."

Joe nodded. "Met him the other day," he said. "Looks like he hasn't ate in a while."

Mrs. Baker gave a short gasp with her hand over her heart.

"Yeah," Joe said.

"Wait here," Mrs. Baker cried with her hands out. She hurried back to her house. Joe put the bag down and leaned against the truck. After a few minutes she came out, running over to Joe with a hot plate in plastic wrap.

"Leftover casserole," she said, bending over and putting it in the bag on top of the produce. "Tell him I can make a fresh plate tomorrow."

Joe picked up the bag and smiled at her. "You truly are a saint, Angela Baker," he said with a grateful nod. He opened the passenger door and set the bag on the front seat, then shut the door and walked to the driver's side. She watched him with clasped hands and worried eyes. Joe started up the truck and backed out of the driveway.

"Tell him I'll make a fresh plate tomorrow!" she yelled after the truck.

Joe turned around and hit the road, easing to a stop in front of the monk's house soon after. He put the truck in park and let it idle for a while. The monk heard the rattling engine but pretended not to notice. Joe finally shut it off and opened his door, circling the truck to grab the bag. The monk opened one eye and stared from his wicker chair, watching with mounting resentment as Joe headed for the porch.

Tat, tat, tat.

Joe knocked on the screen door from the small patch of dirt at the front of the house. The monk closed his eyes tight and tried counting his first breath. Maybe he could meditate him away.

Tat, tat, tat.

Joe knocked again and waited for a few seconds. When no answer came, he peered through the screen and looked around the porch, noticing the monk in a chair. It looked like he was pretending to sleep.

"Hey Bodhi," he called through the screen.

The monk acted like he couldn't hear, counting his second breath in his head.

"Hey *Bodhi!*" Joe shouted.

The monk cringed. He turned his head toward the door, opening his eyes. "Greetings, Mr. Joe," he said.

"Hey man, I, uh," Joe started, feeling awkward now, "brought you somethin'." He lifted the bag for the monk to see. The monk stared back with a blank expression. "It's uh, it's food," Joe offered, raising the bag a little higher and toward the window. "I thought you might like some." He lowered the bag and waited for the monk's reply.

"Many blessings," said the monk, still upset from the day before, "but I've already eaten." His stomach rumbled against his bones, and even Joe could hear it from where he stood.

"Sure," Joe said with a sarcastic nod.

"Truly," said the monk, trying to mask his hunger.

Joe stared at him, marveling at his resolve while feeling annoyed by it. "Well regardless," he said, shaking his head, "there's some good stuff in here." He opened the bag a little wider and peered into it. "Some onions, some squash…"

"Mr. Joe, I—"

"Some casserole…"

"Casserole?" The monk sat up in his chair.

"Yeah," Joe replied, "Mrs. Baker sent me with it."

"Mrs. Baker?" the monk asked, leaning forward with wide eyes.

"Yeah, but I'll just tell her you weren't hungry." Joe turned and took a step toward the truck.

"Wait!" shouted the monk, getting up from his chair. Joe turned around. The two watched each other through the screen for a while.

"Come in," the monk finally sighed, defeated. Joe opened the door and stepped onto the spongy green turf. "Excuse me for a second," said the monk, walking into the house. Joe set the bag down on the floor and looked around. The monk came back a few seconds later with his alms bowl and Tibetan spoon. He sat down near the bag and leaned forward to rummage through it, leaving his visitor standing.

Joe observed him curiously. "There's a chair over there," he said, motioning toward the wicker.

"Strictly for meditation," answered the monk, pulling out an onion.

"Ahh," Joe said with a tinge of sarcasm.

The monk inspected the onion in the waning sunlight, turning his hand back and forth. "Please excuse me," he said, "I do not normally accept the alms in front of others."

"Of course," Joe said with a little more sarcasm.

The monk placed the onion at his feet and lowered his hands to his knees. He closed his eyes and bowed his head. "First, let us reflect on our own work and the effort of those who brought us this food," he said quietly. Joe watched as he mused, then with gratitude in his face he mouthed the words, "I am thankful for Mrs. Baker." He paused, struggling with what to say next. He opened one eye and glanced over at Joe, then begrudgingly added, "I am thankful for Mr. Joe." Joe cocked his head back and smiled. The monk recited a few more lines, then finished by saying, "in order to continue our practice for all beings, we accept this offering." He opened his eyes and grabbed the onion. He sat back in delight and studied it for a second, then took a bite.

"Ooof, buddy," Joe cringed. The monk didn't hear him. He took another bite, then another, indifferent to the sharp sting of raw onion.

"Why don't you try the casserole?" Joe suggested.

"Yes," exclaimed the monk, pointing a finger toward Joe while still holding the onion, "the casserole." He put the onion down and bent over his folded legs to search through the plastic bag. He found the plate and slid it out. He removed the plastic wrap and picked up the plate with his left hand, holding it over the alms bowl and grabbing the Tibetan spoon with his right. He started to scrape the food into the bowl then stopped, remembering the words of the Buddha: "Desire cannot master a man who is self-controlled in his senses, moderate in eating, resolute and full of faith, like the wind cannot move a mountain crag."

Joe watched him pause with food in midair, closing his eyes and reciting more blessings, thank-yous, and devotions. When he finally opened his eyes and scraped the food into the bowl, he did so with care, and when he picked up the bowl and began to eat, he ate slowly. Joe noticed the simple pleasure the monk took with each bite.

"Good stuff, huh?" he said.

"Yes," the monk nodded with his eyes closed, "the best." Joe watched him finish the casserole and put the spoon in the empty bowl, then rest his hands on his knees and take a big, contented sigh.

"You know," Joe said after a while, "she's worried about you."

The monk opened his eyes and looked at Joe. "Mrs. Baker?" he asked, a slight tremor in his voice.

"Yeah."

"She is good," said the monk, nodding slowly then turning his sad eyes to the floor. "I don't like it when she worries."

Joe saw his pain and felt sympathetic. "She worries a lot," Joe offered, trying to make him feel better. "I wouldn't think too long on it." The monk kept his gaze on the floor. "That garden of yours is pretty cool," Joe fumbled, trying to change the subject. "What all flowers you got?"

The monk looked up at him. He was still processing how he felt about the peonies. "I appreciate the food," he said, "I really do. But please do not insult me."

"What? No man, I'm serious," Joe insisted.

The monk studied his face. He felt an urge to yell at Joe, to accuse him of ruining his garden, even though he knew that wasn't entirely true. "Look, Mr. Joe," he began, throat clinching with anger. Joe opened his smiling eyes a little wider, and the monk saw something sincere in them. It made him stop.

Holding onto anger is like grasping a hot coal with the intent of throwing it at someone else; you are the one who gets burned. Accept what is, let go of what was, and have faith in what will be.

"I, uh, what would you like to know about my garden?" the monk asked awkwardly, doing his best to soften his tone. He'd bring up the peonies another time. There was the path of the Bodhisattva to consider, for one; and besides, Joe wasn't that bad—he had brought the monk his first meal in days and some goodwill from Mrs. Baker, after all. And if what the monk witnessed yesterday really was a miracle, he didn't feel comfortable enough with Joe to explain it, even if he was starting to realize the man wasn't altogether terrible.

"What all flowers you got?" Joe asked again.

"Oh, yes. Well, let's see here..." The monk was guarded at first, like a kid that got picked on at school and didn't quite know what to say. But Joe asked good questions, and the more the monk talked about black-eyed Susans and coneflower and sedum, the more excited he became.

"Then in September the hibiscus will bloom, right next to the white asters and pink lilies," he concluded with a smile. "It's hard work, but it brings me peace." He looked at Joe from where he sat. Joe smiled at him. The monk was more comfortable with Joe now but stared a little too long and felt foolish at the sincerity of the moment. "Well," he grinned, averting his eyes to the floor and standing up, "I need to pull the weeds."

"Need some help?" Joe asked, ignoring the cue to leave.

"Thank you, but I—"

"I ain't got nothin' to do," said Joe.

"Well..."

Joe stood up. "C'mon man," he grinned, slapping the monk on the shoulder, "let's pull some weeds."

"Alright," the monk sighed, "thank you." He pushed the screen open and walked outside to the edge of the garden. Joe followed him, stopping about halfway across the yard. The monk bent down and grabbed his watering can, then turned and headed toward Joe.

"Would you please fill this up?" he asked, pushing it into Joe's unsuspecting gut.

"Where at?" Joe asked, grabbing the can.

"The kitchen sink," answered the monk, turning to the garden to go pick the weeds. Joe shrugged and headed for the front door. He didn't know where the kitchen was, but he figured the house was small enough for him to find it.

When his eyes finally adjusted to the darkness of the house, he realized it was even smaller than he'd imagined. He walked across the living room and into the kitchen in just a few steps, but not without banging his lower shin on the coffee table. He rubbed his leg and looked around.

"No fridge, no stove, nothin'," he said to himself. He went over to the sink and put the can in the basin, then pushed the handle. The water flowed from the spout and echoed against the bottom of the can, the sound of it getting higher and higher until the can was full. The water sloshed around as he pulled the can from the sink and headed to the living room.

He noticed a door halfway open to his right. He stopped and took a step toward it, then peered inside. There was a mattress on a box spring and that was it.

"Jesus," he muttered, turning around and heading for the front door, "thought *I* had it rough." He opened the door, crossed over the porch, and stepped outside.

The monk was sweating and pulling weeds near the two peonies. He sprang up when he heard Joe, hurrying to meet him at the edge of the garden.

"Thank you, Mr. Joe," the monk said, doing his best to act normal.

Joe squatted down near a patch of violet flowers, seeming not to notice. "It's just Joe," he said, reaching for a cluster of weeds, "no Mr."

"Oh," said the monk, a little surprised. "Well, thank you...*Joe.*"

"No problem brother," he answered, hand clasped around a big weed. His forearm bulged as he pulled, and there was a little tear as the roots broke and the dirt shook from the plant. He tossed it in a nearby pile the monk had started.

"While we're on the subject," Joe said, grabbing another handful and spitting into the dirt, "what am I supposed to call you?"

The monk worked for a bit longer, looking into the dirt and feeling the sun on the back of his neck. "I told you yesterday. I don't have a name."

Joe ripped another weed from the ground and threw it on the pile, then sat up to look at the monk. "Why not?" he asked.

"Names mean nothing to the void," he replied, sweat dropping from his face to his hand as he uprooted a thistle.

"So one name's just as good as the next?" Joe asked.

"Or just as bad," said the monk. "Names don't mean anything."

Joe chuckled. "So I could call you Mr. Shithead and that'd be the same as, say…Kevin?"

"Well, no," the monk frowned, taken aback, "that's not what I meant."

"What do you mean then?"

The monk sat up. "What I mean to say is that names take what may not be there and make it there, or what may be there and put it somewhere else. The name makes the thing become something it is not."

Joe cocked his head and rested it on his closed hand, thinking. "What's that over there?" he asked.

"Where?" asked the monk, looking around.

"There, that thing with the sunfire buds," Joe pointed.

"That's the butterfly weed," the monk answered.

"And what's that over there?" Joe asked, pointing to a flower with deep blue petals.

"That's the blue iris."

"Are they the same thing?" Joe asked.

"Well, no."

"But both beautiful, right? Both beautiful flowers."

"Yes, but you recognized their beauty before knowing what they were called," the monk replied.

Joe smiled. "I knew I liked you," he said.

The monk smiled too. "Thank you, Joe." He got up and grabbed the watering can, tipping it over the rows. Joe crawled to another patch of weeds and started pulling them. The two worked in silence.

"If you must call me something," the monk offered after a few minutes, "call me Bodhi." Joe stopped and looked at him. "You called me that before," the monk said. "I think I like it."

Joe nodded, then turned back to the flowers and emptied the can.

"Yes, I'll be Bodhi," the monk said to himself.

"It's a lot better than Mr. Shithead," Joe laughed.

"Or Kevin, for that matter," the monk said with a grin.

………..…

Joe picked weeds and Bodhi went back and forth filling the watering can, careful to keep Joe away from the peonies. Night fell and the mosquitoes came out.

"Well Bodhi," Joe said, slapping his forearm to stop the bite, "I got work in the mornin'."

Bodhi stood up. "These things are bad, aren't they?" he said, wiping the sweat off his brow and swiping at his legs, careful not to hurt the mosquitoes. He followed Joe to his truck, watching him climb in.

Joe turned the key. "Be back tomorrow," he hollered over the engine. "Mrs. Baker said she'll have a fresh batch." He shifted into drive and onto the road. "Take it easy Bodhi," he called through the window.

Bodhi smiled and waved humbly. He watched as the truck sped off and around the bend, pondering eternity and whether he could truly name it.

The way is inconceivable, he thought, remembering the fourth and last Vow of the Bodhisattva. *We vow to attain it.*

XVI

Joe turned right at Taco Bell and pulled into the drive-through line. He waited a few minutes in the hot sun for his turn. He crept up to the big menu, scanning over the pictures until the tinny voice of a teenager crackled through the speaker box.

"Welcome to Taco Bell how can I help you."

"Hey, yeah, can I get uhh…" Joe started, looking over the menu. "Let me get a chalupa box and some cheesy potatoes," he said, shifting in his seat and feeling satisfied.

"Any sauce with that sir."

"Fire please."

"Second window."

Joe pulled around. After a few minutes the window flew open and a high schooler handed him a bag of food.

"Thank you sir."

"Thank *you*," Joe said, speeding from the drive and down the road.

Mrs. Baker heard the tires over the gravel and the old truck engine die when Joe turned the key. She ran to her window, touching her chest when he stepped out of his vehicle.

"He's here!" she cried, running back to the kitchen. She checked the timer on the stove, reaching for the knob and turning it down.

"Pretty much done," she said to herself. "We'll let it broil for a bit." She opened the drawer to get some Saran Wrap and turned toward the cupboard for a plate.

Sadie came trotting through the grass and up to Joe's leg when he reached the door.

"Sadie ol' girl," he cooed, scratching her head. The two went inside and Joe fed her, scratching her back as she ate. He stood up and watched her for a while, grinning and listening to her purr. He backed away before she noticed he was already leaving her, then turned to go outside. He was still on the porch when the Bakers' screen door slapped shut and Angela came bustling into the yard.

"Hey Mrs. Baker," he called, stepping into the grass.

"Joe," she cried, "I'm so glad you're home." She handed him the hot plate of casserole. "Now, be sure you tell him it's fresh," she said, one hand still on the plate.

"Don't you worry Mrs. Baker," he said, smiling as he took it from her. "I'm sure he'll like it."

She nodded with a half-smile, exhaling softly through her nose. "Thank you, Joe," she said.

He turned and walked to the truck, opening the passenger door and putting the fresh casserole next to his bag of Taco Bell. He was excited to share a meal with his new friend.

Bodhi was meditating on the porch when he heard the truck pull into the yard. He opened one eye, half contemplating the universe and half watching Joe climb out of his truck with a plate and a paper bag. He closed his eye, said a quick incantation, and stood up to greet him.

"Hey there Bodhi," Joe called.

"Hello Joe," Bodhi grinned from the dirt patch just outside his door.

"Got somethin' for ya," Joe said, handing him the plate of casserole. Bodhi looked down to see his favorite meal through the hot, foggy wrap. "Musta pulled it out right before she gave it to me," Joe added.

Bodhi turned and opened the door, leaving it cracked for Joe to get through. "I need to walk over there and thank her," he said.

Bodhi had brought out the coffee table and the mahogany chair for Joe to sit. There were two glasses of tap water spaced apart with Bodhi's bowl and spoon sitting next to one of them. He motioned to the table. Joe bent over and put the bag on it and sat down in the chair. Bodhi put his plate next to him and crossed his legs to sit on the floor. He unwrapped the casserole and slid it into the bowl, then bowed his head and said his gratitudes. "I am thankful for the saintly Mrs. Baker," he said quietly, "and of course, for Joe." He said it with a little resistance, but not as much as yesterday. Joe grinned and unwrapped his meal. The two ate slowly out of respect for one another.

Joe noticed Bodhi looking at him every few seconds. He'd take a bite of the casserole and peer over Joe's hands to see what he was eating.

"What are you lookin' at?" Joe finally asked, leaning back in his chair with his hands turned open.

"Nothing, nothing," Bodhi said, looking away. Joe went back to eating and Bodhi turned again to look. "It's just," he said, "what is that?"

Joe put his chalupa down on the paper next to his plastic bowl of cheesy potatoes. "What?"

"That," Bodhi said, pointing at Joe's meal.

Joe cocked his head and grinned. "You mean, you ain't never had Taco Bell before?" he asked.

"Definitely not," Bodhi answered.

Joe picked up his bowl of cheesy potatoes. "Here," he offered, leaning toward him, "try some."

"No, thank you," Bodhi said, "that's quite alright."

Joe pushed it a little closer. "Nah," he said, "have some."

Bodhi looked at the bright yellow cheese and the white sour cream over the potatoes. Nothing about it looked natural. He wrinkled his nose. "Okay," he said, already doubting his decision, "thank you." He scooped some up with his Tibetan spoon and put it in his mouth. The warm cheese and sour cream melded on his tongue. "It's alright," he said, working the flavor around in his mouth before swallowing. "I like it."

"See?" Joe smiled. Bodhi smiled back.

They ate the rest of their meal in silence, enjoying each other's company.

XVII

The sky was black with green stars. Bodhi looked down and across the plane.

In the distance, a gray blur stormed through the dark. There was a sound blowing through the ether and this time he knew what it was. Instead of turning and running, he waited for it, even though his heart was pounding. The headlights shone on him and he lifted his hands over his eyes.

The truck screeched to a stop next to him. After a few seconds he put his hands down and looked through the driver's side window. Joe grinned at him with his long graying hair and his Old Milwaukee hat. Bodhi took a few steps then stopped. Joe leaned into the open window.

"Hey buddy," he said, "get in."

………..

Bodhi finished his blessing then reached into the old grocery bag. He grabbed Joe's squash, gave a slight bow and raised it in the air, then bit into it like a banana. It was bitter, but he liked it. He set it down on his knee and gazed upon the lake.

He heard a low rumble and watched Joe pull into the yard. He used to cringe but now he smiled. Joe came up to the door; usually, he had some food or a new, sobering thought, but today he came empty-handed, banging on the screen.

Bodhi got up and went to him. "Hey Joe," he said through the mesh, "is everything okay?"

"It's Sadie," Joe said with fretful eyes. "I can't find her anywhere."

"Sadie?" Bodhi asked, a little confused.

"My cat," Joe answered, "my little tabby girl—I can't find her any-where."

Bodhi saw the fear in his face and felt sympathetic. "Joe, I…" he said. "I'm sure she's around here somewhere."

"She always comes home," Joe said, voice full of worry, "but it's been at least a day, maybe two." A heavy feeling settled over Bodhi's heart. In the short time he'd known him, Joe was a lot of things, but he was never scared.

"I'll help you look," Bodhi said. Joe took a step back from the door and Bodhi came out. "Where was the last place you saw her?"

Joe shook his head with a half shrug and his mouth partway open. "I, I don't know," he replied. "I let her out in the mornin' and she always comes back when I get home."

"Alright," Bodhi said, "she couldn't have gotten far." The two left the yard and went down to the beach. There was a cluster of peppermint bushes near the corner of the sand by the lily pads. Bodhi reached down and parted them with his hands to see the dirt underneath. The fresh mint hit his nose but there was no cat. They combed the green areas down the beach, calling her name and going "tht-tht-tht" with their teeth until they ended up behind Crazy Craig's. Craig saw them from his sliding glass door. There was the sound of it rolling against the frame and the two turned to see Craig standing on his deck in nothing but a velvet blue robe.

"Can I help you boys?" he called.

"Sorry Craig," Joe hollered with one hand up, "just lookin' for Sadie."

"Ahh," Craig answered, nodding in commiseration.

"Have you seen her?" Bodhi asked.

Craig looked into the sky, squinting his eyes and pursing his lips like he was thinking about it. "No, no I haven't," he answered. He paused for a few seconds then looked down at them. "Hey, I ever told ya'll how to make a sparkler bomb?"

They walked through the trees bordering Craig's yard and into the street. They went through the neighborhood calling for Sadie, the sinking feeling of a pet lost pulling their nervous hearts lower and lower into their stomachs.

After a few laps they came back to Bodhi's house. They were ready to give up, and Bodhi prepared to say, "she'll come back sooner or later," when he realized the one place they hadn't looked. "There's a patch of trees behind my house—maybe she's there."

The two of them walked to the side opposite the flower garden and around the house. The back wall was streaked with faded dirt and rain spots. A wild sea of tall grass ran from a few feet up the wall and back into a thicket of trees.

"Jesus Christ man," Joe said. Bodhi ignored him and they waded through the grass, stopping at the mess of thorns that marked the edge of the thicket.

"You ain't got no shoes on," Joe observed.

"The better to feel the earth with," Bodhi replied. He stepped into the bramble and struggled through, the thorns cutting his legs and the underside of his feet until he found the leafy dirt on the other side. Joe laughed in amazement then stepped onto the mess with his big, heavy boots, the bramble crunching under his feet.

"Shoulda let me go first," he said.

"Shh, listen," Bodhi whispered, standing still. "Do you hear it?"

"Hear what?"

"Shh!"

The two stood in silence until the faint cry of a little animal reached their ears.

"This way," Bodhi whispered. The two fought through tree branches and thick, needling shrubs, weak cries growing louder until they pinpointed them under a dark wall of thorns. The little animal cried out in quick, pitiful bursts of suffering. Bodhi bent to the ground, knees and hands on the dirt. Sadie was propped on her side against the trunk of a wild bush, scared and barely visible in the dark. Her left paw seemed crooked and Bodhi saw blood in her fur.

"There she is," he whispered to the plants. "She looks hurt."

"Sadie!" Joe shouted, taking a nervous step and crushing the viny wall. The cat pushed her ruffled body against the bush and hissed.

"Stop!" Bodhi yelled. Joe looked down at him. "She's scared," Bodhi cautioned. "We need to be gentle." Joe nodded and stepped back. Bodhi pushed his stomach to the ground and started crawling through the dirt.

"Here, kitty kitty," he called, "here kitty." Sadie growled quietly in her belly and pushed further against the bush. "Aww, it's alright," he cooed, "it's okay." He crawled further into the brush and reached with his hand, wiggling his finger to signal it was okay. The cat glared with suspicion, then leaned forward to sniff it out. Bodhi worked his hand closer until Sadie let him scratch her side.

"There we go," he soothed, "it's okay." He rubbed his finger against her coat until she was comfortable, then reached his whole hand in and placed it on her side. He felt her purr rumble against his palm, then heard it in his ears.

"There we go," he said again. He pressed his stomach to the ground, working his other arm through the dirt until both hands were around the cat. "Come on now," he cooed, tugging gently, "come on."

He dragged her softly, Sadie making him do all the work as she went limp against the dirt. He got her to the edge of the foliage then scooped her up from the thorns.

"Got her," he said to Joe, wriggling her body as he stood up. The cat squirmed for a bit, calming down when he pulled her close to his chest.

"That's a good girl," Joe cried, scratching her head through Bodhi's arms. She wiggled deeper into Bodhi's chest, then turned to look up at him. Bodhi and Sadie locked eyes and the cat's pupils grew wide and glassy. For a moment Bodhi stared into them, wondering about reincarnation as he felt their souls connect. He shifted her in his arms and looked away. The little cat was too much for him.

"We need to get her home," he said. "She's been hurt."

"Let me get the truck." Joe jogged over and climbed into the vehicle. Bodhi came around the corner of the house, holding Sadie and feeling nervous.

"Come on man, get in," Joe called through the window. Bodhi hesitated. He had had too many nightmares to go anywhere near the truck.

"Let's go man!" Joe yelled.

Bodhi looked down at the poor creature in his arms. He closed his eyes and took a deep breath. "I'm coming," he said. Joe leaned over the seat and popped the passenger door open. Bodhi got in and they sped off, the cat lying between the two men like a little princess. She looked up at her savior and purred the whole way home.

…………

When they got back to Joe's, they nursed the cat as best they could, then fed her and watched her eat.

"I think she will heal," Bodhi said.

"Just look at her eat," Joe exclaimed. "Looks like you with a plate of casserole."

"She's been fasting," Bodhi replied. "She's been scared and alone."

Joe leaned forward in the kitchen chair, arms on his knees. "I just don't get it," he said, shaking his head. "She always comes back after work."

"You let her out and she got hurt," Bodhi answered. "Maybe she should stay inside." Joe looked over and saw the pain in Bodhi's eyes. He sensed there was more to Bodhi's words than simple concern for a cat.

"Welp," Joe grunted, slapping his knees and standing up, "we'll figure it out." He walked over to the fridge and pulled it open. "Wanna beer?"

Bodhi turned in his chair. "A beer?" he asked.

"Yeah man," Joe answered, halfway in the fridge, "a beer, a brew, somethin' to take the edge off."

"I, uh…"

"Here man," Joe said, turning and tossing a can as he shut the fridge.

"Hey!" Bodhi yelped in surprise, fumbling it for a second before it fell squarely in his hands. He turned it over and his eyes fell on the pinup girl. A sudden ache hit his chest. "I, I don't think so," he stammered, growing anxious. "I don't think I like this one." He offered it back to Joe.

"Ffff," Joe chortled, waving it away. "Try it."

Bodhi looked back at the can. The pinup girl smiled at him. "Alright," he conceded. He went to open it but his finger kept slipping, the tab making a *tik, tik, tik* sound against the top of the can.

"Need some help?" Joe laughed.

Bodhi turned his shoulder away from him. "I've got it," he said, feeling defensive. The tab clicked under his finger a few more times before he finally caught it and cracked open the beer. A little vapor poured out and a bready bitterness hit his nose.

"Hell yeah brother," Joe said, immediately opening a beer of his own. Some foam gushed over the top as he clanked his can against Bodhi's. He threw it back without thinking. Bodhi looked at his can.

"It ain't gonna drink itself," Joe choked, heart burning.

Bodhi looked at him, then back at the can. He shrugged. "You only lose what you cling to," he said, taking a sip. It was bitter, skunky, a little sweet, and its carbonation burned as he swallowed. He shuddered, almost gagging.

"I remember my first beer," Joe laughed.

Bodhi smacked his lips softly and worked his tongue around his mouth. He didn't like it all that much, but the aftertaste left a compelling imprint on his mouth. He took another drink. It went down easier. He looked over at Joe. "Is this what you do for enjoyment?"

Joe gave him a quizzical look. "You mean, for fun?"

Bodhi shrugged.

Joe took another swig and sat down. "Well," he said, leaning back, "I suppose most of the time I'm enjoyin' myself, there's a beer in my hand or somewhere close by."

Bodhi frowned. "So this is all you do?"

"Well no," Joe answered, "most of the time I'm workin'." He tilted the side of the can toward him like he was reading it. "And when I'm not workin', I'm havin' fun. I just tend to be drinkin' while I'm doing it."

"Fun—like what?" Bodhi asked.

Joe smiled wide, and the rough skin cracked over his face. "You know, like goin' to parties, seein' a movie, bowling for Chrissake."

"Bowling?"

"Bowling, goin' to a ballgame, playin' cornhole—fuck man." Joe could tell Bodhi was confused. He blew his breath against his teeth and shook his head. "What do you do for fun?" he finally asked. Bodhi looked down at the mouth of his beer.

"Craving pleasure for yourself causes pain to others," he recited into the can.

"Shiiit," said Joe. Bodhi looked up. He could see the joy in his friend's face. Joe tilted his head back and killed his beer, then crushed it in his hand. "Somewhere I read, somewhere somebody said, 'be a light unto yourself.' That's what I remember." Joe stood up, and Bodhi could see the power in his big body. He started to think there was a little wisdom in it too.

Joe opened the fridge and grabbed two more beers, tossing one to Bodhi. He cracked open his and took a long, cold drink.

XVIII

August is the hottest month of the year, even while the days get shorter on their long, slow march to fall. Back to school sales hit the department stores, football teams and marching bands sweat on the field well into twilight, and while the kids dread the inevitable first day of school, the adults look forward to cooler days. It's a time of change, painful for some, but good for most.

Bodhi was changing too. He was getting out of the house more, even going on small trips with Joe. On one of these trips he found himself in the Marathon station, holding a bag of ice while Joe chatted with Mandy about the price of gas.

"Can't believe it went up twenty cents!" Joe exclaimed.

"Oh I know," Mandy said, "had me out at six this mornin', holdin' that stick and changin' the numbers."

"Is that right?" Joe replied, sliding his change into his pocket.

"Yep, yep," said Mandy. She turned and looked at Bodhi. "I don't remember seein' you in here before. What's your name?" Bodhi saw her pretty eyes and her sweet country smile and began to stutter.

"That's Bodhi," Joe answered, "lives down the street from me."

"Please to meet ya," Mandy grinned. "I like your robes."

Bodhi blushed and looked at the floor. "Thank you," he muttered.

Mandy drummed on the countertop and turned her attention back to Joe. "Well, take it easy," she said.

"You too," he answered. He turned and slapped Bodhi on the shoulder, and the bell chimed as the door shut behind them.

"Somebody's gotta crush," Joe chided as they walked to the truck. Bodhi didn't know the term but was able to figure it out.

"I do not!" he cried, placing the bag of ice in the tail bed. He noticed a bucket of baseballs, a wooden bat, and a couple of mitts back there. "What are these?" he asked.

"You'll see," Joe grinned. The two climbed in the truck and sat down on either side of Sadie in the middle seat. She raised her head toward Bodhi and bunted against his left arm until he gave her a scratch.

Joe started the engine and pulled out of the gas station. Bodhi noticed he turned toward the elementary school, which took a little longer to get home when leaving the Marathon. He didn't think much of it until they crossed 150 West, missing the route by Craig and his deer heads. He looked around and through the windows like a dog realizing he was going to the vet.

"Um, where are we…?"

"To the ball diamond," Joe answered with a smile.

Joe passed the fire station just west of town and pulled into the gravel lot at the edge of the baseball field. He shut off the truck and kicked open the door, circling back to the tailgate.

"What are we…?"

"Here," Joe said, throwing a baseball glove at him. Bodhi let out a stilted "oof" when it hit his chest. Joe put his glove in the bucket and hoisted it from the truck bed, then grabbed the bat with his other hand and headed toward the field. Sadie leapt from the truck and onto the gravel, stretching her hind legs.

"Beautiful day for some baseball," Joe said. Bodhi followed him into the dugout. Sunflower shells lay across the concrete floor and under the players' bench, games of tic-tac-toe and schoolyard vows like "I Love Stacey Budd" carved deep into the wood. Joe popped the end of the bat against the dugout wall and walked onto the field.

The infield was a thin pit of sand. The outfield was like a well-kept, Midwestern lawn—mostly green grass with a few weeds and dandelions. Joe put the bucket and bat down by home plate and grabbed his glove, then pointed toward the pitcher's mound. Bodhi put his hand into his own glove and took a step onto the sand. The smell of old leather hit his nose. It was oddly familiar.

"Let's warm up," Joe said. Bodhi walked out to the mound and turned toward his friend. Joe bent down and put his fingers around an old baseball. Sadie trotted into the grass like a veteran outfielder.

"I'm gonna throw it to ya," Joe said. "Open your mitt and use two hands." Joe reached back and lobbed a slow pitch to Bodhi. Bodhi took an impulsive step back, as if afraid of the ball, but something happened on its way there. He repositioned his feet, opened his mitt, and caught the ball. He bobbled it a little but caught it nonetheless.

"Nice work buddy!" Joe shouted. Bodhi looked down at the glove in his hand. The smell of the game, the infield dirt under his feet, the stark red stitches on an off-white baseball—he'd done this before.

"Musta been a ballplayer in your past life," Joe chuckled.

"Yeah," Bodhi said to his mitt. It felt more recent than that. He picked up the ball and threw it to Joe, but it landed in the dirt by his foot.

"Junior varsity, then," Joe quipped, bending down to grab the ball. The two played catch for five minutes or so, Bodhi growing confident and his movements becoming sharper.

After they'd warmed up, Joe tossed the ball back to Bodhi and threw his glove in the sand. He grabbed the bat and took a few practice swings before digging into the batters' box. "Throw it right here," he said, holding the bat over the plate.

"What if you hit it back at me?" Bodhi fretted. "It will hurt."

"I'll hit it over there," Joe grinned, pointing past the fence and to the woods. "Now c'mon," he said, lowering the bat and pumping it over the plate a few times, "don't be a bitch."

Bodhi shook his head and pushed an angry sigh through his nose. He thought about throwing the ball at Joe's head for a moment, then realized things like that are generally frowned upon in Buddhism. He took a deep breath and focused on the spot where Joe wanted the ball to be thrown. He wound up and released the ball.

There was a perfect "crack!" as the ball hit the wood of the bat. Bodhi turned and watched it sail over his head, landing just shy of the woods. The sound rang in his ears. It was sweet, familiar, and it sounded like the *om*.

"Now that's how you hit a baseball!" Joe yelled. Bodhi smiled. He reached into the bucket of balls and threw him another.

Crack!

The ball flew over the fence, but not quite as far as the first. The two laughed as they played, Bodhi throwing pitch after pitch until Joe got tired.

"Alright buddy," he said, dropping the bat and wiping the sweat off his forehead, "you're up." They traded places and Bodhi picked up the bat, digging into the batter's box and doing his best to imitate Joe's powerful stance.

"Here comes the ol' heater," Joe joked. He reared back and threw the ball. Bodhi swung as hard as he could, missing the ball by at least a foot before the bat flew out of his hands and crashed against the dugout fence on the third base side. Sadie shot away from the sound like a nervous, feline rocket. Joe burst out laughing. Bodhi shook his head and walked with his head down to retrieve the bat.

"Okay, okay," Joe chuckled, hands on his knees and trying to stifle his laughter, "let's try this again." Bodhi trudged back to the batter's box and dug in. He gripped the bat so hard his knuckles turned white, determined not to throw it again. The pitch came in, and he swung.

The ball squibbed off the end of the bat, rolling into the dirt. It stung his hands. "Ow," Bodhi said to himself, dropping the bat and looking down at the handle.

"Loosen up a bit," Joe called from the mound, "and keep your weight back." A wave of déjà vu washed over Bodhi. He looked up at Joe, half expecting to see someone else on the mound. He dropped his eyes to the bat, gazing over its smooth, light grains. He knew Joe was right, and somehow, from somewhere far away, he remembered that the power in a good swing came from the legs. He kicked some sand and set his feet in the box.

KROK!

A towering fly ball came off the bat and over Joe's head, hanging in the air for what seemed like eternity before plopping just shy of the fence.

"Alright buddy!" Joe exclaimed. Bodhi grinned and dug back into the box. He was proud of himself—but he didn't get all of it, and he knew he could do better. All he had to do was rotate his hips a little more and keep his front shoulder down. He wasn't sure how he knew, but he knew.

CRACK!

Bodhi smoked a deep line drive through the air and over the fence.

"Holy shit!" Joe cried, watching it go, "now I *know* you've done this before."

"Yeah," Bodhi said, smiling, "me too." He kept his left hand on the handle and slid his right under the barrel, staring at the bat. He could smell the grains on the bat, the leather on the ball as it popped against the glove, the sunflower seeds on the ground and the buttered popcorn in the stands. He could see the shadows on the grass as the sun went down over the field, the pitcher's glare and his own spit turn dark in the sand in front of the batter's box. He could hear the announcer through the tinny speaker, the fans yelling and his teammates cheering from the bench. He turned toward the dugout and saw one of his teammates, sitting back from the rest and beaming with pride. Bodhi looked into his eyes, and for a second he knew him.

Two kids came shrieking down the road, snapping him from his reverie. Big sister and little brother saw Joe and Bodhi from their bikes and turned toward the field.

"Hey Mr. Joe!" they cried in unison as they shot down the small, grassy hill behind the third base dugout. "Can we play?" They were now off their bikes and to the fence, faces pressed up against it and their fingers gripping the wire.

"Sure," Joe cried, "always happy to see two little sluggers excited about the game." Bodhi looked at him in protest. The two kids raced through the dugout and to the batter's box, pawing at Bodhi's robe to get to the bat. Bodhi held it high over his head. He wasn't ready to relinquish his daydream.

"Aww," Joe said, "let 'em play."

"But," Bodhi began. He looked at the kids jumping up and down, little hands miles away from the bat. He saw their eyes, and he knew their happiness in the present was more important than a memory in his head.

"Here." He smiled reluctantly, handing the bat to big sister. "She gets to go first."

"No fair!" cried the boy.

"Come on," Bodhi said, bending his knees, "I'll race you to the outfield." Like any kid, little brother couldn't turn down a challenge. He turned and sprinted toward the grass, Bodhi trailing behind in his clumsy, brown-robed stride. Sadie saw them coming and bolted away in frantic, catlike circles.

Joe pitched to the kids, and Bodhi ran after their little grounders in the grass. Their laughter echoed from midday to twilight.

"One more swing, one more swing!" little brother cried.

The sun was setting. Bodhi gazed over the field. He felt good but there was something missing.

"It's right here," he said to himself, "I, I can feel it—I try to touch it and it's gone." The streetlights came on, and the kids got on their bikes. Sadie, Joe, and Bodhi hopped in the truck and went home.

XIX

Joe came to the screen and balled his fist to knock. He saw Bodhi meditating and lowered his hand, studying him for a moment. His brow was furrowed and there were sharp wrinkles around his eyes. He looked like he was trying to rid a thought by closing his eyes real tight.

Joe turned and took a few quiet steps, looking around for something to do. He cocked his head and stared out onto the lake, pretending he was deep in thought. A few of Bodhi's neighbors passed by and he acted like he didn't see them. After a few minutes he scratched his head and walked over to the flower garden. A man can't look awkward if he's working.

Many of the midsummer flowers had wilted, but the blooms of late summer were doing well. He knelt under a patch of gold petals and began to pull the weeds.

Bodhi stood next to the ghostly tire swing, its green fire blazing in the dark. He reached for the rope, slowly extending his hand to test the heat, but a mad impulse overcame him and he snatched it in his fingers. It didn't burn him; in fact, the fire receded from the rope and rubber, leaving each with their frayed yellow and black colors. He inspected the rope in his hands, then put one foot into the bottom curve of the tire. He shifted his weight to his back foot, still on the floor of the void, then with a rush of glee pushed his weight forward and jumped on. He laughed as he swung back and forth in the cosmos.

The swing took him higher and higher, as if some cosmic hand pushed the tire, and he soon realized he'd lost control. The rope cut into his palms as he gripped it tighter, euphoria turning to nausea. He swung down hard from the rope's zenith and back to the cosmic hand, and there was one last push that sent him flying off the swing and

104

landing on his back. He lay there for a few terrifying seconds, unable to breathe, when a voice cried out to him in the dark.

"…" it said, calling him by name, "remember?" He recognized it from previous dreams.

"…" it insisted, "remember?" He tried to sit up, but the nausea clenched his stomach, pulling him into the blackness. He struggled against it, seeing a dying glimpse of the swing, the tree, and a new image behind them: an old country house with faded paint, tall windows, and a big summer porch. It all disappeared and the darkness swallowed him whole.

Joe lost track of time and had worked his way to the center of the garden. He wrapped his bare hands around a group of weeds and tore them from the dirt, then threw them down and parted the last row of flower stems.

"Holy shit."

The two peonies appeared before him. They were perfect in their beauty. He stood up to inspect them, in awe of such a miracle. Even he knew peonies didn't last this long.

"Hey, what—hey, wait."

Joe spun around to find Bodhi at the edge of the garden.

"Oh, uh, hey there Bodhi," he said, sidestepping to cover the peonies with his back. He felt like he'd stumbled upon some mystical secret, one that Bodhi didn't trust him enough to share. He needed to hide his intrusion.

"What were you looking at?" Bodhi asked.

"Me? Oh, uh, nothin'," said Joe. "I, uh, pulled some weeds for you."

Bodhi decided to believe him. His dream had left him too disoriented to be suspicious. "Thanks, brother," he said.

"A'course," Joe grinned, relieved he'd gotten away with it. He walked over to Bodhi, trying to think of a joke to change the subject. He looked at his friend and could tell he was already distracted. "Hey buddy, everything alright?"

"Yeah," Bodhi answered, looking past him. He shook his head as if sweeping out a troubling thought. "Uhk," he shuddered, clearing it away. "Yeah, I'm fine."

"Well alright then," Joe said, slapping him on the shoulder as he emerged from the last column of flowers, "let's get somethin' to eat." Joe walked past him. Bodhi paused for a second, still a little disoriented, then turned to follow.

"Thought I'd take you out. Applebee's got some real nice food," Joe said, climbing into the truck. "Then maybe we could do some bowling."

Bodhi stopped at the door. "Apple what?" he asked.

Joe chuckled. "Come on man, get in."

"I don't know," Bodhi said, afraid to venture out too far, "can't we just eat here?"

"You and I both know there ain't shit in there," Joe chided, pointing at the house.

"What about your house?"

"There ain't shit in there neither."

"What about the gas station?" Bodhi asked, getting desperate. "There is food of all kinds in there."

Joe laughed. "You just want to see Mandy."
"No!" Bodhi cried. "Really, there's a lot of food there."

"I ain't had a gas station dinner since I was nineteen years old," Joe scoffed, "high as fuck." Bodhi had no idea what that meant. "Now come on," Joe cried, slapping the side of the truck, "let's go!" Bodhi bounced his head around a little and moped into the passenger seat.

"You ready to see the big city?" Joe grinned, leaning toward his friend.

"No."

Joe started up the truck. The engine roared and the radio blared. Bodhi didn't know what made him most anxious—the loud music, the trip to town, or the dream he just had.

………

Bodhi was quiet down Old 27 as the truck cut through the sweet, sticky dusk. Joe tried to talk to him, shouting over the radio instead of turning it down, but Bodhi was too deep in his thoughts to respond.

When they got to The Mound, Bodhi's thoughts left him and his eyes lit up. First, it was the monument—its sheer height amazed him, and he marveled at the green statue at the top. Then, the old movie theater caught his attention. Joe chuckled and did another circle through the roundabout, Bodhi's hands and face pressed up against the window as the neon of the marquee reflected in his eyes. Joe peeled off and went north down Wayne, Bodhi looking left and right at each small business and historic home.

"Where are we?" he asked in wonder.

"New York City," Joe snickered. He never thought anyone could be so impressed with Angola, Indiana.

The pale red lamplight fell on Bodhi's face as they turned into Applebee's. Joe circled around the lot, looking for a spot to park. It was Friday night, and the restaurant was packed.

Joe pulled open the glass door and they stepped into the restaurant. The hostess looked at Bodhi then set her menus down and ran to get the manager.

Bodhi looked around. The walls were dark red with light wood paneling. Hung on them were pictures of state and local sports teams with banners and plaques, as well as random celebrity photos; for some odd reason, an old picture of LeAnn Rimes was part of the decor. The dining area ran along the walls, its red leather booths full of parents drinking mudslides and margaritas, kids scarfing appetizers and downing pops, and hapless young couples on very bad dates. In the center was a sunken bar, shiny glassware hanging above its light wooden top. Townie drunks sat around calling for tall boys and liquor. The bartender poured drinks and spent the rest of her time scooping ice. Every now and then a young waiter would drop off a plate of boneless wings for the happy drunks.

Bodhi felt overwhelmed, but there was a familiar warmth to the place. He peered over his shoulder and saw a couple of families sitting on the cushioned bench in the waiting area, looking hungry and listless.

The manager came around the bar. Joe hit Bodhi on the shoulder to get his attention.

"Fix your robe," he said from the corner of his mouth, "cover your feet." Bodhi gave him a confused scowl, and Joe pointed to the "no shoes no service sign" on the hostess stand. Bodhi rustled the folds of his clothes over his feet.

"Howdy neighbors," the manager said, grabbing the menus and shuffling them against the stand, "how can I help you?"

"Table for two," Joe answered. Bodhi looked at the floor and messed with his robe some more, anxious about his feet.

"Oh, I'm sorry partner," said the manager with a fake frown, "we're all full."

"How about that high top, next to the bar?" Joe asked, pointing to an empty spot. The manager looked over his shoulder and saw the table, feeling annoyed. He turned to face his guests.

"Right this way gents," he grinned. Joe and Bodhi followed him down the steps and to the high top. The manager clicked the menus on the table twice more and set them down.

"Amber will be right with you," he said over his shoulder as they settled into their chairs.

Joe drummed his fingers on the table and smiled at Bodhi. "Well, whatcha think?"

Bodhi glanced over at the bar and saw a townie in a Cabela's hat, bill bent so hard it looked like a lower-case "n." He talked too loud, pointed too much, and spilled his beer without apologizing. It was barely seven o'clock.

Bodhi looked down at his menu. "It's a lot to take in," he said.

"Might help if you open it," Joe replied, thinking Bodhi was referring to the menu only. "They got it broke down in little sections."

Bodhi flipped through the pages, scanning over bright fonts and poorly cropped pictures of bar food and flavored drinks. "Is there a vegetarian section?" he asked.

Joe laughed. "Even the salad has chicken in it," he said. He took his hand from his menu and rubbed his chin. "Though I suppose you could get it without. Might be some appetizers for ya too."

"Appetizers?"

"Yeah, you know—quesadillas, fried food, snacks. Should be able to find somethin'." Bodhi flipped through the laminated pages until he found the appetizer section. He put his finger down on the first appetizer and read the description carefully, then slid it from item to item, murmuring to himself and furrowing his brow.

A college-aged waitress came to the table with a notepad and a couple waters. "My name's Amber and I'll be takin' care of you tonight," she recited, setting the glasses down in front of them. "Can I get you somethin' to drink 'sides water?" She looked up at them and noticed Joe. "Well hey Joe," she grinned, putting one hand on her hip and the other on the table, "didn't see ya there."

"I'll forgive ya," he chided, "if you bring me a beer."

"If you tip me well enough," she shot back.

"Always do," Joe said with a smile. "Got any Old Milwaukee?"

She laughed and shook her head. "You know we ain't got that shit," she said. "People like you get PBR." Joe cocked his head with mock disappointment.

"Unless," she went on with a twinkle in her eye, "you want one of them IPAs." Joe shuddered.

"Let me get two tall boys, PBR," he said. Bodhi gave a worried look, suspecting one was for him. "And I think we're ready to order," Joe went on, "if you're ready for us."

"Alrighty," she answered, raising her notepad, "what're we having?"

"I'll have a Whiskey Bacon Burger, fries," said Joe.

"You know that sauce is cooked—you can't get drunk on it," Amber chided.

"Well, shit," Joe laughed.

"And for you?" she asked, turning to Bodhi.

"Hmmm, can I please have, uh," he said, moving his finger back over the menu. The mozzarella sticks looked intriguing, but he remembered how much he liked the onions in Joe's garden. "Can I please have these onion rings?" he finished, stopping his finger on the picture.

"Going for the healthy option, I like it," Amber joked.

"Yes, I am a vegetarian," Bodhi replied, missing the humor.

"Okay then," she said with a wry smile as she grabbed the menus from the table, "let me get that started for ya." Bodhi watched her head toward the wait station before looking around the restaurant. The lights, faces, and smells of this new experience stirred his anxiety. He brought his hand to his chin and returned his gaze to Joe, not seeing him but looking past, his mind on the tire swing, the old country house, the voice that knew his real name.

The beer glasses clinked against the table and Bodhi came back to the restaurant. He half-waved and gave a soft "thank you" to Amber as she receded toward the kitchen.

Joe grabbed his glass and saluted him with it. "Drink up," he said. Bodhi didn't want to drink all that much, but he wanted to think even less. He took a small sip of PBR, shuddered a bit—although beer was starting to taste better to him—and looked over at Joe. Half his beer was gone already.

"C'mon brother," Joe cried, "we're gettin' drunk tonight!"

Bodhi wondered what the Buddha might do. He shrugged his shoulders, titled his head back, and downed half his beer.

. . . .

Amber placed the onion rings in front of him, and he tried not to slur as he thanked her. She went over to Joe and cleared four empty glasses from the table before setting his burger down.

"You boys let me know if you need anything else," she said. She turned to Bodhi. "Maybe eat some of them before you get another beer." He gave her a thumbs up and a tipsy grin with his eyes closed.

"Thank you Amber," Joe said, smiling. She walked away and he picked up his burger, taking a big, juicy bite. The bacon and beef went perfect with the whiskey glaze. Bodhi picked up an onion ring and inspected it.

"Dip it in the secret sauce," Joe said, swallowing a bite and nodding toward a ramekin. Bodhi reached over and dunked the end of the onion ring, then took a small bite. The crunch of the breading, the sweetness of the onion, and the warm tang of the sauce swelled into an explosion of flavor unlike anything he'd ever tasted. He closed his eyes and worked it over slowly, savoring the flavor.

"Cosmic," he said.

"Glad you like it brother," Joe said after swallowing his food. He reached for the fifth and only glass their waitress hadn't cleared from the table, still about half full, and took a gulp. He set the glass down on the table and wiped his mouth with his sleeve. "Glad you're havin' a good time."

Bodhi popped the rest of the onion ring in his mouth, relishing it for a second. "You know," he said, swallowing it, "I really am."

Joe smiled. "I'm happy for you buddy. Glad you like the big city." He took another drink and looked up at a baseball game playing on TV near the bar. "You really hit that ball the other day."

Bodhi chuckled, already chewing on a second onion ring. "Yeah, I don't know what that was," he said with a small mouthful. "I had the strangest feeling, like I knew exactly what to do." He thought about his dream for a second, then shook his head. "It didn't mean anything," he added.

"Oh, come on now," Joe choked in disbelief.

"No, really," Bodhi said, even himself doubting his next words. "The universe is emptiness. Good or bad, nothing really happens."

"But I saw you hit the piss outta that ball," Joe insisted, pointing at him with a French fry. "I saw you smile."

"Irrelevant to the eternity of the void," Bodhi answered, reaching for another ring.

"No, not irrelevant," Joe said, still pointing with the fry and raising his voice. "It has meaning, and you know it." Bodhi put the onion ring down and leaned back in his chair, crossing his arms. He didn't know what to say.

"Look," Joe said, "when I first met you, you told me some far-out shit, like, you were this guy that traveled through infinity. I don't know if I believe that or not. In some ways I do." He finally ate his fry and washed it down with the rest of his beer, then leaned in closer and folded his hands. "But if what you say is true, then that means you, Bodhi, traversed the fabric of the entire universe so *I* could watch *you* hit *that* baseball over *that* fence. Believe what you want, but that's pretty fuckin' cool." Bodhi uncrossed his arms, leaned forward, and rested his head on his chin, thinking about what his friend was saying.

"And you know it, too," Joe went on. "You about killed us both over a fuckin' beer can."

Bodhi laughed. "Maybe you're right. Or at least, half right."

"Put the two of us together, we could get some real thinkin' done," Joe said. He looked up and waved at Amber for more beer. Bodhi could tell he was done with philosophy.

"When was the first time you hit a baseball?" Bodhi prompted.

"Oh, I don't know," Joe answered, half looking at Amber. He raised his head and put two fingers up to get her attention. She nodded and headed to the bar. "I guess when I was a kid," he said, turning back toward Bodhi.

"Yeah?" Bodhi asked.
"Yeah."

Amber set the beers down in front of them. Joe thanked her and took a sip, then set the glass back down and stared off. A smile crept to his lips.

"I'll tell ya the first time I hit a baseball," he said, feeling nostalgic. "Couldn't've been more than three, maybe four years old. My old man used to mow baseball lines in the backyard. He'd keep the rest of the grass a bit longer but cut a little ball diamond out. I had this wood bat I had to choke up on. He pitched underhand and I hit a little grounder, might've went ten feet. Goddamn was he happy."

Bodhi felt a wave of emotion for his friend. "That is very beautiful," he said.

"Thanks," Joe said. Both men grabbed their PBRs and took long, thoughtful drinks. Behind them the Cabela-wearing townie was getting louder and drunker.

"Well come on now," Joe cried, reaching across and slapping Bodhi on the arm, "there's gotta be somethin' like that you remember, somethin' from your childhood." Bodhi sat back in his chair and furrowed his brow. He thought about his dream—the tree, the tire swing, the farmhouse. He thought about the voice. He thought about his name.

"You know, there really isn't," he replied. The Cabela-wearing townie was up out of his chair now, screaming at the TV. His favorite college football team had lost. Bodhi started to look over his shoulder but decided to ignore him for the time being.

"There's gotta be somethin'," Joe insisted. "Reincarnated or not, you didn't just pop out of thin air." Bodhi tried to sort it out in his head. He didn't know what was real, what was fake, and how much of any of it he wanted to share with Joe. It's also hard to concentrate when a drunken hick gets to screaming in the Angola Applebee's.

"Well," Bodhi started.

"Our boys got screwed by them refs!"

"I have this…"

"*Absolutely fucked!*"

"This dream…"

"Cheaters, all of 'em!"

"This dream where…"

"Just like the demo'*rats!*"

"I see this tree—"

"*Nancy Pelosi!*"

Bodhi gave up and turned around, offering a glance that was equal parts annoyed and confused.

"What? You got somethin' to say over there?" the townie demanded. Bodhi snapped back around, feeling anxious.

"Aw don't worry about him," Joe advised. "That's Clint Toucher. Always mad, usually drunk. Wish he'd stop fuckin' with Mandy though." He shook his head. "Now, what were you sayin'?"

"Nothing," Bodhi said, "it's just a dream." He grabbed his PBR. Behind him, Clint Toucher snarled and pushed some air through his nose, giving a little nod to show how tough he thought he was. Amber came over to tell him to calm down, and he turned back to the bar.

"How's Mrs. Baker?" Bodhi asked, changing the subject.

"She's doin' alright," Joe answered, seeming not to notice. "Invited me to dinner the other day. You should come along. She'd love to see ya." They talked about Jim and Angela for a few minutes, then moved on to other points of conversation. After a while they finished their food and only their beers were left. A few minutes later, those were gone too.

Joe settled the check and prepared to leave. "Welp," he said, standing up, "better get goin'." Bodhi stood up too. Clint watched them over his shoulder. Joe moved toward the door and Bodhi followed. They got a few feet from the steps leading up out of the bar when Clint Toucher jumped from his chair and cut them off.

"Hey buddy!" he cried, getting close to Bodhi's face. Bodhi took a few steps back. Clint looked him up and down, teetering on his feet. "You ain't from around here, are ya?"

Bodhi stammered, growing anxious. He was a pacifist by nature but was beginning to wonder if that was just a convenient excuse to avoid people like Clint Toucher. The drunken hick stepped closer, jamming his finger into Bodhi's chest.

"Answer me, boy!"

Joe stepped between them and snatched Clint's finger, throwing him back a step. "That'll be enough outta you, Clint," he said.

"Well if it ain't Big Joe," Clint sneered. "I ain't scared of you neither."

"Don't have to be," Joe said, nodding his head toward the bar. "It's Amber you should be worried about."

"Clint Toucher!" Amber cried, coming toward him. "Pay up and get out!"

"Yes ma'am," he muttered, embarrassed. He clenched his teeth and shook his head, giving a foreboding glare before walking to the bar with his tail between his legs.

Joe put his hand on Bodhi's shoulder. "C'mon buddy," he said, "let's go bowling."

XX

The breeze blew cool on Joe's skin from the open truck window. He slowed down and turned into the bowling alley.

Outside, a haggard old bowler stood by the brick wall smoking a cigarette. He nodded at the boys as they headed in.

The sweet, nostalgic smell of faint sweat and old popcorn greeted them, accompanied by the thud of a heavy ball and the sharp crashing of pins. Joe walked by the broken Ms. Pac-Man machine and up to the counter, Bodhi close behind.

"Hey Joe," the attendant greeted.

"Hey Lenny," Joe said. "How's the wife?"

"Oh you know," Lenny said, grabbing a pair of dirty shoes and spraying the insides, "wants me home. Got another kid on the way."

"Well congratulations there bud," Joe said.

Lenny pulled his lips against his teeth and shrugged. "Ain't happy when I'm workin'," he replied, "ain't happy when I ain't. Three games? Size twelve?"

"You know it," Joe answered. He turned to Bodhi and waved him to the counter. "This is my friend, uh, Bodhi," he said. "Bodhi, tell him what shoes you want."

"Shoes?" Bodhi asked, confused. He looked to his feet. Joe and Lenny looked too, wondering how he could walk on the beer-stained carpet.

"Looks like a ten," Lenny said, pushing a pair to the edge of the counter. "Thirty bucks Joe. Lane one." Joe gave him thirty-five, feeling generous.

The boys turned from the counter and headed toward the far end of the alley. Bodhi felt the grime of the carpet give way to the cool polish of laminate wood and sat down on a vintage, hard plastic alley chair near the scoring table.

"Gonna get some beer," Joe said, turning back toward the counter as Bodhi struggled to put his shoes on. He couldn't remember the last time he'd worn any, but after a while he got them on and figured out how to tie the laces. He stood up and took a few paces, slapping the soles against the wood. A few of the other bowlers looked at him and he sat back down. He surveyed the alley to avoid their glances. The walls were white brick; in between them were twelve polished lanes of a light wooden color. An American flag hung over lane four and the Indiana flag over lane five. Behind him was a long bar that stretched most of the width of the alley, Joe leaning on it to ask Lenny for drinks. Above them hung a line of faded, multi-colored pennants for each person who'd ever bowled a 300; to the side of them was a receded corner with a broken popcorn machine and a working game of crane for the kids. There was a small kitchen with a deep fryer and a pop fountain back there too.

"Here we go," Joe muttered, returning with a pitcher of amber beer and two plastic cups. "It's Yuengling," he said. "Only non-union beer I'll drink. Try not to, but goddamnit it's good." He set it down on the table and picked out a ball from the bowling rack. "Grab a ball," he told Bodhi. Bodhi got up and grabbed a navy-blue ball, almost dropping it on the ground.

"Try somethin' a little lighter," Joe advised. Bodhi picked out a jungle-green ball with the number "12" etched into its face. He turned it over in his hands, wondering what to do next.

"Come over here," Joe motioned, walking up to the lane. "You put your fingers in it like this." Bodhi mimicked him, his arm bending a little from the weight. "Now, take a few steps back, bring your left hand up like this, size it up." Joe paused, looking at the pins. Bodhi set his feet next to him. "Now, stay there; watch what I do." Joe stepped toward the pins and released the ball with good form. The ball rolled across the lane with a slight hook and crashed into the pins for a strike.

"Boom," Joe said, walking past Bodhi and pouring himself a drink. Bodhi sidestepped to where Joe had stood, still struggling with the weight of the ball. He took a deep breath and stepped forward, doing his best to imitate Joe.

The ball soared from his waist in a clumsy, two-foot arch and smacked the middle of the lane, almost hard enough to crack the wood. Lenny scowled from the bar. The other bowlers turned in surprise, and the ball rolled into the left gutter.

"Released it too late," Joe laughed, taking a swig of beer. "Just let it roll off your fingers." Bodhi stood alone, embarrassed and confused. Joe pointed to the return rack. "Try again," he encouraged.

Bodhi took his ball from the rack and repositioned himself. He went into motion, trying his best not to repeat his mistake. The ball rolled off his fingers and into the lane, careening to the left and finding two pins.

"There it is!" Joe yelled. He set his cup down and walked up to the rack. Bodhi headed for the pitcher and poured himself a beer. When the foam settled he put it to his lips. It was smooth, a little dark—not at all like the other beers Joe had him drink. He liked it.

They finished their game and bowled another, drinking beers between throws. By the start of the last game they'd finished two pitchers and were working on a third. Joe had hit a 196 and a 214; Bodhi had a 28 and a 32. Bodhi wobbled up to the starting line and set his feet. Joe walked over to him.

"Be the pins," Joe said with a hint of mysticism.

"The what?" Bodhi asked.

"The pins, be the pins," Joe repeated.

Bodhi lowered the ball to his stomach and turned toward him. "How is that going to help?"

"See them in the void, visualize them as one, see them falling down," Joe answered. "Be the pins."

"Wouldn't it make more sense to be the ball?" Bodhi asked.

"Look man, I don't fuckin' know," Joe snapped. "You're always on that hippie shit. I was just tryin' to help." Bodhi shook his head and reset, staring down the lane.

"Be the pins," Joe whispered.

Bodhi looked at them. His vision was a little blurred from the alcohol. He relaxed his mind and imagined them all together, but each separate, like a field of dandelions blowing in the wind. He started his motion.

The red and white of the pins ran into each other, but just before he threw he saw each individual pin, the 1 and 3 pins standing in the exact spot where the ball should go.

Strike.

"Hell yeah!" Joe bellowed. Bodhi turned from the lane with a big grin. Joe held up his hand for a high five, and though the greeting seemed primitive to Bodhi, he slapped it as hard as he could.

Joe and Bodhi hung around the bowling alley, staring at the empty lanes and drinking more Yuengling. Lenny hopped around, cleaning the lanes and wiping down the bar. Before he could tell them to leave, Joe came to the counter.

"Five Buds Lenny, cans," he said, putting his bowling shoes by the register.

Lenny eyed him for a second, then bent down and grabbed the beers. "What're you gonna do with these?" he asked.

"Drink 'em, a'course," Joe answered.

"Alright, be quick. Wife's not too happy." Lenny slid the beers over. Joe responded with a twenty.

Bodhi finished his cup. He offered a confused smile to Joe as he scrambled over with his armful of cans.

"Quick, put these under your robes," he ordered.

"What, why?" Bodhi asked.

"Just do it—here," Joe said, shoving them toward him. Bodhi started to protest but was too drunk. He took them in his arms and hid them under his robes. Joe poured another drink from the pitcher and quickly killed his cup. "Let's get outta here."

The two friends headed toward the door. Lenny was too busy to care.

Outside, the air was balmy and the sky was dark. Bodhi dropped one can, then another trying to pick up the first one. They cracked against the pavement and rolled away from him.

"Jesus man, get it together," Joe admonished, scooping them up. "Let's go." They climbed into the truck. Bodhi set the remaining cans on the floor by his feet. He noticed he'd walked out with his bowling shoes on.

Joe started up the truck and put the radio on low. He edged up to the exit, then turned down Wayne Street.

"Have a good time buddy?" Joe asked.

"Yes, except I accidentally stole something," Bodhi answered. He lifted his right foot and pointed at the bowling shoe. Joe burst out laughing.

"Grab yourself a beer then," Joe chuckled. He handed Bodhi one of the beers he'd picked up in the parking lot. Bodhi struggled to open it, then the tab cracked against the metal and the beer exploded all over him.

"No, oh no!" Bodhi cried, writhing in his seat.

"Holy shit, holy shit!" Joe laughed, pounding on the steering wheel. The fizz settled and Bodhi managed to laugh it off, shaking his head with his eyes closed.

"Jesus Christ pal," Joe chuckled, shaking his head. Bodhi wiped his face, grinned, then took a drink. They continued down the road, Joe slowing up as they noticed the flash of red and blue lights by the Taco Bell.

"Keep it low," Joe warned. Bodhi put his can down as they passed two cop cars behind a lifted truck.

"Poor bastard," Joe muttered, speeding up with the scene in his rearview.

Vacant streets made the trip easy, and soon the truck reached The Mound. It was dark, except for a weak beam of streetlights and the lights of his own truck, and it was quiet. Joe took a moment to admire its solitude before rounding The Mound and heading east. Bodhi didn't know where they were going, and he didn't care. He was having a good time.

They got a mile out of town when a big square building and a dark hill rose from the nothingness of Indiana grass.

"There she is," Joe whispered with a gleam in his eye. He pulled into the high school and worked his way to the back of the lot. "Had some of my best days here," he said, killing the engine.

"What're we doing?" Bodhi asked.

"Nothin'. Just reminiscin' I guess," Joe said. "Grab those beers." Bodhi gathered the Buds by his feet and climbed out. They shut their doors, and the sound echoed across the field below.

The gate to the football field was open. Bodhi followed Joe through, and they descended the path through the practice fields. The game had ended a few hours ago. They could almost hear the happy ghost of the crowd.

"This'll do," Joe muttered, plopping down with the grunt of an old man. Bodhi sat in the grass next to him. Joe cracked open a beer. "Cheers," he said, tapping Bodhi's unfinished can. They both took a drink. "Had my first kiss right over there," Joe reminisced, pointing toward the stands, "right under them bleachers."

"A kiss?" Bodhi asked.

"Well son," Joe chided, impersonating a father, "when two people like each other, they put their lips together, and well, they kiss."

"Stop it!" Bodhi laughed, feeling embarrassed.

"Okay, okay," Joe promised. He took another drink. "But really though—you ever think about stuff like that? I know you're a monk and all, probably against that sorta thing." Bodhi thought about it for a second, then fell backwards into the grass.

"Mandy is soo pretty," he said drunkenly to the sky. Joe chuckled. "But how would you say it?" Bodhi grinned, mocking Joe, "Mandy is so *goddamn* pretty." Bodhi giggled at his own impression, and Joe chuckled some more. A few minutes went by; Bodhi laid in the grass looking at the stars, Joe stared out across the field, thinking about something.

"You know," Joe finally said, swallowing some beer, the carbonation making his throat a little raspy, "you're about the best friend I've had in a while."

"Aww, thank you Joe," Bodhi said, still looking at the sky. "I like you too."

"'Bout the *only* friend I've had in a while," Joe said.

Bodhi sat up in disbelief, wobbling. "Nooo," he said loudly, "that can't be true."

"Yep," Joe swore. "I gotta couple friends, Sadie a'course. I gotta lotta people I like talkin' to, and they like talkin' to me. They say, 'Hey, Big Joe,' shit like that, you know. I'm the fuckin' life of the party. But by and large, I'm alone." He killed the can and crushed it in his hand.

"Why?" Bodhi asked.

"Oh, I don't know," Joe sighed, tossing the can aside. They sat in silence for a while. Bodhi could feel the giddiness of a drunken night fading into the sad reflections of two in the morning.

"Took a girl to prom up there," Joe said, pointing up the hill to the faded square building. "Hardly knew each other, but we decided to go. Thought it'd be fun." He cracked open another beer. Bodhi sensed Joe's sorrow and it reminded him of his own.

"Picked her up in my uncle's Chevelle. Goddamn was she beautiful." Joe took a swig of beer and set the can down by his feet. "She wore a hazel dress, same color as her eyes. Went to the dance, had a good time, went to a party, had a few beers, you know. Took her home after a while. We didn't do nothin'; I don't think I even kissed her. We just talked." He grabbed his beer and took a long drink, staring across the field. "I remember how she looked, standin' on her porch in that dress. And I remember how sweet the air tasted, the sky gettin' lighter like that bluish gray before the sun comes up, my shoes gettin' wet from the dew in the yard but I just keep talkin' 'cause I don't want it to end."

"What happened?" Bodhi asked, eyes wide.

"It ended."

"What? How?"

Joe gave a melancholy shrug. "Fall came, she went off to school. I stayed here, worked at the factory." He lifted a corner of his mouth and shook his head a little. "Never saw her again."

Bodhi sighed. "The only constant is the void," he said.

"Don't give me that shit right now," Joe said. He spit into the grass.

"Joe, I'm sorry," Bodhi pleaded. Joe didn't respond. Bodhi turned his eyes to the ground, then sighed again. "Look," he said, struggling with what he was about to say. "I have this dream. I started to tell you in the restaurant, but I stopped." Joe looked at his friend and felt the weight of his struggle.

"I have this dream," Bodhi went on, "and there's this tree. It's tall, leafy, with a lot of branches, looks good for climbing. Hanging down one of the branches is this rope, and hanging from that is this tire, like a swing. And I run and I jump on it." He looked up at Joe, pain in his eyes. "And after a while, someone's pushing me. I don't know who, but I'm not swinging by myself. Someone's pushing me higher."

"Yeah?" Joe said, leaning toward him.

"And there's this, this house. I hardly get a glimpse, but it's big, and white, with faded paint and big windows, and a big porch." Bodhi had tears in his eyes. They spilled in long, slow streaks down his face.

"What do you think it means?" Joe asked.

"I think it's where I'm from," he declared. "I have a name." Joe's heart raced as he stared at Bodhi with quiet sympathy. "I have a name," Bodhi repeated. "I have a name, and it isn't Bodhi." He looked down into his lap. He wiped his face but more tears came.

Joe hugged his friend.

XXI

Bodhi stared down his legs and saw the bowling shoes on his feet. He groaned, feeling pain in his body he never thought possible. He was hungover.

He rolled off his mattress and tried to stand up, quickly sitting back down. The midmorning sun ran through his window, and the birds chirped happily in the breeze. He put his head in his hands and rubbed his eyes.

Some sounds came from the kitchen. Confused and nauseated, he trudged into the front room. Joe walked in holding the watering can.

"Morning, sunshine," he grinned.

"What're you doing here?" Bodhi said, rubbing his head with his eyes to the floor.

"Thought you might need some help," Joe chuckled. "First one is somethin' else." Joe passed through the doorway and went to the screen, pushing it open. It shut behind him, its loud crack echoing in Bodhi's brain. Bodhi got up and headed for the door.

He fumbled for the handle, then clutched it in his fingers. It swung open and he almost fell, stumbling into the hot morning sun. He put his hands up to shield his eyes.

Joe made his way to the middle of the garden. Bodhi's achy eyes adjusted to the sun and he saw Joe crouched over the two surviving peonies.

"Wait," he tried to shout. He went to run but fell into a half jog. "Wait," he panted when he got there, keeling over.

"When were you gonna tell me about these?" Joe asked, sprinkling a little water over the peonies and caressing their petals.

"They're just flowers," Bodhi mumbled, trying to sound coy.

"Oh come on," Joe cried, "even I know they're two months past bloom."

Bodhi rubbed his head. "It's not like you didn't know," he muttered, a little annoyed. "I saw you out here yesterday."

Joe grinned like a mischievous kid. "Still, woulda been nice of you to share," he said with a shrug. "Friends don't keep secrets from each other, you know."

"I thought I shared enough last night," Bodhi answered. The romanticism of late-night drinking and vulnerability was gone; now, he felt embarrassed and hungover.

"Well, what do you make of it?" Joe asked, turning into the sun to look up at Bodhi.

"I don't know," Bodhi said, easing himself down next to Joe. He stared at the two peonies and their magnificent blooms, thinking of the Lotus Sutra. He reached out and touched their perfect petals. "I was so mad at you," he said. "You, your beer can." He let his hand fall to the dirt. "I locked myself in the house, and I missed their bloom. And I ran out here, and I fell to my knees. I was so mad at you, and I was so scared. Scared of you, scared of everything." He picked his hand back up and cupped one of the flowers. "But here they were, two perfect blooms. Two perfect blooms in the middle of the madness." He looked at the folds of the peony without speaking for a while. "It's like some kind of miracle," he whispered.

"I think you're right," Joe agreed. They sat in silence, contemplating it. Joe picked at a weed without the intention of pulling it. "Do you think it has somethin' to do with your dream? With your name?" he finally asked.

"I don't know," Bodhi answered, sitting back and putting his hands on his feet. "I suppose it could."

Joe watched him with compassion. "So, what is your name?"

"I don't know," Bodhi answered. "I hear it but I don't remember. I hear it but it's gone."

"Is it Kevin?" Joe grinned.

"God, I hope not," Bodhi muttered, grabbing his head.

XXII

Bodhi was still hungover the next day. It wasn't as bad, but the sun was hot and he felt weak in the garden. He was sweating a lot.

Joe stopped by in the heat of the day and took note of how depleted Bodhi was; he invited him to the movies to cool off. Bodhi didn't know what a movie was, but Joe insisted it was cool, dark, and there was plenty of water and other things to drink. Bodhi had also been impressed with the bright lights of the movie marquee on their way to dinner the other night. He put his things away and climbed in the truck.

"Yep, two classics," Joe said as they barreled down Old 27. "*East of Eden* and *Rebel Without a Cause*."

Bodhi stared at the trees and the windblown grass on the rolling hills. "What are those?" he asked, without looking from the open window.

"The movies we're gonna see," Joe said. "Two of my favorites."

"What's in them?" Bodhi asked. Joe was a little surprised that Bodhi didn't ask "who's in them," but remembered he was an interdimensional monk cut off from the day-to-day vices and pleasures of Hoosier society.

"A lot," Joe answered.

They eased into the quadrant of The Mound that held parking for the Brokaw Movie Theatre. They exited the truck and walked inside. Bodhi smiled and closed his eyes when the cool blast of the air conditioner hit his body. Joe walked past the old 27"x40" movie posters and up to the counter.

"Two, please," he said to the teenager who ran the ticket counter. The teenager looked at him and Joe realized he hadn't specified what showing. "For the matinee double feature," he added. Joe paid him and they walked into the lobby, Bodhi intrigued by its black and white tile, its high, cathedral-like ceiling, and its red carpeted walls adorned with more old movie posters. Joe went up to the concession stand and squinted at the black rubber letters arranged on the soft, white glow of the sign. Bodhi followed him, stopping to stare at the large, red popcorn machine to Joe's right just behind the counter.

"I'll take a chili dog and a light beer," Joe said to another teenager. "Oh, and better get him a water." Joe reached into his wallet and pulled out a few dollar bills, then turned over his shoulder. "You want anything else?" he asked his friend. Bodhi was mesmerized by the vintage red machine. "Better get him a large popcorn," Joe laughed, reaching back in his wallet to grab another bill. "Thank you."

Joe found his seat in the theatre, Bodhi sitting down next to him with his arms around a box of popcorn about the size of his torso. He tried his first bite; soon after, he ate it by the handful.

The previews started and Bodhi fell back in his seat, almost spilling the box. He turned to Joe with fear in his eyes.

"Relax," Joe assured him, waving one hand while finishing a bite of chili dog with the other, "it's not real." Bodhi reached out and tried to grab the image, realizing Joe was right.

"Why do people go to see something that's not real?" he asked, inspecting his empty hand and feeling unnerved.

Joe took a slug of beer. "You're always talkin', 'the universe is an illusion,' shit like that," he grumbled, using finger quotes and waving his hands. "Movies are a more comfortable illusion for some of us." Bodhi thought about it for a second, then nodded his head and reached for another handful of popcorn. He ate half the box before the overture finished.

The music ended and a young, tortured man ambled onto the screen. Bodhi was so taken aback he lowered his handful of popcorn.

"Who is that?" he asked with a mixture of dread and wonder.

"That," Joe said, "is James Dean." Bodhi watched him move across the screen. "Born here in Indiana," Joe added, "grew up in Fairmount, actually." The word hit Bodhi in the chest, making his heart pound.

"Fairmount?" he asked, a little afraid.

"Yep," Joe said, eyes on the screen.

"Fairmount?" he asked again, the word becoming more real to him.

"Uh huh," Joe grunted.

"Where is that?" Bodhi asked.

"A little over an hour from here," Joe grunted. "Now shut up, I'm tryin' to watch this."

Bodhi sat back in his chair and let the movie wash over him, eyes glued to the screen. He watched as the boy roamed the countryside, grappling with lost innocence and completely unable to connect with people. He teared up when he smiled his "aw shucks" smile and his family rejected his gift. He cried when the boy's brother went off to war and never came back. Joe thought he took it oddly personal.

The second movie started and Bodhi didn't realize it was separate from the first. He noticed the boy wore different clothes and tried a little harder to connect. He noticed he wasn't as naïve, but his fate was still the same. He cried then, too.

They stayed in the theatre until the credits finished and the lights came on. Joe hit Bodhi on the shoulder to break his trance.

"C'mon man, let's go," he urged.

"What? Oh, right," Bodhi said, a little disoriented. He stood up and followed Joe out of the theatre and into the truck.

Bodhi was silent for the first few miles, watching the town fade into the rolling countryside of Old 27. "Whatever happened to him?" he finally asked, somewhere down the road.

"Who?" Joe replied.

"Cal, Jim, whatever he's called," Bodhi sputtered. "The boy from the movie."

"He died," Joe said quietly. Bodhi's chest tightened.

"Yep," Joe sighed, "died a long time ago. Real young. Pretty sad." Up until today, Bodhi hadn't thought about death too much. His tradition told him all things were temporary, life and death were relatively meaningless, to not get attached. Now he wasn't so sure.

"They do a car show in his memory. Me and the boys go every year," Joe said with a twinkle in his eye.

"Car show?"

"Yeah," Joe said. "People from all over, showin' off their classic cars—like the ones from the movie. Drink beer, look at cars, get a little nostalgic. It's a good time."

Bodhi thought about it for a moment. "Where?" he asked.

"Well, there's two, actually. One in Fairmount, one down the way in Gas City. We go to Gas City." Bodhi winced at the word *Fairmount* again. The other town sounded familiar too.

"We drive over to Fairmount at night, past his childhood home, past the place they buried him, pay our respects, you know." It all felt so heavy to Bodhi.

"You should go with me this year," Joe offered. Bodhi looked out over the road. He felt something missing from his own life, and for once he didn't want to avoid it.

"I think I need to," he said.

XXIII

"When's it supposed to start workin'?"

Bodhi side-eyed Joe from where he sat on the porch. The two were meditating in the heat, and Joe was drenched in sweat.

"It doesn't really 'work,' as such," Bodhi replied, a little annoyed. "You just sit, close your eyes, and empty your mind." He sat back in his chair and refocused. Joe grumbled a few words and did the same.

Bodhi took a deep breath and let it out slow. He felt a heavy wave from the crown of his head dip into the pit of his stomach and release itself. He forgot about his fears—the darkness, the tree, his family. He just simply was.

A mosquito came and buzzed by his forehead. He didn't hear it. He was one with the cosmos again, adrift on a river with his eyes to the stars. Not even the mosquito wanted to disturb him. It buzzed over to Joe and landed on his neck.

Bodhi heard a loud *SLAP* followed by more grousing from Joe. "Goddamn mosquitoes."

Bodhi tried to ignore it. "Every living thing has its purpose," he offered quietly, keeping his eyes closed.

"Not mosquitoes," Joe grumbled. "Only thing they gave us was *Jurassic Park*."

"Just focus," Bodhi said. "It helps if you count your breaths."

Joe settled back in and closed his eyes. "One," he said with his first exhale. Bodhi decided to count with him. They got to nine and stopped counting. Both men were in deep meditation.

After about an hour Joe shook with a bewildered "Huhh!" as if startled awake. He stood up and stretched. Bodhi looked up at him.

"Jesus Christ man," Joe muttered, shaking his head, "that was somethin' else."

"Yeah?"

"I can see why you do it," he answered. "Pretty refreshing."

Bodhi smiled. "You ready to go out?"

Joe lifted his hat and scratched his head. "I am," he grinned. Bodhi stood up with excitement and went inside to get his alms bowl.

"You know, normally at this point I'd say somethin' like, 'Jesus pal, I ain't beggin' for no food, let's get some fuckin' Taco Bell,'" Joe called through the open door, "but I'm not gonna say it. This meditation shit really works."

Bodhi came back outside. "I only have one bowl," he said, "so we'll have to share."

"Fine by me," Joe said. Bodhi pushed the screen door open. Joe followed him across the yard and onto the lake road.

It was only mid-morning, but the air was hot and humid. Bodhi was glad he had his bowling shoes to protect his feet from the sun-drenched asphalt. After a minute of walking they came upon Crazy Craig's and his deer skull-covered garage; Bodhi thought it best to avoid his door.

They turned up the road toward the elementary school and came to a row of houses just past it. The first house had faded yellow paint with a stone porch and some crumbling statues keeping guard. They made their way to the door and Bodhi lifted his hand to knock.

"So we just, uh," said Joe, feeling out of place.

"We say, 'Many blessings, Mr. or Mrs. So-and-So,'" Bodhi said over his shoulder, "and then we hold out this bowl."

"Alrighty then," Joe shrugged.

"If they're really confused," Bodhi continued, gently rapping on the door, "we ask them to drop a lump. It's tradition."

In a bay window to the right, both men saw two bony fingers make a slit in the vinyl blinds. A cautious eye appeared for a second and the blinds closed. They waited a while for someone to come to the door. Nobody came.

"Happens more often than not," Bodhi shrugged, turning around. They went back to the sidewalk and tried the next house. Nobody answered there either. They continued on, knocking all the doors on one side of the street without any luck.

"May we fare better on the other side," Bodhi offered. They crossed the street and walked up to a large brown house that, while a little rundown, had a lot of historic charm and a nice, covered porch.

The front door was old and made of wood, with a large, elliptical glass window in the middle. There were two bay windows on either side of the door. No light penetrated any of the glass and the inside was dark. Bodhi knocked on the door, which made a deep, rich sound against his knuckles.

There was a low rumble from inside the house, followed by a slow, soft, shuffling noise. Bodhi waited at the door for over a minute.

"C'mon, man," Joe whispered, "let's g—"

The door opened with a painful creak. An old figure hunched in the crack of the doorway, obscured by the shadows of the house. Joe shot Bodhi a sideways glance. Bodhi lifted his bowl. The door opened a little wider to reveal a woman. She looked to be a hundred years old.

"Many blessings, Mrs., uh," Bodhi started to say.

"Hello boys," she croaked, "just a minute." The door closed and the two men looked at each other. A full three minutes passed before it cracked open again and her bony hand reached out to drop something in the bowl.

"Happy Halloween," she said. Bodhi started to thank her in the way of the Bodhisattva, but she closed the door.

"What'd we get?" Joe asked, peering over. Bodhi lowered the bowl. They looked inside to find two pennies and a piece of hard candy.

· · ·· ·· ···

Joe and Bodhi tried a few more houses before they made their way around the lake, stopping at a muddy one-story with a Trump flag and a dirt bike in the yard.

"This oughta be good," Joe snickered. Bodhi didn't know what he meant. He reached up and knocked on the screen door.

"Who is it?" a man's voice boomed from behind the door. Bodhi felt threatened.

"Many blessings, sir," he began.

"The fuck are you talkin' about?" he yelled, getting up and marching to the screen. He threw it open and Bodhi stepped back to avoid being hit.

"The fuck do you want?" he demanded. He didn't have a shirt on, and his belly hung over the waistband of his shorts. He had big shoulders and strong arms, but was out of shape from the corndogs that were likely his main source of protein. He glared at Bodhi with angry eyes and screamed at him through his scraggly beard. "Jesus Christ boy! You deaf?" Bodhi took another step back and timidly raised his bowl.

"Get that shit outta my face before I—"

"Listen here you country-fried fuck," Joe yelled, stepping in front of Bodhi, "you touch my friend, I'll knock your teeth out!" The hillbilly reeled for a second, caught off guard. He sized Joe up and realized he couldn't win.

"You're not worth it," said the man, knowing he'd get his ass kicked but wanting to look tough anyway. "Now both of you git, before I sick my dogs on you!" Joe flexed and opened his mouth, but Bodhi grabbed him and dragged him away.

"Many blessings to you, sir," Bodhi offered, raising one hand in apology and using the other to hold Joe back. The hillbilly grumbled something like, "Yeah, that's what I thought," in order to maintain appearances. Joe cursed all the way back to the lake road.

"You shoulda let me whoop his ass," Joe lamented.

Bodhi frowned. "Hatred will not cease by hatred, but by love alone," he quoted. "This is the ancient law."

Joe scoffed. "I'll be damned if any law keeps me from knockin' out a piece of shit like that."

"Joe, I've been doing this for a long time," Bodhi said. "This isn't the first time one of these poor souls misunderstood me, and it won't be the last."

Joe shook his head. "But he—"

"When we seek alms," Bodhi interjected, "we do so not with expectation, or out of fear of hunger—we do so for the connection of spirit. It is as much for them as it is for me."

Joe furrowed his brow. "So, in other words, fuck that guy?" he asked.

Bodhi winced a little. "Yes, if you want to look at it that way, fuck that guy."

…..…..

They were tired, hot, and ready to quit when Joe's house came into view. The only alms they'd received had been the strange and mostly inedible gift from the old woman.

"She gave what she could," Bodhi said, feeling grateful. "May she be blessed." Still, they had nothing to eat after knocking almost every door in town.

"I knew we shoulda just went to Taco Bell," Joe panted, sweaty and starved. "Let's find the truck, I'll take us there."

"Strive on diligently," Bodhi quoted, "don't give up."

"C'mon man, I'm serious," Joe wheezed.

"So am I," Bodhi said, "look." They stopped.

Joe looked to where Bodhi was pointing. "Aw, not there," he complained.

"Why not?" Bodhi asked.

"They're my neighbors."

"All of them have been our neighbors."

"Yeah, but next door? I don't know man." Joe shook his head.

"Mrs. Baker always drops a lump," Bodhi reasoned.

"Yeah, but—"

"But what? You said you wanted to seek alms. This is seeking alms."

Joe looked around. He let out a deep sigh. "Alright," he said. They walked up the porch and stopped at the door.

Tat, tat, tat.

Nobody answered. Joe pleaded with Bodhi to leave.

"Hold on," Bodhi urged.

Tat, tat, tat.

A few seconds later they heard loud, rumbling footsteps, and the door burst open. "I thought I told you..." Jim Baker started to scream. "Oh, hey Joe," he said, seeing his neighbor over Bodhi's shoulder, "what're you doing here?"

"Oh you know," Joe shrugged, "just hangin' out."

"Yeah?" Jim Baker smiled, somewhere between a grin and a sneer. "With this guy?" He thumbed toward Bodhi.

"He's a good kid," Joe said.

"I don't know about all that," Jim grunted, sticking his thumbs in his waistband to accentuate his gut.

"Bit eccentric is all," Joe said, falling into colloquialism. Catching himself he added, "He's a monk, ya know."

"He's a gotdamn—"

"Is Mrs. Baker here?" Bodhi interjected. Jim was taken aback, and his eyes widened a bit. He wasn't used to being interrupted.

"She's at church, actually," he replied, "helpin' out again."

"Do you know when she'll be back?" Bodhi asked.

"Not for a couple-three hours," Jim grumbled. Bodhi looked to the floor. He sighed, then lifted his bowl.

"What am I supposed to do with that?" Jim asked. He scowled at Joe. "You believe this guy?" he asked.

"Just give him some food," Joe said, "he hasn't eaten all day." His stomach ached when he said it.

"Big Joe's getting soft in his old age, eh?" Jim sneered. He motioned to Joe with his right elbow as if to needle him in the ribs.

"C'mon Jim," he said. "It's the Christian thing to do."

"Teach a man to fish..."

"Jesus'll still take what he caught and feed 5,000 people with it. C'mon man."

Jim's eyes widened again. He wasn't used to being pushed around. "Now listen, Joe," he said, shaking his head, "I like you and all, but you can't talk to me that way, least of all not on my property."

"You're right," Joe agreed, feeling his stomach suck against his bones, "you're right."

Jim Baker surveyed both men. He didn't know if it was Christian morality or a feeling of superiority, but he decided to help. "Give me the bowl," he groused, snatching it from Bodhi's hands. He stomped into the kitchen. "You ain't getting no three-course meal!" he hollered through the screen door. "Best I can do is instant rice." Bodhi's eyes glimmered. Traditional alms usually called for rice, and he hadn't eaten any in a long time. They heard Jim's grumbling over the sounds of the microwave, and after two minutes he returned with a steaming bowl of Uncle Ben's. He passed it to Bodhi.

"Many blessings, Mr. Baker," he cried, feeling ecstatic. "May you be well, may you be peaceful—"

"Yeah, yeah," Jim muttered, waving his hand.

"Thank you Jim," Joe said, "means a lot."

"Just don't make a habit of it," he said, knowing Bodhi already had. He turned to go. His neighbors thanked him and started down the porch steps.

Jim was halfway through the threshold when he remembered something his wife had asked him to do. He stopped in the doorway. He didn't want to do it.

"Hey listen," he said, turning to face them. Joe and Bodhi stopped and spun around. Jim tried to fight it, thinking, *Christ, am I really about to do this?*

"Angela wants you two boys over for dinner," he grumbled, almost choking.

"Both of us?" Bodhi asked with excitement.

"Yes," Jim answered, clenching his teeth.

"When?" Joe asked.

"Believe she said next Thursday."

"What time?" Joe asked.

"Six o'clock."

"Alright," Joe said, smiling his big country smile, "see you then." They turned and walked through the yard toward Bodhi's house.

"That's *next* Thursday," Jim Baker hollered after them, "not this Thursday, but the next!"

"Alrighty Jim," Joe called, waving his hand without turning around.

"Show up this Thursday there won't be nothin' for ya!" he yelled.

"Thanks Jim," Joe answered, waving his hand again.

Jim Baker put his hand on his forehead. "Jesus Christ," he muttered to himself.

XXIV

"Thing about Hoosiers," Joe said, "they love their basketball." He threw a chest-pass to Bodhi. His catch was mostly clean, but part of the ball thudded against his upper abdomen. He didn't complain.

"I've seen some of the neighborhood kids play this at the elementary school," he replied, throwing it back to Joe, "could be fun."

"Could be," Joe said, "except some of the geezers we're playin' take it too seriously. Gotta be on your A game." He caught the ball and paused for a second. "Now, this is a bounce pass." He pushed the ball and it bounced on the road a little over halfway between him and Bodhi. Bodhi caught it cleanly at his waist. "Now you try," Joe said. Bodhi followed along, and his pass went right into Joe's hands.

"Not bad," Joe said. "Let's hit the road. We'll take some shots when we get to the gym." They climbed into the truck and headed for town.

Retirees, college kids on break, the unemployed, and old men on salary with long, overdrawn lunch hours gathered at the local gym every Wednesday at noon for a very intense, albeit sloppy, round of basketball. Joe rarely made it, but he had enough sick time saved up over his dutiful factory career to call in every now and then. Plus, he was really enjoying spending time with Bodhi.

The guys were warming up when they walked into the gym. Jimmy Docker stood at the three-point line with two knee braces and a weightlifting belt, calling for the ball with his hands out and draining every shot. Gregg Price worked on his layups, grunting with every attempt and huffing and puffing after his own rebounds. On the baseline, one of the younger guys practiced his skills by dribbling a ball as quick as he could in each hand. Others were doing ridiculous stretches and half-assed calisthenics they'd learned sometime in the seventies, and there was a guy with one leg who laid on his back with his prosthetic in the air, waiting for a partner stretch and shouting, "Little help?" at anyone who walked by.

Joe led Bodhi into the middle of the fray and cleared his throat. "Hey guys," he said, "this is my friend, Bodhi." The commotion stopped as everyone assessed the newbie in brown robes and bowling shoes.

"Little help?" said the guy with one leg. He noticed the gym was quiet and put his leg down, then sat up to stare with the rest of the crowd.

"Hey guys," Joe said again, "this is Bodhi." Bodhi gave a slight bow. The gym was silent. "He's a monk," Joe added.

Greg walked up in his old man short-shorts and tank top. He looked Bodhi up and down. "He's on your team."

The group shot for captains. Jimmy and one of the college kids made their shots and chose teams. Joe and Bodhi were picked last.

"You get Gregg," Jimmy said to Bodhi as they lined up on defense. Gregg scoffed, feeling insulted. "Don't embarrass me out there kid," Jimmy added before turning around and checking up.

Gregg blew past Bodhi and the point guard tossed it to him as soon as the ball was checked for an easy backdoor layup. Greg celebrated like he'd won the NBA finals. Jimmy shook his head.

"It's alright," Joe shouted, clapping, "you'll get him next time."

Jimmy brought the ball up and his team settled in on offense. Bodhi stood at the wing, confused and a little depressed at how the game was working out. Gregg played him unnecessarily tight, elbowing him in the ribs and talking trash. The ball went around the horn a few times until it somehow landed in Bodhi's hands. Greg stole it immediately and, too lazy to run, threw the ball to half-court where one of the college kids took it and scored.

"Booya!" Gregg yelled, getting in Bodhi's face.

"Not the NBA Gregg," Joe hollered. "You sell insurance for a living." Gregg scrunched his face and mocked Joe before settling in on defense.

The game continued with Bodhi's teammates refusing to pass him the ball and Gregg dominating him on offense.

"Time out," Joe called after a while.

"There's no timeouts in rec ball!" Gregg caterwauled.

"Fuck off, man," Joe said, waving his hand. He called Bodhi over. Bodhi trotted up with his head down, covered in sweat.

"Look," Joe said, putting his hand on Bodhi's shoulder, "you gotta toughen up out there." His teammates mumbled in agreement. Bodhi looked at Joe with pain in his eyes. "Don't give me that shit," Joe said, both forceful and calm. "I want you to stick on him. From now on, he doesn't touch the ball." Bodhi nodded. His team walked back and set up their defense. Bodhi took a deep breath and walked right up to Gregg, bending his knees and resting his forearm on Gregg's torso.

"Watch it, bud," Gregg snapped, his angry enunciation making "bud" sound like "bahd." Bodhi narrowed his eyes and pressed harder. The ball came into play and Bodhi stuck on him. Gregg ran around sweating and complaining that Bodhi was fouling him between grunts and odd guttural noises. Now that Bodhi was playing hard "D," his team started coming back.

After a few times back and forth, Gregg finally caught the ball down low. He faked once and went for the shot. Bodhi checked him with his body and put his hands up to defend the ball.

"Gaawwww!" Gregg cried as he threw his arms up toward the rim and his body out of bounds, bricking the shot completely. One of Bodhi's teammates caught the rebound and threw it downcourt to Joe for an easy bucket.

"We're in his head now boys!" Joe yelled in delight, clapping his hands in Gregg's face as he ran back on defense.

"Watch it bahd!" Gregg warned, slapping Joe's hands away.

The game went back and forth until the last shot, Bodhi's team on defense. One of the college kids dribbled up and motioned something with his hand.

"Watch the pick!" Joe cried.

"The what?" Bodhi said, right before the guy with one leg crashed into him, knocking them both down and leaving Gregg open. The college kid tossed Gregg the ball, who licked his lips in anticipation. Bodhi sprang to his feet and ran toward him. Gregg paused for one second to savor the victory, then shot. Bodhi leapt from behind and snatched the ball out of the air, Gregg feeling the breeze of his opponent rushing past. Bodhi landed on his feet and fired it to Jimmy at the opposite three-point line. Gregg dove out of bounds for some reason, ragdolling around and crying that he'd been fouled. Jimmy shot.

Swish.

Being a rec ball game with most of his teammates over the age of forty-five, nobody ran and carried Bodhi off the court. Instead, Jimmy pointed at him then thumped his own chest and pointed at him again. His other teammates gave a mixture of masculine head nods and hand gestures. Joe smiled and slapped him on the back.

"You're a real Hoosier now," he said with a smile.

"Thanks brother," Bodhi grinned. He was happy that he'd earned his team's approval and proud that he'd earned Joe's respect.

·····.··

"One more game?" Jimmy asked at the end of the third, like he did every Wednesday. Most of them were too tired. Some of them had to get back to work, others had to take a nap or go home to their wives.

"Sorry bahd," Gregg said, "have to head back to the office."

"We gotta get somethin' to eat," Joe said. "You're welcome to come."

"I'm good," Jimmy said, turning to the basket to shoot. The guy with one leg and two of the younger kids stuck around, hoping to play two on two.

"Alright then Bodhi," Joe said, putting his arm around him, "let's get goin'." Bodhi wiped the sweat off his forehead and they headed out to the truck.

The lunch crowd had cleared out when they walked up to Pizza King. Joe grabbed the door and held it open for one of the last people to trickle out, an old man with a John Deere hat and a toothpick in his mouth. They nodded at each other, Joe waiting for him to pass before leading Bodhi inside.

Joe walked through the foyer and stopped at the old arcade machine near the counter. Bodhi fixated on the lights and colors of the machine as Joe waved to a woman by the register. She was tired and covered in flour from the lunch rush. She motioned them to sit wherever they'd like, then turned to help her coworkers clean and pull the last few orders from the pizza oven.

Joe tapped Bodhi on the shoulder, who broke his stare and followed Joe into the main dining room. Everything was red—red carpet, red trim, red booths. They sat down and Joe grabbed two red menus next to a red phone mounted on the wall.

"What's that?" Bodhi asked.

"What?" Joe asked, looking around before seeing Bodhi staring at the phone.

"Oh, that's the phone," Joe answered. "You pick it up when you're ready to order. Kinda weird, but I like it. It's old school." He grabbed his menu and looked at it for a second.

"Ahh, the Royal Feast," he said, "best pizza in town." Bodhi looked down and saw a picture of it next to the description. It was covered in meat.

"Can we, uh, get something else?" he asked.

"What?" Joe asked, incredulous. "Oh, right, the vegetarian thing." He surveyed the menu with a frown. "Know what, you go ahead and order. Just get a fourteen inch." He put his menu down and pushed it to the middle of the table. "Guess I could stand a little less meat."

Bodhi reached for the phone and pulled it off the hook. Joe motioned for him to put it to his ear. "There'll be a voice on the other end," he said, "just tell 'em what we want."

"Hello, hello?" came a tinny voice from the phone. Bodhi scrambled to hold it up to his ear.

"Yes I," he said, then froze. Joe swirled his hand as if to say, "go on." Bodhi paused for a second. "Greetings," he said, "how are you today?" Joe put his face in his palm.

"Fine. What can I getcha," said the voice without inflection.

"Yes, I would like the, uh..." Bodhi slid the menu back under his eyesight. "I'll take the Veggie Feast."

"Add jalapeño," Joe whispered.

"With jalapeño," Bodhi added, feeling flustered.

"And beer," Joe whispered.

"And beer," Bodhi added.

"What kind?" the voice asked.

Bodhi pulled the phone away and looked at Joe with worried eyes. "What kind of beer do you want?" he whispered.

"Get me a pitcher of domestic," Joe whispered back.

"Pitcher of domestic," Bodhi said.

"Got Michelob, Bud Light, Coors Light…"

Bodhi got nervous and tried to hand Joe the phone.

"Jesus Christ," Joe whispered, "just get a pitcher of Bud or somethin'." Bodhi grabbed the phone and put it back to his ear.

"The pitcher of Bud Or Somethin'," he said with confidence. Joe put his face in his palm again. The server on the other line closed his eyes and rested his head on his hand, the thumb and forefinger pinching the bridge of his nose.

"So Veggie Feast with Bud Light," he grumbled. "Table number?" Bodhi's eyes searched frantically until he saw a black number "27" under the phone.

"Uh, 27."

"Thank you."

"Thank you," Bodhi said. "Goodbye. Take care now." Bodhi hung up. Joe shook his head in disbelief.

The waitress came to the booth after a few minutes and set down two ten-ounce mugs with the pitcher of Bud Light. Joe picked one up and looked at it, confused as to why anyone would drink a beer so small. He half offered it to Bodhi, who put his hand up and shook his head. Relieved, Joe filled both up for himself. He drank the first in one take, then set the empty mug down and gazed around the dining area.

"Used to come here a lot," he reminisced, eyes getting red from the fizz of a chugged beer. "There was always somethin' playin' on that jukebox." He nodded toward a dusty corner of the restaurant. Bodhi turned to look at it.

"One time some little snot-nosed kid kept playin' Chumbawamba," Joe said. "I don't know where that little fucker got so many quarters—I probably heard that song thirty times." He grabbed the other mug and downed it, too.

"I don't know what you mean," Bodhi said.

"It was this song in the nineties," Joe said, "you never heard—ah hell." He got up and fished in his pocket for some change, then crossed the room and punched some numbers into the machine. When he came back he sat down with a satisfied grunt and filled up his mugs. "To good times at the Angola Pizza King," he grinned, toasting himself.

The song came on and Joe pointed up to the ceiling as if to say, "There it is, yep, wait for it, right there." Bodhi nodded along. It was somehow equal parts annoying and fantastic.

When it was over, Joe stood up and fed the jukebox more quarters. He played song after song, telling a story for each.

"Remember comin' here and seein' the high schoolers get breadsticks and pay with exact change, little shits..."

"Used to have the high score on that arcade machine back there 'til some punk named AJP broke my record. Never could catch the fucker..."

"Dated a gal that had a little boy. We took him up here for his fifth birthday. Always wondered what happened to them..."

He played at least ten songs and finished two pitchers before the pizza came. The waitress dropped it down in front of them and Bodhi's eyes got big. It was covered with cheese and savory vegetables, and a little steam rolled off it and filled his nostrils with a tantalizing smell.

"Thank ya kindly," Joe said to the retreating waitress, slurring a bit. Bodhi grabbed a slice and took a bite, and the flavor exploded in his mouth. The jalapeños burned, but all things considered, it was the best thing he'd ever eaten.

Pizza King cuts giant pizzas into a series of seemingly manageable rectangles, so it's easy to overeat. Every time Bodhi told himself he was finished, he'd wait about ten seconds and grab another slice. Twenty minutes later the pizza was gone, and Joe was trying to order another pitcher.

"I think you've had enough," the waitress said flatly.

"No, look," Joe pleaded, "he's been helpin' me." He slid one of the mugs over to Bodhi, who furrowed his brow.

"Is that so?" she asked, looking toward him. Bodhi could see Joe behind her, nodding and urging him to lie.

"Yes," he lied. "I sure love Bud Light." Joe grimaced at how awkward it was.

"Okay," she said, knowing better, "but this is the last one." When she came back a few minutes later, Joe grabbed Bodhi's mug and tipped the contents of the pitcher into it until she turned away.

"There you go pal," he chided, sliding no more than five ounces of beer toward his friend. Bodhi caught the glass and looked down into it. He felt guilty for lying, and he was a little worried about Joe. He stared at his beer for a while.

XXV

There was a blinding flash of light and Bodhi's nausea disappeared. He rubbed his eyes and looked up from where he lay.

His eyes met the undersides of leaves, lightly kissed by the sun and woven in a beautiful green tapestry. He brought his hands back and rested his head on them, contemplating underneath the tree.

After a few minutes he sat up. A gentle breeze blew through his hair as he gazed across the lawn and saw the farmhouse. It had white faded paint and tall windows, and a big summer porch. He got up and stood on his feet.

He could feel the breeze blowing through his clothes, and he realized he wasn't wearing his normal robes; he wasn't barefoot or bowling-shoed either. He returned his gaze to the house. He studied it for a second, then went toward it.

A sense of calm washed over him as he walked through the grass. He got to the old wooden porch and lifted his foot to take the first step. He knew how it would sound before his foot came down, the tired creak of the warped wood under his shoe. It made the same sound in his ear as he stepped on it and ascended the stairs.

He stopped at the door and reached out to touch it. He felt each grain against his hand; one or two sticking out could maybe cause a splinter, but otherwise it was smooth in his palm. He lowered his hand and felt the worn-down iron of the knob. He turned it and pushed.

The lights were off, but the sun came through the windows and lit the dust that hung in the air. He stepped inside and looked around. There was a large front room with high ceilings, wooden floors, and an old sofa. Straight ahead was a wide entryway that led to a country kitchen. He took a few steps toward it then stopped. There was a low murmur coming from it.

He stayed in the middle of the room, feeling indecisive. His curiosity got the better of him and he took a few careful steps toward the kitchen entryway and slowly peeked inside.

His eyes met the back of a woman, standing at the sink and talking aloud. Her hair was dark and tied up; a few loose strands fell down her neck and onto a white blouse that covered her shoulders. She wore bright blue jeans.

He contemplated her for a while, trying to make out what she was saying. He decided she must've been talking to someone else. At that moment he felt eyes on his back and spun around.

Sitting on the old sofa was a young man, staring through Bodhi and answering the woman's call from the kitchen. Bodhi looked down at his own stomach to make sure he wasn't a ghost, rubbing it and expecting to find a hole there. He found his body intact and returned his gaze to the young man. His dark, piercing eyes met Bodhi's, and he realized he wasn't talking to the woman at all—the young man was talking to him.

"You made it," he said, voice full of warmth and love, eyes softening.

"I hope you're hungry," the woman called from the kitchen.

"Who are you?" Bodhi asked.

The young man stood up. "Don't you recognize me?" he asked. Now his voice was full of hurt. "I'm–"

Tat, tat, tat.

"And you're–"

Tat, tat, tat.

Bodhi's eyes darted to the door. He couldn't hear anything over the knocking.

"What?" he asked.

"I'm–"

Tat, tat, tat.

"And you're–"

Tat, tat, tat.

"What?" Bodhi asked again. His eyes were wild and full of fear.

"Listen," the young man said, walking toward him and reaching out his hand. "I'm–"

Time suspended for a moment and Bodhi saw the young man's fingertips within grasp. He lifted his own hand to touch them as he anticipated the young man's final words.

Tat, tat, tat.

A sudden, violent force pulled him backwards, and it all began to fade. He cried out and everything went black.

Tat, tat, tat.

Bodhi came to on the old wicker chair. Through the window he saw Joe rapping at the door.

He sighed and stood up, then went over to let him in. He reached for the handle and saw Joe holding a beer in the midmorning sun.

Who is this poor creature? He thought to himself. He started to pull the door open, then caught his own sad reflection in Joe's eyes. *Better yet, who am I?*

XXVI

September comes to northeastern Indiana, and at first it feels like August. Nothing much changes until Labor Day.

In north Angola and Fremont, where the big boating lakes are, people throw Labor Day parties and cling to the last remnants of summer. Kids play water sports and parents show off their boats one more time before a long winter of storage. Somewhere a drunk uncle floats in a tube, using a belly full of beer as a coaster for his drink.

In the rest of Angola and its outlying towns the parties are the same as the Fourth, only tamer. Joe sneaks off with Crazy Craig to see how much beer they can drink; the unofficial record is a case apiece. The Bakers throw a small barbeque; Jim has too many cocktails and traps a young, unsuspecting church couple, demanding to know their stance on the national debt crisis. Bodhi notices one of his neighbors is having a party; he walks over but only stays for a beer and a cup of potato salad, then heads back to his drab little shack to meditate.

The day after Labor Day is when September actually starts. Each day gets one degree cooler and hoodies make their way out of closets. The varsity football team fights hard under the lights every Friday night and their classmates prepare for homecoming. Some skip the big dance and stay home to get high with their friends, listening to their favorite vinyl records. Cigarette smokers cling to porches, happy it's not so hot but quietly dreading winter. You can see their embers glowing in the twilight as the days get shorter. They put them in the ashtray and go inside to watch black and white movies, falling asleep to 1950s space-men and waking up to cold dew on the grass.

....

"Oh I'm so happy you came," Mrs. Baker gushed. "Come in, come in." She pulled the door open and stood by it, beaming. Joe walked through first, wearing a collared shirt and his only pair of khakis.

"Hey Angela," he said, smiling as he kissed her on the cheek. She grinned even harder, scrunching her face toward him. Bodhi took a step toward the entryway, looking awkward as he held a bottle of wine Joe had bought for him to give to the Bakers. He lifted it toward her.

"Oh, how sweet," Mrs. Baker cooed, pulling him in for a big hug.

"Greetings, Mrs. Baker," he managed to choke.

She stepped back and her eyes sparkled with joy. "Well come in, come in," she cried. "Jim's in the other room."

Angela hurried toward the kitchen and her two neighbors walked through the main room. The wooden floors were nice and polished, and a gorgeous dining room table was set with tablecloth, fine china, and sparkling glasses. Bodhi looked around as he walked, amazed at the beauty and comfort of their cozy little home. There were family pictures on the wall next to oil paintings of Jesus, and a cross hung over every entryway.

Jim grunted as they made their way into the TV room. He was watching baseball with a beer in his hand and couldn't be bothered.

"Greetings, Mr. Baker," Bodhi offered, standing in front of the TV.

"Goddamnit, move!" Jim shouted. Bodhi stumbled backward, flustered by the reply.

"No goddamnit, away from the TV!" Jim yelled, motioning toward a sofa against the wall. Bodhi stumbled over and sat down, still clutching the wine bottle.

"Hey Jim," Joe laughed. He walked over and sat down next to Bodhi.

"Hey Joe," Jim said, momentarily taking his eyes from the game, "wanna beer?" Joe opened his mouth to respond, but something happened to the Cubs that Jim didn't like. "Ahh, goddamnit!" he cried.

Joe waited a few seconds. "Yeah, I'll take a beer," he said.

"Angela!" Jim bellowed.

"Yes dear?" she called from the kitchen.

"Can you get me a beer?" he asked.

"You already have one, dear," she answered.

He let out an annoyed sigh. "Joe wants one," he called.

"Oh," she cried, "yes dear."

"I'll get it," Joe said, feeling awkward and standing up.

"She'll get you one," Jim promised. "Sit down."

"I got it," Joe said, taking a few steps.

Angela rushed from the kitchen with an open can. "Please," she assured him, handing him the beer, "sit, sit." Joe took the beer and went back to the sofa.

"Thanks," he said awkwardly, sitting down. Bodhi watched it all unfold, feeling uncomfortable.

"Sox are about to win the division," Jim grumbled.

"Yep," Joe answered, taking a sip, "shame how your boys fell apart." He hated the Cubs but was just being polite.

"Yeah," Jim muttered, "need to fire the front office, every one of 'em."

"What're you talking about?" Bodhi asked with genuine interest. Jim shot him a look of disgust. Joe opened his mouth to say something but decided against it.

"Dinner's ready," Angela called. "Jim, shut off the TV, will you?"

Jim let out another annoyed sigh. "Yes, dear," he said. He stood up from the couch and looked at Bodhi. "You heard the woman," he barked. The men got up and went to the other room. They sat down at the dining table as Angela rushed in and put the last dish in the center.

"Alright," she said, smiling as she sat down. She held her hands out and closed her eyes, quietly inviting everyone to join hands and pray. Jim and Joe instinctively followed, each grabbing one of her hands and holding the other out for Bodhi, who sat clutching the wine bottle with a bewildered look on his face. Jim shot him a disgusted look and muttered something under his breath, then withdrew his hand. Joe raised his and put it awkwardly on Bodhi's shoulder, trying not to laugh as he closed his eyes. Angela squeezed Jim's hand to start the prayer, pressing harder than normal to remind him to be kind to their guests.

Jim frowned with his eyes closed and let out a sigh that could've been mistaken for a deep, prayerful exhale. "Dear Lord, thank you for this food we are about to receive," he began. Bodhi looked around. Everyone but him had their heads bowed and their eyes closed, and they all seemed to be in some form of meditation. "And bless the hands that made it," Jim continued. Bodhi noticed Angela blush a little. "May we find favor with you, Lord, and may we always strive to carry out your will on this Earth." Jim stopped. Bodhi could tell that he wanted it to be over, but that he knew he'd be in trouble with either the "Lord" or with Angela if it wasn't. Bodhi saw Angela squeeze Jim's hand.

"And thank you for our guests," he grumbled. "Amen."

"Amen," repeated Joe and Angela.

"Amen!" Bodhi shouted, too loud and too late. Jim rolled his eyes, then noticed the wine bottle in Bodhi's hands.

"Gonna share that with the rest of us?" he barked. Startled, Bodhi drew back and pinched his shoulders against his neck, lifting the bottle.

"Oh Jim, stop it!" Angela said. "Here honey," she added, patting the table, "set it right here. How thoughtful." Bodhi set it next to two large dishes of casserole. Both looked and smelled delicious. "Here we go," Angela said, standing up and grabbing a serving spoon, "I'll start with our guests." Jim grunted. "Now Bodhi," Angela went on, ignoring her husband, "Joe tells me you're a vegetarian. Why didn't you tell me before?"

"Your kindness is a virtue," Bodhi said, "I didn't want to reject it."

"Aww," she blushed, bringing her hand to her heart. "Well, you shoulda told me sweetie. I've fed you enough chicken to start a farm."

"Hard to complain when it's free," Jim scoffed.

She shot him a quick look then grabbed the serving spoon. "Anyway," she said, digging the spoon into the dish, "this one here is veggie casserole. Had to call up my niece in Denver for the recipe—people in this town gotta have their meat." She served him a big, cheesy portion.

"Thank you," Bodhi said, his mouth watering.

"You know, sometimes I don't want to eat so much meat myself," she replied, putting the spoon down and moving toward the chicken casserole, "so I just have a little fish with my salad." Bodhi wanted to tell her that fish was still meat but thought better of it. She grabbed a second serving spoon and heaped a big, meaty pile onto Joe's plate.

"Thank you kindly," Joe said.

"Now I know my Jim can't survive without his meat." She smiled as she served him.

"Thank you dear," he replied.

She finished with him and got a small portion for herself. She sat down, feeling content. "Thank you both so much for coming," she said. "Jim and I are just so delighted to have you, aren't we hon?"

"Yep," Jim replied through a mouthful of food.

"Here, take some bread," Angela added, picking up a basket and passing it around the table. They each took a piece. Angela waited until the basket came back to her to grab the last one. Everyone ate in silence, thoroughly enjoying the meal.

After a few minutes Angela set her fork down. It made a small clank against her plate and signaled that she was ready for conversation. "So, Bodhi," she said after swallowing some casserole, "I'm really interested to learn more about your religion."

Bodhi looked up at her with confusion and a mouthful of food. "My religion?" he choked, trying to swallow as fast as he could.

"Yeah, you know," she replied with a smile, "the robes, the alms. When we first met you told me you were a monk."

"Oh," he said, finishing his food and taking a quick drink of water, "that. Well—"

"Gold tablets and the sanctity of Utah, honey," Jim said through a mouthful of chicken, "what else is there to know?"

"Don't listen to him," she snapped. "Now go on. You were saying?"

"Well, it's less of a religion and more of a universal truth," Bodhi said. "I am a Bodhisattva."

"A what now?" Jim scoffed.

"A Bodhisattva," he answered. "In my tradition, we believe that all beings cling to impermanence, which leads to unsatisfaction and a constant cycle of pain and rebirth."

"Uh huh." Angela smiled, nodding her head and trying to follow.

"The only way out is Nirvana. And the only way to that is a series of deeds that improve your cosmic standing."

The Bakers gave him puzzled looks. "Started as a bug and now he's here," Joe offered. The Bakers pursed their lips and nodded with their gaze turned upward, as if they understood but didn't quite agree.

"Well," Angela said, her Christian sensibilities reeling a little, "there's some similarity there."

"What do you mean?" Bodhi asked.

"Well," she said, looking at him in earnest with her hands folded, "we believe that humans are born in sin, and they cling to things they shouldn't cling to either, but the only way out is accepting Jesus Christ as Lord and savior."

"Amen," Jim said.

"Is that who you were talking to earlier?" Bodhi asked. Jim choked on his food. Angela's face went white for a second.

"We pray, yes," she said, recovering quickly.

"Pray?" Bodhi asked. Jim fidgeted in his seat and prepared to respond in anger.

Joe saw it and came to Bodhi's rescue. "It's kinda like meditating," he said. "Sometimes you ask for things, sometimes you say blessings—you've said blessings before."

"Ahh," Bodhi said, leaning back in his chair to ponder for a second. "I like it," he concluded with a smile.

The tension broke and the others were relieved. Angela chalked it up as a small victory and planned a full conversion for another day.

"So Joe tells me you're going to the car show at the end of the month," she said, changing the subject. "That'll be fun."

"Gas City or Fairmount?" Jim asked. A small ping hit Bodhi's chest as he recognized both places again.

"The boys set camp in Gas City," Joe answered, "usually hang there. You goin'?"

"Not sure this year," Jim replied. "Angela gets too excited, starts begging me to get her something."

"I really want a car from the '30s or '40s," she said, her eyes lighting up. "Like a mobster car you see in the movies."

Joe laughed and shook his head. "Now why on earth would you want somethin' like that?"

"I don't know," she said, smiling and wrinkling her nose, "sometimes I'd like to be bad."

"That's impossible," Bodhi said. "You are the kindest being I've ever known." The words were sincere, and it moved them a little. A tear came to Angela's eye.

"Thank you Bodhi," she said. Jim reached over and put his hand on top of hers. Bodhi debated on whether he should add a joke.

"Of course, you'd 'bout have to be," he heard himself say, sounding a lot like Joe, "to put up with a piece of shit like him." He motioned toward Jim with a grin on his face.

Angela choked out something between a gasp and a hiccup. Joe's eyes widened as far as they could and he turned away. Jim cocked his head and gave Bodhi a look that was equal parts bewildered and amazed. Bodhi's grin vanished into a nervous, dropping jaw as even he couldn't believe what he'd said. Then he saw Jim laugh.

It started as a reluctant grunt at first, followed by another, and then a series of grunts turned into a few solid chuckles. Angela put her hand on her chest and sighed with relief. Joe turned back toward the table with a big, beaming smile. Bodhi looked around the room and chuckled softly.

Jim grinned and laughed and shook his head. "You know somethin' kid," he said, "you're alright."

XXVII

Flowers die.

The bright orange of the butterfly weed fades to pale gold, shrivels, and passes. The deep indigo of the wild iris loses its color and goes underground. The sedum's pink gets lighter and lighter until it shines no more. They all die first in Bodhi's garden, sometime around July or August.

The black-eyed Susan is next. Its petals grow pale and weak; some fall off, some cling until death. Then comes the balloon flower; its big, vibrant bloom slowly recedes inward into oblivion. They die in late August or early September.

Now, it's up to the white asters, pink lilies, and hibiscus to keep color until frost. They stand in a spectral wave of white and pink, blowing gently in the mid-September breeze. They look beautiful in full bloom; they give Bodhi's shabby yard a bit of pride, and they give his neighbors a sense of hope. But the cold will kill them too.

But flowers live again.

The perennial's life force finds itself in a bulb in the dirt. It sits there like the singularity point at the center of the universe. And when the sun shines again, it bursts and pushes through; the green stalk grows and blooms into the big, colorful flower it's supposed to be. The life of the annual spills its seed, and either the dirt takes it and makes it grow, or a bird eats the seed and shits it into a field; suddenly, there's a sunflower in the middle of some godforsaken farm. Either way, life goes on.

But Bodhi's peonies were the real miracle. They'd have their time too, to die and be born again. But the last two in his garden were hanging on, as pink, intricate, and beautiful in mid-September as they'd been in June. By all accounts they should have withered and run underground. But they were clinging to something—a different resting place maybe, or perhaps they had one more sutra to teach.

XXVIII

"We're gonna raise hell is what we're gonna do," Joe grinned. "But first, we gotta get you cleaned up."

Bodhi looked down at his robe then lifted his arms to inspect them. He looked up at Joe.

"I think I'm alright," he said.

"Dude," Joe laughed in disbelief, "you bathe in lake water, and Lord knows the last time you got a haircut. Get in the truck."

Bodhi shrugged and climbed in. Joe corralled Sadie into the house and gave her some food. Bodhi looked at himself in the side mirror, running his hand through his hair, jutting out his chin and running his fingers through his scraggly beard until the front door slammed and Joe came outside. Joe got in, fired up the engine, and they headed to town.

There's a little salon on Wayne Street, right by the new Mexican restaurant everyone was excited about. They do stylish cuts and dyes for women; they do nice and cheap haircuts for men. Joe walked in behind Bodhi and the bells on the door jingled as it closed behind them.

A row of black chairs stood to the right of the counter, populated by two middle-aged women and a middle-aged man getting haircuts in black salon capes. One of the stylists looked up and toward the door.

"Be right with you," she called. She looked down, then her eyes shot back to Bodhi. "Uhh, have a seat," she added.

Bodhi and Joe sat down in the hard plastic waiting chairs by the door. Joe opened up a magazine from the strewn pile of *Cosmo, Good Housekeeping,* and *People,* thought to himself, *Wow, she* does *look good at fifty-five,* then realized what he was doing and threw it back on the table. Bodhi watched him and then looked around the room.

The stylist came to the counter. "How can I help you today?" she asked.

Joe stood up. "This young man needs a haircut," he said, motioning toward Bodhi. The man in the salon chair looked in the mirror, turning his head and running his fingers over the sides of his hair. He nodded to himself, stood, and came to the counter.

"One second," the stylist told Joe. The man paid and left. She thanked him and looked back toward Bodhi and Joe.

"What're we thinking?" she asked while messing with the register. Joe looked toward Bodhi with raised eyebrows and pursed lips. Bodhi didn't know what was happening.

"You know," Joe answered, "just give him a nice, clean cut. Nothin' fancy."

"Alright then."

"Oh, and a shave," he added.

The stylist nodded then took a few steps. "Right this way," she said.

"Go on," Joe urged, giving his friend a nudge. Bodhi got up and followed her. Joe grabbed the magazine again and crossed a leg over his knee as he read it.

"Have a seat," she said. Bodhi sat down and caught a glimpse of himself in the mirror. He saw his tired eyes, messy hair and beard. He didn't recognize himself, but he didn't know who else he could've been. The water from the spray bottle hit his hair and broke up his musing.

She combed out his gnarly hair and prepared to cut. Bodhi looked with trepidation at the scissors in the mirror.

"Ow!" he cried. A small piece of hair fell to the ground. In the lobby, Joe looked up from his magazine.

"I'm sorry, did I get you?" she asked.

"No, it's just," he said, rubbing his head. "It's been a while." He also feared change, but he didn't tell her that.

"Just relax," she said. "We'll go slow, and I'll take care of you." She went back to work. It took her a while, and Bodhi winced a few more times, but she did a fine job. When she was done she shaved his beard. She didn't even ask how he wanted it done—she decided to take it all off.

Bodhi looked at himself in the mirror when it was over. The face staring back at him was one he recognized, but not fully, like one he'd seen in a photograph. There was still a little fear in his eyes, but he felt good. "Thank you," he told the stylist.

Bodhi came around the corner and Joe put down his magazine.

"Jesus Lord Almighty," he exclaimed, "now there's a good-lookin' guy!" Bodhi smiled sheepishly and looked at the ground.

"I ain't kiddin' ya buddy," Joe cried, slapping him on the shoulder, "you look good." He thanked the stylist, paid for the haircut, and gave her a good tip. "Now let's get you some clothes."

There's a chain department store in town where people shop when they want a nice outfit. When it first came to Angola, everyone went berserk: Hoosiers back to school shopping, Hoosiers buying Christmas clothes, moms screaming "cash back" on every purchase and yuppies fiending for every sale. By now it'd settled down, and its allure had worn off, but every once in a while it convinced the townies it was still cool by stocking retro video game and classic rock t-shirts. Joe and Bodhi went inside, and Joe bought him a Thin Lizzy t-shirt and a few pairs of jeans.

When they got back to Joe's, Bodhi took a shower and put on his new clothes. He came out of the bathroom, fidgeting a little.

"Ooh! Someone's goin' to Jonesboro tonight!" Joe exclaimed.

"What's that?" Bodhi asked, tugging at his shirt collar, then at the waistband of his jeans.

"Nothin', just an expression," he said. "Let's get some food and hit these bars."

....

It started off at Applebee's, as most good nights in Indiana do. They had a nice meal and a couple beers apiece.

From there they went to the seediest bar in town, down the street from the factory.

"Joe!" the people cried when they walked in. Bodhi smiled at every-body and followed him to the bar. It looked more like a makeshift table that a shop class had built around some liquor store coolers. They took their seats on two shoddy stools and prepared to order drinks.

In the corner of the place was the punching-bag game, where hyped-up men took aggressive shots at a punching bag and tried to impress people with their high scores. Bodhi contemplated the weird machine for a second before noticing a woman at the edge of the bar. She was eying him but looked away every time he turned toward her. She was wearing an old hoodie and pajama pants, and her face was worn from cigarettes. She was the queen of the bar to anyone who cared to notice; she was beautiful but hardly tried.

Bodhi turned back toward Joe, who slid over a shot and a beer. Joe had already killed his shot and had a can of his own in hand.

Bodhi looked down at the liquor in the shot glass. He'd seen Joe take shots many times but had never tried one himself. He grasped it in his fingers and threw his head back. The foul burn of the liquor hit his mouth before scorching his throat and curdling his stomach. He gagged loudly and it came back up his throat.

The bartender glared at him and his cheeks full of liquor, ready to punch him if any came out. Bodhi turned toward Joe with pleading eyes and was met with a stern look and a solemn shake of the head. He choked it down, feeling the burn all over again. The bartender snorted and turned away. Joe smiled and slapped Bodhi on the top of the back. Bodhi hiccupped, feeling drunk already.

"Chase it down," Joe said, nodding toward the beer. Bodhi reached for it and took a drink. His mouth was relieved and his stomach settled a bit, though there was still a nauseating burn underneath the new beer in his gut. He shook his head and tried to get his bearings.

Bodhi took a few more sips of beer and the queen of the bar drifted to the seat next to him. She bent over the bar and gave a wry smile to get the bartender's attention, half-turned from Bodhi as if she didn't notice him.

"Jack and Coke?" the bartender asked her.

"Yep," she said. He made her the drink and slid it across the table. She put a five-dollar bill down.

"Thanks Charlene," he said.

She sipped her drink and studied Bodhi out of the corner of her eye. When she realized he wasn't going to initiate, she said, "Haven't seen you in here before."

Bodhi spun to look at her, feeling drunk. "Can't be seen in a place I've never been," he said.

"True," she replied, taking another drink.

"That wasn't rude was it?" Bodhi asked. "I don't mean to be rude— I'm not used to liquor."

"Not at all," she said, smiling as she touched his arm. Bodhi looked down at her hand where it touched him. It filled him with a warm rush of excitement.

"We must be careful with our words," he said, preparing to take a risk by quoting the Buddha to an Indiana barfly. "Words have the power to both destroy and heal. When words are both true and kind, they can change our world."

"You're not like the other guys that come in here, are you?" she asked, leaning closer and putting a hand on his leg.

"No, I guess not," he answered, feeling full of himself.

"I like it," she said. She downed the rest of her Jack and Coke and then leaned in to touch his leg again. "Buy me a drink?" she asked seductively.

Bodhi stuttered, feeling hot and excited. At that moment the door to the bar flew open, cracking against the wall from a forceful, drunken push, and in stumbled Clint Toucher.

"Hey motherfuckers!" Clint yelled. Joe rolled his eyes. Bodhi sat back in his chair and Charlene took her hands off him.

"Goddamnit I need some whiskey!" Clint hollered at the bartender. He lumbered up to the bar, noticed Charlene, and put a drunken arm around her. "Charly! Give me a kiss!" She turned away from him as he planted a big, sloppy kiss on her cheek.

"Hey Clint," she muttered.

"Aw what's the matter?" he asked, taking a shot of whiskey from the bar. "Gotta new boyfriend?" He turned toward Bodhi with a sadistic smile. Because of his new haircut and clothes, Clint didn't recognize him.

"We were just talking, Clint," she muttered. Then she turned to Bodhi. "Look, I'm gonna go."

"Alright," he said to her back as she left. Bodhi didn't know what made him feel worse—his fear of Clint, his anger that Clint had violated Charlene, or his own failure to do anything about it. There was a hot, smoldering shame that settled over him as he turned away.

"Aw look buddy, you made her leave!" Clint yelled. "Hey buddy," he added, putting his hand on Bodhi's shoulder, "I'm talkin' to you."

Joe got up and pushed Clint off his friend.

"Don't touch him!" he bellowed. "And you better apologize to Charlene the next time you see her."

"Ah, Big Joe," Clint grinned with malice. The bartender looked up, ready to kick people out.

"It's alright," Joe said, "we're leavin'." He tapped Bodhi on the shoulder. "C'mon man, let's go."

Clint watched them leave, smiling to himself like an animal that'd just proven he was king of the pride. "Pussies," he said under his breath. He took another shot from the bar then looked back at the door. It suddenly dawned on him who Bodhi was, and his smiling, drunken hubris turned to anger and violence.

"That's that same motherfucker from the other night!" he screamed, marching over to the punching bag machine. A group of hypermasculine country boys were there to greet him. He put a quarter in the machine and got ready to wallop the bag.

"When I catch 'im I'm gonna beat that little fucker senseless!" He hit the bag as hard as he could. Even his macho friends were impressed. He dug in his pocket and put in another quarter. "Him and his stupid fuckin' bodyguard!"

XXIX

Bodhi was silent in the truck. Joe tried to help him forget.

"Don't worry about him," Joe said, fishing under his seat and grabbing Bodhi a beer. "He's a dumbass."

Bodhi took the beer and sighed.

"Drink up man," Joe urged, "it's Saturday night."

Bodhi cracked the beer open and took a drink. Joe cranked up the radio, and Bodhi felt a little better by the time they got to the next bar.

They parked a few blocks away because the bar was right on The Mound, near the police station, and everyone knew Joe's truck. There was live music spilling from the door and a group of twenty- and thirty-somethings smoking cigarettes and vape pens out front. One of them had snuck a weed pen into the circle.

"Hey man, how you doin'?" one of them slurred, putting their arm around Bodhi.

"Um, hello," Bodhi answered.

"I remember you," he said, his eyes hardly open. "Here, hit this." He stuck his weed pen in Bodhi's face. Bodhi tried to refuse but the guy was persistent, and all his townie friends seemed excited. Even Joe wore a grin like he wanted to see what would happen next.

Bodhi left it in the guy's hand but craned his neck and put his lips around the end of the pen. He took a deep, meditative inhale. The dab set his lungs on fire and he started coughing.

"There you go!" hollered one of the townies as the rest started laughing. Bodhi couldn't stop coughing.

"Class of '09 baby!" the guy added, punching Bodhi on the arm. Bodhi had no idea what it meant. He just wanted to stop coughing.

"Thanks guys," Joe chuckled. "Let's get you inside," he said to Bodhi, putting his arm around him.

The inside of the bar was a blur of bright lights, dark shadows, giddy people, and loud music. Bodhi couldn't tell if it was always this way, or if whatever he'd smoked was disorienting his brain. He got a little nervous and tugged at Joe's sleeve, who yanked his arm away to pay the cover.

"Grab that booth over there," Joe shouted over the music, pointing.

"I am the void," Bodhi shouted back.

"Let me get you some water," Joe answered. Joe went over to the long wooden bar and Bodhi floated to the booth. He fell in and started rubbing the vinyl seating, wondering why it felt so appealing. He inspected his hands and enjoyed how unique the cracks in his palms looked, then suddenly started worrying about how dry his mouth was.

Joe returned with two pitchers: one of water, and one of beer. He slid Bodhi an empty cup. Bodhi tried to say something but his mouth was a desert. He poured himself a cup of water and drained it.

"Thank you," he choked.

"Welcome," Joe said, grabbing his beer. He started talking again, but Bodhi poured himself more water and let his mind and eyes wander away.

The band had taken a break and the frontwoman was leaning over the stage to speak with some fans. The guitar player turned to his half-finished beer on the amplifier, killed it, and motioned to the bar for another while the drummer fidgeted on his stool. On the dance floor, college kids stood in various cliques: frat boys huddled together shouting things like "bro," laughing at their own bad jokes while working up the courage to talk to disinterested townie women; a group of engineering students stood sipping craft beers in the corner, trying to forget about upcoming exams; a drunk older couple slow-danced in the back of the crowd, unaware that the band had stopped playing.

At the bar, people of all ages swarmed the countertop to call for drinks over the heads of either geniuses or fools who'd claimed seats hours before. The bartenders hustled about, pouring shots and beers in between jokes to customers, quick eye rolls, and sarcastic comments to one another. One old regular sat with his third pitcher, long crusty hair over his eyes, shoulders hunched, sipping beer and pretending it was still the same old bar that he loved.

"I said are you feelin' okay?" Joe yelled over the din of the place. Bodhi jerked out of his trance and looked at him.

"Yeah," Bodhi answered, "yeah! I feel pretty good."

The music started back up and he looked toward the dance floor.

"Feel like dancin'?" Joe grinned.

"I don't think so," Bodhi answered without turning around.

"We'll see," Joe snickered, finishing his cup and heading to the bar. He got in line and waited a few minutes for the bartender to notice him.

With his back turned and his mind on alcohol, Joe didn't see Clint Toucher stumble in. The security guard was flirting with a college girl so he didn't see Clint either; otherwise, he would've taken one look at him and tossed him out. Drunk as he was, Clint still recognized his own good fortune and hobbled up the stairs to the bar on the second floor.

Joe came back with two pitchers of beer this time. "I think you've sobered up enough," he said, leaning over and placing one in front of Bodhi. He moved toward his end of the booth and let out a grunt as he sat down. Bodhi watched the dance floor a little longer then turned back and looked down at the table with a smile.

"Go on," Joe laughed, waving his hand, "you know you want to."

"No, no," Bodhi grinned, shaking his head. "It's just nice to see them having fun."

Upstairs, Clint found a group of hicks that liked drinking and fighting as much as he did. They bragged about their exploits and drank shot after shot of Fireball.

Bodhi had drunk half of his pitcher by the time Mandy came in. She smiled at the doorman and headed to the bar. A group of her girlfriends had just ordered shots, and a row of glasses lined the counter. She leaned over and put a friendly hand on her girlfriend's shoulder.

"Mandy!" she cried, surprised to see her there. "Here, take a shot!"
"I gotta work tomorrow," Mandy answered, grinning and shaking her head.

"Oh come on. You always gotta work tomorrow."

Mandy thought about it. "S'pose you're right," she said, grabbing a shot glass.

"Thatta girl," one of them said as Mandy threw it back.

"Oooh, that's my song," another said, getting up and grabbing Mandy by the hand. "C'mon!"

Bodhi took another drink of beer, feeling drunk.

"Hey," Joe said, "look." He motioned with his thumb toward the dance floor.

Bodhi looked over and there she was. She was done up and out of her work clothes. The lights from the stage hit her long blond hair and she smiled her sweet country smile. His heart skipped a beat.

"Go talk to her," Joe suggested.

"No," Bodhi muttered, taking another drink.

Upstairs, Clint threw back another shot. "Charlene, that bitch," he slurred.

"Thought you was with Mandy," one of the country boys said.

"They're all the same," Clint answered, motioning for more liquor.

Bodhi watched Mandy dance with her friends. She was having a good time, and it made him happy. She looked over and saw him sitting there. He looked away. She blushed and tucked her hair behind her ears, then went back to dancing.

"I'm tellin' you man, go talk to her," Joe urged.

Bodhi ignored him and finished his pitcher. He was nervous, but the alcohol gave him a little confidence. "I don't know," he said.

The song ended and the crowd cheered. After the clapping faded the lead singer took to the microphone. "Thank you, thank you," she said. "Right now, we're gonna slow it down a little." The guitarist slid into a wavy, melodic rift. The band came in behind, and soon the bar was filled with the tune of a sweet, nostalgic song from the 1950s. It was perfect for slow dancing.

"I'm gonna sit this one out," one of the girls said. Mandy's friends left her on the dance floor. She stood there, swaying and looking nervous.

"Now's your chance," Joe said.

"I don't know," Bodhi said. He could feel his confidence work up his chest into a heavy fever pitch. He watched her for a second, then turned back to Joe with a drunken grin.

"C'mon man!" Joe cried, reaching across and slapping him on the shoulder.

Bodhi stood up and took a step toward the dance floor. "I'm gonna do it!" he cried, smiling. Joe took a drink of beer then raised his glass to his friend's hubris. With the encouragement from both Joe and a beer-marijuana buzz, Bodhi stumbled onto the floor. He got a few steps from Mandy and his nerves kicked in. He looked back to the booth. Joe gave a thumbs-up. Bodhi turned toward Mandy and saw her swaying. She looked like a peony in the sunlight, but more beautiful—more beautiful than anything he'd ever seen. "Um, hi," he choked.

Mandy spun around and saw him standing there. "Bodhi?" she cried. "Bodhi, is that you?"

"It is," he said, standing there like an awkward teenager.

"I almost didn't recognize you," she said, tucking her hair behind her ears again.

"Yeah," Bodhi muttered, palms sweaty as he stared at the floor and kicked at nothing. He was going to say how Joe made him get a haircut, buy a pair of jeans, wear a rock n' roll t-shirt, but nothing came out.

"Do you wanna dance?" Mandy finally asked, a little more excited than she let on.

Bodhi looked up into the prettiest eyes he'd ever seen. "Uh, sure," he managed to say. He shuffled his feet in front of her in an awkward wobble. She giggled, putting her hand in front of her mouth.

"Here," she said, grabbing his hands and putting them on her hips, "you go like this." He felt her slender curves and his heart started racing. "And I go like this," she said, putting her hands on his shoulders. His heart beat even faster.

They swayed in time with the music; Bodhi stared into her eyes and he knew he was in love. Mandy smiled and giggled.

"Hey, isn't that Mandy down there?" one of the hicks asked, back-handing Clint on the shoulder.

Clint took another shot of Fireball. "Where?" he demanded.

"Down there."

Clint peered over the railing and saw Mandy smiling at Bodhi. His eyes lowered and he got mean. He was ready to fight.

"Yep."

Time seemed to slow down for Bodhi, and yet he was afraid for the moment to end. Mandy's heart was happy and she wasn't aware of time at all. The romantic melody of the band washed over them as they danced.

Clint marched toward the stairs with violence in his eyes. The country boys spit on the floor and cracked their knuckles. They followed him down and onto the dance floor.

The song was coming to an end. Bodhi's heart raced and he wondered if he should kiss her.

"Mandy," he said.

"Yes Bodhi?" she said, looking at him with big, beautiful eyes.

"Mandy, I—"

There was a vicious tug on his shoulder and Bodhi fell to the floor. He looked up and saw Mandy standing there with her hands out, eyes wide with worry. Clint stood over him with a malicious grin on his face and grabbed Mandy for a dance.

"What's a matter baby?" he smirked, trying to pull her closer. Mandy pushed him away. Bodhi sat for a second, helpless and disoriented.

"You can dance with this faggot but not your man?" Clint demanded.

"Clint, leave me alone!" Mandy cried.

"Oh, come on," he said with a sickening darkness in his voice. Bodhi stood up.

Clint grabbed Mandy again and pulled her in. She tried to fight but he wouldn't let her go.

"Leave her alone!" Bodhi bellowed, surprising himself with the force of his voice.

Clint pushed Mandy away and turned toward Bodhi. "What the fuck are you gonna do about it?" he yelled. The country boys moved in and surrounded them.

"I shouldn't have to do anything about it," Bodhi said, trying to reason with him. "You should just treat her with respect."

Clint laughed and turned toward Mandy. "C'mere baby," he grinned, reaching for her, "that guy's a pussy."

"Get away from me!" she cried. Bodhi moved in between them, shielding Mandy from Clint's advance. Clint tried to brush Bodhi aside and grab Mandy.

"C'mere you little bitch!" he yelled. Bodhi's body swelled with rage. He pushed Clint back and clenched his fists.

"You gonna hit me?" Clint asked. He turned to the country boys. "Is this little pussy gonna hit me?" They responded with sick, dark smiles and moved in closer. Joe got up from the booth.

Clint turned back to Bodhi. "You ain't nothin' but a little, wannabe chink." Bodhi couldn't control his rage anymore. He reached back and threw his best punch at Clint's face, connecting flush with his jaw. Clint stumbled backward for a second, then gathered himself and prepared to knock Bodhi out.

Bodhi froze, feeling overwhelmed. He felt a tremendous amount of guilt for breaking the most important rule of the Bodhisattva: never resort to violence. But he hated Clint for what he said, and he felt the need to protect Mandy. He stood his ground in front of her, but his shame wouldn't allow him to throw any more punches.

Clint reached back with all his might. The last thing Bodhi saw was the hate in Clint's eyes before he closed his own and prepared for death.

Joe stepped in and punched Clint so hard that he crumpled to the floor in a pathetic, lifeless heap. Bodhi opened his eyes and regarded Clint's body with a mix of excitement and horror. The country boys dashed in, ready to fight.

The first, a wiry hick with dirty fingernails, swung at Joe's face. Joe saw it coming and ducked underneath. Then, he shot upward, hooked the guy's underarm over his shoulder, and sent him flipping over his back and crashing through a table. Two big hosses came at Joe next and he jabbed one in the face, but the other got behind him and pinned his arms back. Joe struggled as the first recovered and pummeled him in the stomach. Bodhi stood protecting Mandy, trying to back her away, but she broke free and ran to help Joe. She grabbed the boxer by the shoulders and spun him around, then drove a knee into his stomach. Bodhi was both afraid of her and a little turned on. Joe headbutted his captor then elbowed him in the chest, sending him backward. Mandy's foe stood up, clutching his gut. He saw her standing there, and although it was against the Hoosier code to hit a woman, he reached for her throat. Joe grabbed him and spun him around, knocking him out with a heavy right.

Another country boy snatched a cue from a hapless pool player and closed in on Joe. Bodhi realized Mandy was caught in the crossfire. He ran in and grabbed her, pushing her to the safety of a nearby booth. He fell on top of her and squeezed her tight. He wouldn't let anything happen to her.

The redneck swung the pool stick; Joe caught it in his hand. He yanked it toward him and the redneck stumbled forward, then Joe hit his nose with another headbutt. He ripped the cue out of the redneck's hand and smashed it over his head.

The bartender called the police, and the security guard stopped flirting and rushed the floor. He saw Clint and his boys on the ground and smiled a little. They were always starting fights. Only one was still standing, and he was squaring up against Joe. The security guard decided to wait and see what Joe could do.

The last redneck hit Joe with a strong jab, sending him back. He hit him with another, and the barflies rushed out of the way as Joe fell into the stools. Joe sat like a boxer with his arms in the turnbuckle ropes, thinking his time was up.

The country boy trudged over with angry confidence in his step and violence in his heart. He grabbed Joe by the collar and pulled him up against the bar. "You're fuckin' dead," he spat, reaching back for the haymaker.

Joe turned and noticed a half-finished cocktail near his open hand. He grabbed it and threw the liquor in the aggressor's face.

"What the fuck!" he screamed, clawing at his eyes. Joe grabbed the back of his head and smashed his face into the bar, then picked him up and threw him over the rail and into the liquor shelf. Glass shattered and liquor bottles rained over him. He was finished.

Police sirens wailed and the security guard ran toward the bar. "You got ten seconds," the guard told him. Joe gave him a grateful nod. He dug in his pocket and slapped a few hundred dollars on the bar.

Joe ran toward the booth and pulled Bodhi and Mandy up. "Let's get the fuck out of here," he said.

Bodhi nodded, still in a stupor from everything that'd happened. He followed Joe to the truck, clutching Mandy's hand behind him. They got to the door and Mandy pulled her hand away.

"I gotta go," she mumbled.

"Are you sure?" Bodhi asked.

"Yes," she mumbled, "thank you." She jumped in her car and drove off. Bodhi watched her go.

"C'mon buddy," Joe said, grabbing his shoulder, "let's go." Bodhi climbed in the truck, feeling sad and confused. Three cops drove past them before Joe turned his lights on and slid away undetected.

The truck was silent as they cut through the night.

"You did the right thing back there," Joe finally said.

Bodhi burst into tears. He wept for humanity; he wept for the universe. He couldn't understand why life had to be so hard. "Just take me home," he said.

XXX

At first it was just a sad, dark blob. Bodhi squinted to see better. The kitchen doorway formed in his vision and he realized he was in the farmhouse.

He saw the lady at the sink, but something was wrong. There were a bunch of different pictures of her in his head, all cut into trippy, geometric shapes. He went to rub his eyes but his arms were too short. He stretched them as far as he could and felt the fuzzy membranes of his thin little limbs brush across a pair of delicate, glassy eyeballs. He blinked a few times but the images remained.

He became aware of some loud noises behind him, but there was a heavy buzzing in his abdomen that rattled his brain. He spun around quicker than he knew he could, and the sight of something hit his kaleidoscope eyes before he should've been able to see it. It sat in the dark on the living room couch, talking to him.

Bodhi tried to shut out the buzzing in his head. "Hello?" he managed to ask.

"Hey buddy," it said, "come and sit down."

Bodhi moved closer, and he felt his body scuttle over. He was moving fast but it took forever to reach the couch.

"Use your wings there pal," it told him. Bodhi was confused, but he heard a series of flaps and he suddenly reached the thing on the couch. He almost threw up when he saw it.

A giant centipede in an Old Milwaukee hat sat deep in the couch, its buggy beer-belly poking out. "Take a load off," it said. It tapped on a nearby spot with one of its only legs that wasn't holding a beer.

Bodhi sat down next to it.

"Sorry bud, we really fucked up this time," the centipede said, taking a drink. "Here." It extended one of its slimy legs to offer Bodhi a beer.

173

Bodhi reached for it and saw a pair of hairy, insect legs come from his own body to grab the can.

"Welp," the centipede said, clanking its can against Bodhi's. Bodhi went to take a drink and saw his reflection in the can—his big buggy eyes, his disgusting mouth, his hairy abdomen, his large, transparent wings.

He was a fly.

The buzzing boomed in his head and his legs grinded together in fear. He spat on the floor involuntarily.

"Oh come on," laughed the centipede, "it ain't that bad."

The image of the grinning bug refracted in his eyes. There were at least eight different cuts of it crashing together in his brain. It was like a psychotic carnival in his head and it made him sick.

"Joe!" he shouted at the centipede. "Joe, why'd you make me do it?"

The centipede took a slug of beer. "Purity or impurity depends on oneself," he answered, tilting his can toward the fly. "Drink up."

Bodhi woke with a gasp and shot up in his bed. He was happy he wasn't a bug, but his immediate relief soon gave way to a heavy, burning dread. The world was still cold and violent, and he was still living in it.

He looked down at his bowling shoes on his feet, then at his jeans, and finally at the Thin Lizzy logo on the chest of his t-shirt. He sighed and took everything off, wadded it up, and threw it into the corner of his room.

He rose slowly and put on his robes, walked out to the porch, and sat down to meditate. Beer, bowling, being in love—he wanted to erase it all. Then the world couldn't corrupt him anymore.

He took a deep breath.

One.

He just wanted everything to go back to normal.

Two.

XXXI

Tat, tat, tat.

Bodhi cracked open his eye from his meditation chair. It was Joe. That was the last thing he wanted to see.

A few days had passed since the fight at the bar. Joe had come by every morning, but Bodhi refused to answer. He shut his eyes and went back to his routine.

The next day Joe went to Mrs. Baker.

"He won't talk to me," he said.

"Oh dear," she sighed, frowning.

"Maybe you can go over there, bring him some food? It's been a few days since he ate." Mrs. Baker nodded with good Christian spirit, made her best casserole, and went to Bodhi's door.

Tat, tat, tat.

He opened his hungry eyes and saw her standing there. His heart ached when her worried face peered through the screen. He closed his eyes and ignored her. She set the dish down and walked home.

Tat, tat, tat.

On the fourth day Joe had had enough.

"Open up goddamnit!" he yelled.

Bodhi looked up from his chair and tried to meditate him away.

"Open up you son of a bitch!" Joe bellowed, kicking the spoiled casserole into the yard. Bodhi sighed and closed his eyes, waiting for him to go away. Joe seethed for a few seconds and then waved his hand in disgust, turning and walking down the street. Halfway to his house, he realized yelling and kicking had been a mistake. When he opened his door, he felt embarrassment and remorse.

"Just have to try again tomorrow," he sighed.

Joe got up early the next day to catch Bodhi before work. The sun was still fresh and pale when he knocked on the door. Bodhi hadn't moved from his chair.

"Bodhi, hey buddy, open up," he said. Bodhi pushed his eyes shut even harder.

"You really oughta go to this car show bud," Joe said. "It'll be good for you." Bodhi's stomach sucked against his ribs. He opened his eyes for a second.

"Look man, I—I'm sorry, okay? I'm sorry." Joe had one closed fist raised against the top of the door and his other hand open and pressed against the frame near the handle. His eyes were to the ground.

Bodhi felt a sharp pang in his chest. He cared about Joe, and he felt sorry for him. He stood up.

"I'm sorry buddy," Joe said, eyes still down and shaking his head, "I really am."

Bodhi came to the door and looked at Joe through the screen. "It's okay Joe," he said, "just go away."

Joe looked up at him. He was surprised Bodhi had answered at all. "Hey buddy," he said, "hey, I—"

"Joe, please, just go away."

"What for?" Joe asked.

"I don't want to see you anymore," Bodhi stated.

Joe felt like he'd been punched in the chest. He tried to hide it, but Bodhi noticed pain all over his face.

"Okay," Joe said, turning away. He took a few steps into the yard and stopped. "What about Mrs. Baker?" he asked.

Bodhi's heart sank. "No," he said, standing his ground.

Joe came back to the door. "And Mandy?" he pleaded.

Bodhi's heart sank even lower. Joe watched him through the screen and noticed he was struggling.

"C'mon man," Joe said, reaching for the door handle and trying to pull it open.

"Joe, stop."

Joe put his hands in his pockets, looked down at the ground, and spat. "So that's it?" he asked. Bodhi didn't respond. "You get into one little fight, and you throw it all away?"

"The world made me impure," Bodhi said. "I had it all figured out before I met you."

Joe laughed, indignant. "You didn't have shit figured out," he said.

The anxiety in Bodhi's chest turned to anger. He gritted his teeth and pushed hot air through his nose. "Listen," he began, pressing his finger against the screen. He could feel his voice rising and knew he wanted to yell. He sighed instead and took a step back. "I'm not going to the car show with you."

"Unbelievable," Joe scoffed, turning away. He took a step toward the street then turned back around. He still wanted to save him. "I'll go," he promised, "but I have more to say first."

Bodhi crossed his arms. He'd let Joe say what he had to say, then kick him out for good.

"Mrs. Baker's always tryin' to drag me to church," Joe began. Bodhi squinted his eyes, wondering where he was going. "And I always tell her no. I invent some reason not to go." Joe spat on the ground, then turned and looked off into the distance. "Maybe I pick up a shift, maybe I'm too drunk the night before. But I never wanna go." He took off his hat and ran his fingers through his hair, then placed it back on his head. "Last time I went with her, God, it's been a few years now. Last time I went with her, the preacher was talkin' about peace. He was talkin' about this dove. This beautiful, white dove in the middle of a hurricane." He turned and looked Bodhi straight in his eyes.

"What's that got to do with anything?" Bodhi scoffed.

Joe shook his head. "Can't you see it?" he cried. "The dove in the hurricane, the peonies in September, the beer can in your garden?"

Bodhi looked at him. He knew there was some wisdom in what Joe was saying, but he also knew he was a deeply flawed human being.

"Joe," Bodhi heard himself say, "you're addicted to alcohol." Joe reeled backward for a second. "You're addicted to alcohol, and you threw a beer can in my yard," Bodhi said. "That's it."

"But you picked it up!" Joe cried. "You picked it up and held it right in my face. You damn near killed us."

"I was trying to help you," Bodhi stated, repressing his feelings. "I tried to help you, and it didn't work."

"Help me?" Joe scoffed. "Help me?"

"It is the duty of the Bodhisattva to help all others reach enlightenment before they help themselves," Bodhi recited.

Joe laughed, shaking his head in disbelief. "So that's it?"

"That's it."

Joe started to say something, then stopped. "Alright man," he sighed. He shook his head and walked to the truck. Bodhi watched as he climbed in and drove away. He went back to his wicker chair and sat down, wondering if he'd done the right thing.

………..

Joe drove past Crazy Craig's and turned right down Main Street, silent and bitter. He prepared to turn at the fork and noticed his gas was running low. "Goddamnit," he muttered. He kept past the post office and toward the Marathon, crossed the four-way stop, and pulled in. He eased up to a pump and stepped out of the truck, mumbling to himself as he dug in his pockets for some gas money.

The chimes on the glass door rang when he pulled it open, then rang again when it closed behind him. Mandy looked up from the counter. Joe's eyes were down until he got there. He lifted them up and saw her.

"Hey Mandy," he said, a little surprised.

"Hey there Joe," she said, friendly but less lively than usual, "what can I do for ya?" She was hoping to avoid mention of the brawl at the bar.

"How ya been?" he asked.

"I been alright," she said, "workin' workin'."

"I guess," Joe said. "I'm surprised to see you here."

"Where else would I be?"

"I'm just glad to see ya is all," he said.

"Why's that?" she asked.

"Well, you know, it got so fucked up the other night."

"Yeah," she sighed, "you'll have that."

They looked away from each other. Joe's guilt and Mandy's sadness intensified the silence in the store.

"How's he doin'?" Mandy finally asked.

Joe shook his head. "Not good," he said. "Won't even talk to me."

Mandy offered a quaint frown. "Poor guy," she said.

"Him or me?"

"Him," she answered.

"Oh," Joe replied, "a'course." The quiet resumed. Joe looked at Mandy and saw all the warmth and sweetness in her face. An idea came to him.

"Do you think," he started, getting excited but still meek and subdued by his guilt, "maybe, maybe you could talk to him?"

"Oh, I don't know," Mandy sighed, closing her eyes and shaking her head.

"Please?" Joe begged, growing more convinced that it was the best way to get through to Bodhi.

"I…" she began, looking up at the ceiling and shaking her head some more. "I just don't know," she answered, looking back at Joe.

"Please," Joe begged harder, now sure it was the only way, "he really needs it. He's convinced he's done some kinda evil."

"Bodhi?" Mandy asked, furrowing her brow.

"Yeah." Joe shrugged, commiserating with her disbelief. "Got some notion that the world made him wicked."

"Wicked? Like how?"

"I don't know," Joe said. "But the man hates violence, I know that much. And sometimes the world's too cold for him. I think it all came to a head the other night."

"Yeah," she muttered, "did that to me too."

"So you'll talk to him?" Joe asked.

"Well," she said, looking away, "Frito truck's comin' later, got some stockin' to do. And the pop run out again." She stopped to think about it. After a few seconds she looked back at Joe. "But if I can get me a break, I'll go see him."

Joe responded with a solemn nod. In all the time he'd known her, she'd never taken a break. "Thank you," he said, feeling empty. The silence came back, and it was heavier than before.

"Alright," Mandy finally said, settling back into her work persona, "what can I do for ya?"

Joe reached into his pocket. "Thirty on three," he muttered.

….….…..

Bodhi was so hungry he could feel it in his soul. He stared out the window, waiting for something to come.

He heard the rumble of an engine. For a moment he feared it was Joe, but this engine sounded a little different. A few seconds later an old red Jeep eased to a stop in front of his house.

He squinted through the window, trying to see who it was. The Jeep door opened and a sweet country blond stepped out, straightened her hair with her hands, then dusted her clothes off. His heart leapt into his throat. It was Mandy.

She shut the door and made her way across the yard. Bodhi's chest got tight and he went to hide in the other room.

"Bodhi, is that you?" she called through the screen. He froze. After a few seconds of silence, he turned around and crept to the door.

"Bodhi, I can see you through the window," she said.

He tried to make it look like he was doing something else, then looked up through the screen. "Oh hi," he said, smiling awkwardly.

"What're you doin', ya big weirdo?" she laughed.

He tried to think of an excuse. "Uh, nothin'," he said, attempting to play it cool.

"Come out here," she grinned, waving him outside. "It's too dark in there." Bodhi wanted to tell her to go away, but he found himself opening the screen door.

"You got your robes back on," she observed.

"Yeah," he replied, standing on the step with the door open.

"Will you come down and talk to me?" she asked.

Bodhi stepped into the yard and let the door shut behind him. "Uh, sure. Do you want to go somewhere?" he asked.

"I was thinkin' maybe the beach," she offered. "I'm always workin', don't get to see it much."

"Okay."

The two started across the grass. Bodhi hadn't felt it on his bare feet in a long time. They stopped at the road to make sure no cars were coming, then crossed the asphalt and made their way down the hill. Mandy stopped at the reeds that ran along the edge of the water and sat down. Bodhi watched her do it first and then sat down next to her.

They gazed over the dying September reeds and out onto the cold, clear water. A few minutes passed without words until Mandy finally said, "So Joe come into the store today."

"Yeah?" Bodhi said, picking at a blade of grass. "What did he want?"

"Gas mostly," she replied, dusting off her pant leg. "But he was talkin' about you. Seems pretty worried."

Bodhi felt both grateful and annoyed. "He should worry about himself," he muttered, tossing the blade of grass.

"Prolly should," she agreed, "but still."

"I wish he'd go away," Bodhi said. "I was a lot better off before I met him."

"How so?" Mandy asked.

"I didn't care about earthly things," Bodhi replied, trying to sound wise.

"What else is there to care about?" she asked.

The simplicity of her question caught him off guard. He thought about the cosmos, the void, the everlasting cycle of pain and death, how it all went away when he realized the world was transient, constantly changing, soulless. But having eaten well, having bowled a strike and slammed a beer at dawn, having loved—he wasn't so sure anymore. He stuttered and looked into her eyes. They were blue, and bright, and honest.

He looked down. "I don't know," he answered. He started picking at the grass again.

Mandy watched him with a sympathetic curiosity. She could tell he'd placed a great weight on himself.

"I used to say," he said, somewhere between a scoff and a chuckle, "I used to say, 'the root of suffering is attachment.' It was easier then." He plucked a few blades of grass and tossed them aside, hoping that'd solve his problems.

Mandy waited for him to go on, some of the pain in his face absorbed in her own. "Just because it was easier don't mean you were better off," she finally said.

"Maybe," Bodhi sighed, folding his arms on his knees and looking onto the lake. Mandy's eyes stayed with him.

"You're a good person Bodhi," she said, "and you got some good ideas. They're just a little mixed up is all."

Bodhi didn't answer her for a while. He stared at the lake, contemplating the universe and his place within it. He sighed. "I thought I was enlightened," he said. "I thought I could help people." He dropped his eyes toward his lap and lowered his head. "I can't even help myself."

Mandy's eyes filled with compassion. "You helped me," she said.

"With violence," Bodhi lamented. "People got hurt."

"They're fine," she said. "Only thing hurt is their pride." Mandy waited for him to look at her, but he kept his eyes lowered. "Bodhi," she said, quiet but strong, "you did the right thing." She reached out and grabbed his hand, holding it in her own.

A rush of excitement ran through him when he felt her touch. He looked up into her eyes.

"You're tryin' too hard to figure it all out," she assured him. "Cut yourself some slack."

Bodhi smiled, and some of his sadness lifted. He leaned back and turned his eyes toward the lake, keeping his hand in hers.

They sat in peace for a while, holding hands and staring at the water. Bodhi was one with her and the universe, and the sun faded from bright yellow to gold. He never wanted it to end.

"Welp," Mandy sighed after a while, "shelves ain't gonna stock themselves." Bodhi felt the moment slipping away.

"Mandy, wait," he urged, holding her hand tighter.

"Yeah?" she asked. Bodhi looked down at the grass for a second then turned his eyes toward her. His heart pounded and his chest sank into his stomach.

"Can I kiss you?" he asked.

She looked down at their hands locked together.

"No," she replied, letting go and standing up. Bodhi felt her hand break from his, and his sadness returned. She took a half-step toward the hill, then stopped.

"Take care Bodhi," she said, kneeling down and kissing him on the cheek. His whole body flushed with warmth.

Mandy stood up and walked away, making it halfway up the hill before turning around. "Hey Bodhi," she called.

"Yeah?" he replied, turning toward her.

"Cut us regular people some slack too," she said, smiling her big country smile.

"I will," he grinned. He waited until she left before falling backwards into the grass. In all his lives it had never felt so good.

XXXII

Quitting time came and first shift headed out the door. Joe waved good-bye to the cigarette smokers and climbed into his truck, pulling around the factory and onto Wayne Street.

Bodhi lay in the grass, watching the clouds. He thought about Mandy and what she'd said to him. He knew somewhere down the line he'd find something to worry about, but right now the world was beautiful, and he was content.

The lakes get cold, the lakers go home, and traffic lightens up in September. Joe cruised down Wayne Street, making it to The Mound in a few minutes; a few minutes after that, his truck climbed the small hill where Wayne became Old 27, and soon he hit the open road. The last song on his tape was slow and sad. He fished under his seat for a beer and cracked it open, taking a nice, long drink. He set it down in the cup holder and put his foot on the gas.

Bodhi exhaled, long and blissful, then thanked the sky for its beauty. He got up and turned to the lake, thanking it for its wisdom. He turned and walked up the hill, thanking the grass for its embrace.

Joe approached the speed trap at the fork and faded right past the cemetery. He slammed the rest of his beer before reaching the stop sign, signaled right, and turned down Main Street.

Bodhi reached the top of the hill and stopped. He gazed at his flower garden with a renewed sense of joy. Much of it had withered or died, but the hibiscus, white asters, and pink lilies were in full bloom. He crossed the street to look at them.

Joe passed the elementary school, signaling left. He was anxious about driving by Bodhi's house, but he was a creature of habit, and he wasn't going to change his route for anybody.

Bodhi bent down to feel the hibiscus. He had its soft petals in his hand when he noticed something in the center of the garden. There, surrounded by all the dead flowers from summer past, were the two miracle peonies. He let the hibiscus fall from his hand.

Joe rolled by Crazy Craig's and gunned it up the hill. He usually didn't drive fast on the lake roads; for one, there were often kids around, and secondly, Old Man Halsteder would come running out of his big blue house to yell at any and all reckless drivers. But Joe didn't want to see Bodhi, so he made sure to pick up plenty of speed as he approached his house.

The peonies looked as perfect in late September as they did in June. Bodhi took a step toward them when he heard the unmistakable sound of a beat-up S10 engine. He looked up and saw the horrid gray thing speeding around the bend. He ran into the street and threw his hand up.

A disheveled young man in dirty brown robes invaded Joe's vision.

"Holy fuck!" he yelled, slamming the brakes and yanking the wheel to the right. There was a terrible sound as Joe skidded into the yard, missing Bodhi by inches and coming to a screeching halt just shy of the garden.

Smoke poured from the truck, ratty engine still running. Joe clenched the wheel with his left hand, throwing the truck in park with his right. He turned to look out the window. Bodhi stared at him with intention.

"What the fuck man?" Joe yelled.

"I'll go to the car show with you," Bodhi stated.

"What?" Joe scoffed.

"I'll go to the car show with you, but I'm wearing my robes," Bodhi answered.

"Jesus man," Joe grumbled, angry and confused. He shook his head and thought of something spiteful to say. He looked Bodhi up and down and realized he was being genuine. "Alright," Joe sighed, giving in, "come here."

Bodhi walked up to the truck. Joe turned away from him and dug around the floor. Bodhi waited at the window, wondering if Joe was about to reach out and punch him.

Instead, he turned and handed him the empty Old Milwaukee can. "Throw this away for me," he grinned.

XXXIII

"So what're you gonna do with 'em?"

"I don't know," Bodhi replied, looking at the peonies, "I think they're waiting for something." They stood in the garden, contemplating for a while.

"Better get goin'," Joe said. "Promised Ray I'd help him out, then we gotta come back and pack up the coolers."

"Okay," Bodhi said. It was Friday morning. Joe and the old-timers had taken off work to get ready for the car show. The day was cool but the sun was bright, and there was hope in the air. They climbed into the truck and headed over to the Washingtons'.

They pulled into the driveway, and Ray was already outside with a couple buckets, wax, and some engine cleaner. A mint condition 1967 Ford Galaxie Fastback was parked next to him.

The truck doors echoed as Joe and Bodhi pushed them shut and walked across the driveway, gravel crunching under their feet. "Lookin' sharp buddy," Joe hollered.

"Hey Joe," Ray called. He looked at Bodhi. "Who'd ya bring with ya?"

Joe and Bodhi made their way to Ray, and Joe extended his hand for a shake. Ray smiled and took it.

"This here is Bodhi," Joe said, thumbing over with his free hand. Ray looked over at Bodhi. Bodhi thought he might squint his eyes and make a comment about his robes, but he just grinned and stuck out his hand.

"Pleased to meet you brother," he said.

"Many blessings Ray," Bodhi replied, shaking his hand.

"So what d'we got?" Joe asked.

Ray stepped back and led them around the car. "Gotta get her washed and waxed, scrub the tires, detail the engine," he instructed. Bodhi followed Ray from end to end, marveling at the beauty of the car.

"Is this yours?" he asked.

"Shiiitt, I wish," he said. "Belongs to Julie. Used to be her old man's, got it when he passed."

Bodhi thought about how death was an illusion, and how he'd normally tell someone so. He shook his head. "I'm sorry to hear that," he offered.

"Thank you Bodhi," Ray said. "It happened a while ago. But this is her baby. It's real important to her."

"I can understand why," Bodhi replied. Joe looked over with a quizzical grin. Bodhi had come a long way, and he was proud.

"Welp, let's get started," Ray said. He headed over to the side of the house and picked up the hose. "Grab that bucket over there," he directed, motioning with the nozzle. Joe took a soapy rag from the bucket then lifted it toward Bodhi to indicate that he should do the same. Ray turned the hose on and sprayed down the car. Joe waited for him to finish before showing Bodhi what to do.

"Like this," he said, moving his hand in circles. "Start with the top and work your way down."

Bodhi placed his rag on the dome of the car and slid it across the metal in a series of slow, smooth circles. It felt very Zen.

The screen door smacked against the pane and Joe and Ray looked up to see Julie on the porch. "I know that ain't Joe touchin' my baby," she griped at Ray. She still didn't trust him after his behavior on the Fourth.

"He offered to help," Ray said.

"Hi Julie," Joe said sheepishly.

Julie rolled her eyes. "He better not scratch it," she warned Ray, going back inside. Bodhi was so engaged in the meditative nature of the work that he missed the whole exchange.

They finished washing the car and moved on to waxing and drying. Bodhi got even more fulfillment out of that. When the exterior of the car was done, they started detailing the engine. A lot of gearheads were going to be at the car show; Julie wanted her 390 done up nice.

"That'll do her," Joe said after a while, wiping the sweat from his brow. Bodhi stayed inside the hood for a few seconds more, wiping the last bit of grease from the engine block. He finished up and stood back, joining the other two men in admiring their work.

The screen door smacked against the pane, and Julie came outside to have a look. She stood behind them with her arms folded. "Looks good boys," she said, "thank you." She went back inside for a minute, then came out with three beers. She handed one to Ray first, then Bodhi. She turned to Joe with the last one and gave it to him. "Here ya go. Thank you."

"This mean you're not mad at me anymore?"

"Just means you're less of a dumbass than I thought." She smirked.

"Fair enough." Joe shrugged, taking a swig of beer.

"So you can follow us down?" Ray asked, changing the subject.

"Yep," Joe answered. "Gotta little room in the truck bed too, if you need."

"Might take you up on that," Julie said, "I hate havin' anything on that interior."

"I don't blame ya," Bodhi said with a little twang.

Joe noticed him trying to fit in and flashed him a smile. "Sounds like a plan," he said.

They finished their beers and loaded up a few folding chairs, a couple blankets, a picnic basket, and a cooler. Ray got an old tarp from his garage and fit it over the truck bed.

"Catch ya here in a bit," Joe said with a wave. He started up the truck and headed back to Pleasant Lake.

....

Sadie burst through the foliage behind Joe's house when she heard his truck pull into the driveway. She ran up to Bodhi as he exited the truck and nestled her furry head against his shin. Bodhi smiled and bent down to give her a scratch. She purred louder than normal, and she had an earnest look in her eyes—she was excited to see them and wanted attention, but she sensed they were leaving, and she was afraid. Bodhi picked up on it. He turned to Joe but kept petting her.

Joe was already on the porch, mumbling to himself and calculating how much alcohol everyone would drink in proportion to how much he could bring. There was also a little geometry involved in trying to pack the coolers with as many beers as possible while still fitting all the food inside.

"Hey, what're you going to do with Sadie?" Bodhi asked.

"What?" Joe replied. "Oh, she'll be fine." He went inside and came back out with two cases of Old Milwaukee. He set them on the porch, then went inside again. Bodhi scratched the cat under her chin.

"You're such a beautiful creature," he cooed.

The door swung open and Joe came out with a case of Miller Lite and a bottle of Wild Turkey. Sadie hopped onto the porch and rubbed against his legs, purring loudly.

"Jesus Christ!" Joe cried, stumbling over her. "Oh, hi pretty girl," he added, catching his bearings. He set the alcohol down and knelt to pet her.

"She doesn't want us to go," Bodhi said. "You sure she'll be alright?"

"Angela's takin' care of her," Joe answered, still looking at Sadie and scratching her head. "She'll feel like a queen." Sadie closed her eyes and wiggled her head a little.

"Help me with these coolers would ya?" Joe said, changing the subject. "There's two in the house and some food in the fridge."

Bodhi walked past Joe and into the house. He made his way to the kitchen and found the two coolers stacked on top of each other by the fridge. He grabbed the handle of the bottom one and used it to drag both across the tile and through the living room, using his lower back to hit the latch on the screen door that led to the porch. He struggled with the half-open door on his butt for a second, thinking Joe might help him. He didn't. Meanwhile, the coolers got caught and wobbled on the doorframe, but Bodhi wrenched them free and dragged them onto the porch stone.

Bodhi turned to scold Joe but saw him petting Sadie with more attention than usual. He gave a curious smile and went inside to get the food.

Bodhi grabbed two meat and veggie party trays and a Ziplock bag of cheese from the fridge. He used his hip to push the fridge shut then went to the screen and used the same to pop it open. He stepped onto the porch in time to see Joe kiss Sadie on the head before rising to his feet.

"Alright," Joe said, "let's finish her up."

They packed the coolers with Joe giving plenty of direction; they were able to fit sixty-three beers and all the food. They hoisted the first cooler onto the truck bed, grunting loudly as they did so. Joe pushed it deeper under the tarp and turned to the one left on the ground.

"Wait," Bodhi said. Joe straightened up and looked at him. "Don't load that up yet," Bodhi added, "I'll be right back." He took off toward his house. Joe stood alone, scratching his head.

A door opened and Joe turned to see Mrs. Baker step outside. She smiled at him, coming down her porch stairs and across the yard. "Getting ready for the show?" she asked.

"Yep," Joe said with a smile, "'bout to head out soon."

"Bodhi going with ya?"

"Thought so," Joe said. "He just run off somewhere."

Bodhi sprinted down the road, his flower garden getting larger and larger in his vision. His heart raced as he cut through his yard and into the dirt of the garden bed. He stopped and knelt by the peonies, panting with excitement.

There was hope in the air from the car show. There was love in his heart from Mandy's kiss on the cheek. He gazed at the peonies and was reminded of the Lotus sutra. He realized that the Buddha had to pick the Lotus from the water for it to bestow its lesson.

Bodhi reached out and plucked the first peony bloom, cupping it in one hand; he reached out and plucked the second bloom, cupping it in the other. He paused for a second, contemplating the miracles he held, then rose to his feet and headed back to Joe's.

"You boys need any food?" Angela asked.

"Think we're good," Joe said, "got two coolers packed."

"Seems to me they're mostly packed with alcohol," Angela replied.

"Ah geez, Mrs. Baker," Joe grinned, taking off his hat and scratching his head. Her eyes were full of reproach.

"You're being reckless with all that beer," she said, sadness in her voice. "I don't want anyone getting hurt."

"They won't," he said, "I promise."

Bodhi walked up behind Joe and sensed something was wrong. He cleared his throat. "Greetings Mrs. Baker," he said.

"Hi Bodhi!" she exclaimed. She came over and squeezed him tight. Bodhi thought it was a little strange.

"Ah good, you're back," Joe chided. "Now help me load this cooler." Angela took a step back to give them room.

"Wait, I want to put these in there," Bodhi said. He slowly unfolded his fingers, revealing the simple beauty of the peonies.

"Won't fit," Joe replied. Bodhi furrowed his brow.

"We've got a small cooler inside," Mrs. Baker assured him. "I'll go get it and you can put them in there." She turned and walked back to her house.

Joe turned to Bodhi. "Finally decided what to do with 'em, eh?" he asked.

"Not exactly," Bodhi said, "but they need to come with us."

"They are beautiful," Joe observed.

There was a low rumble of a 390 engine and the Washingtons came around the bend. They pulled up next to the house and honked the horn. Joe gave a quick wave to acknowledge them.

Mrs. Baker came outside with a small cooler and walked over to the boys. "I put a little ice in there," she said, opening it up. "They should keep for a few days." Bodhi thanked her and placed the peonies inside. Mrs. Baker shut the lid and handed the cooler to him. "You boys be careful now," she urged.

"We will," they answered. Bodhi put the flowers in the cab and then helped Joe heave the last cooler into the truck bed. They shut the tailgate and climbed into the truck.

"God bless you," Mrs. Baker said, teary-eyed.

"May you be well," Bodhi said, smiling as he waved goodbye. Joe signaled to the Washingtons to go ahead, then started up the truck and backed into the street.

Mrs. Baker watched them go. Sadie sauntered up to her feet and watched with her. First the Galaxie disappeared around the lake, then the truck.

They reached Old 27 and turned south toward the interstate. "Let's have a beer," Joe said. Bodhi rummaged through the open box of Miller Lite and pulled out two, passing one to Joe.

The spirit of the weekend hit Ray and he pushed the pedal to the floor. The engine cracked and roared and the Galaxie shot ahead.

"Be careful with my baby!" Julie cried, punching his leg. Ray laughed and eased off the gas.

Joe cranked up the radio and rolled his window down. Bodhi rolled his down too, and the September air rushed inside. They each took a long slug of beer, feeling the sun on their faces.

XXXIV

Coach's best time of the year was cruising down the highway in the '66. He used to think it was when he got a fried tenderloin at the park and loaded it with pickles, mayo, and mustard; or when he saw an old high school buddy and they drank a few beers and reminisced about the girls they'd kissed and the cars they drove; or when the baseball team beat Dwenger in the bottom of the ninth. He looked over at his son in the passenger seat, singing along to the Rolling Stones on the radio. He felt the steel in his hands and the wind in his hair, mile markers dropping one by one as the engine screamed toward Gas City. This was his favorite day.

Even Don smiled as he raced down the highway in his old Mustang. He usually had something to complain about, but not today.

Ray and Julie, however, took it slow. Julie was constantly worried about reckless drivers and uneven lanes. Joe followed close behind, wondering how anyone could be so careful. "If I had one of them we'd be doin' 85, at least," he said.

Exit 59 came and they pulled off the interstate. Joe followed the Galaxie as the Washingtons signaled right and turned down the long road to Gas City. The sun was just beginning its descent toward the horizon. Everything looked gold. Old Chevys, Pontiacs, and the occasional Ford Coupe drove past on their way to the Mexican restaurant or the hotels between Gas City and Upland.

Joe smiled and drank it in. "The boys are back," he said.

The car registry was at the fire station on the outskirts of town. The Washingtons pulled into the parking lot and Joe followed them.

Ray and Julie got out and walked inside to get their official car show placard. Joe and Bodhi stepped outside to stretch their legs. They shut the truck doors and Joe took a deep breath of Indiana air. He let it out and looked over at Bodhi. "So, what d'you think?" he asked.

Bodhi saw how the sun fell on the old cars in the parking lot. "I like it." He smiled.

They waited outside for about ten minutes before Joe got bored. "Bet Julie's talkin' someone's ear off," he joked. "Let's go inside and check on 'em."

Bodhi followed Joe through the lot and into the fire station. It was big and open, with high ceilings and an antique fire truck parked in the back. In front of the truck were plaques and signs from car shows past; in front of those were long tables covered with t-shirts, hoodies, and hats with this year's logo on them. A group of pleasant, older women and a few men were at the table running registration and selling clothes. Joe and Bodhi spotted the Washingtons in conversation with a nice woman in a Gas City sweater and an outdated haircut.

"There they are," Joe said, leading Bodhi over.

They got closer and heard them talking about how well the high school football team was doing.

"'Bout ready Julie?" Joe grinned. The Washingtons turned around. The lady stopped what she was doing and Julie rolled her eyes.

"Hey Joe," Ray said, "this pretty lady was just tellin' us how her son got the most interceptions in Mississinewa history."

"Once you get him goin', he don't stop," Julie muttered. Bodhi noticed a middle-aged man a few feet away smiling and talking to a lady behind the table.

"We were liable to leave you here," Joe said.

"Alright," Ray said, starting the Midwest goodbye.

"Live in Fort Wayne now, but I grew up on H Street," Bodhi heard the middle-aged man say.

"Oh, that's right," the woman behind the table replied.

"You mighta known my sister," he said. "She was younger than us, but you mighta seen her around." The man paused, and his voice got soft. "She died in a car wreck," he said. Bodhi found himself walking toward him.

"That was so sad," the lady sympathized. "I remember seein' that in the paper."

"Hey Bodhi, you comin'?" Joe called. Bodhi didn't hear him. He stepped behind the middle-aged man and cleared his throat.

"Excuse me," he said. The man turned to look at him. "I'm sorry for your loss," Bodhi offered.

"Thank you," the man said, "it's been a while now." Bodhi looked into his eyes and couldn't tell if it made him happy or sad to talk about her. "Did you know her?" the man asked with excitement.

"I, uh, no—I don't think so," Bodhi answered.

"Oh," he said, a little defeated, "well, you're about the same age." Bodhi didn't know what to say. He just nodded his head and offered a solemn smile.

"You do look familiar," the man went on. "You from around here?"

"I'm not sure," Bodhi answered.

The man gave him a quizzical look. He tilted his head and studied Bodhi a little longer. "You know, you look like a guy that was in her class, lived in a farmhouse out toward Fairmount."

Bodhi's eyebrows lowered and his lips parted, and he stood there with his mouth open. His heart raced, beating hard against his chest. How did he know about the farmhouse? The room seemed to shrink, suffocating him.

Joe came up behind him and put his hand on his shoulder. "You ready?" he asked.

Bodhi heard the muffled echo of Joe's words in his head.

"She sounded wonderful," Bodhi heard himself say to the man. He swallowed, trying to get his bearings. "I'm really sorry she's gone."

"Miss her every day," the man answered, nodding slowly with a faraway look in his eyes. He shook his head and gave a wry smile, then looked back at Bodhi. "You take care now," he said. He turned and waved goodbye to the ladies at the table, then left the firehouse.

"What was that about?" Joe asked.

"What?" Bodhi said, starting to come back to reality. "Oh, I don't know."

"You ready?" Joe asked.

They left the fire station and found the Washingtons outside.

"Follow me to Terry's," Joe directed. "We'll park the truck there and jump in back with you, then head to the park." The Washingtons nodded and walked over to the Galaxie. Joe and Bodhi headed to the truck and climbed inside.

"Best time of the year," Joe said, starting up the truck. Bodhi didn't respond. Joe backed out and turned down the road. "You're gonna love this shit man," he added, trying to get Bodhi to say something. "There's nothin' like it."

Bodhi kept his eyes on the road. Joe knew something was wrong but didn't want to get into it. "Hey man, it's Jimmy Dean, Friday night. Whatever's goin' on with you, figure that shit out later."

Bodhi knew he was right, even if cavalier. He chuckled. Joe always knew how to pull him out of his head.

XXXV

Terry lived with his wife Kate in a nice, big house. The neighborhood was quiet, well-kept, and away from the madness of the car show.

He was outside when Julie and the boys pulled up, trying to look like he was doing chores. In reality, he'd been waiting all day for his friends to come.

"Terry, you lame bastard! Get over here!" Joe cried, jumping out of the car. The two did that mix of handshake and hug that Hoosier men do when trying to simultaneously show and suppress emotion.

"Good to see ya Joe," Terry said. "Drive okay?"

"Nice and easy," Joe replied. The Washingtons shut their car doors and walked up.

"How ya been?" Terry said to them, shaking their hands. "How're the kids?"

"Fine," Julie said before Ray could say answer. "How's Kate?"

"Fine, fine," Terry replied. "She's out back doin' some gardenin'." Everyone smiled and nodded. Kate wasn't into the car show, but she'd never make them feel unwelcome. They knew she needed her space.

"Terry, I wanted to introduce my friend Bodhi," Joe interjected.

Terry looked Bodhi up and down, then stuck out his hand. "Quite a get-up ya got there," he said, referring to his robes.

Bodhi took his hand and shook it. "Thank you," he said. Everyone stood there looking at each other for a second.

"Well, should we go inside?" Terry asked. He turned and they followed him through the open garage door. "Can I get you anything? Beer, bottled water?" He motioned to the fridge in the garage. "Bouchard's out back, got some whiskey."

"Danny Bouchard?" Joe asked, a little excited. "Been at least twenty years."

"He's back on the patio, got these little bottles. Tryin' his best to host a tasting," Terry chuckled.

"Sounds like him," Joe said. They went through the back door and crossed over the kitchen floor. Terry opened the sliding door and they stepped onto the patio. Bouchard was out there, leaning slightly on a high-top chair.

"Joe!" he hiccupped, trying to stand.

"Nah, don't get up," Joe exclaimed, walking over to him. "How ya been?" he asked, slapping him on the shoulder.

"Fine, fine," Bouchard said, giving Joe a sloppy handshake. "And who are these beautiful people?"

"This here is Ray and Julie," Joe replied, motioning to them. Ray came in for a handshake.

"How do you do," Julie said, nodding.

"I remember you," Bouchard said. "Been coming here for a while now."

"Least twenty years," Ray answered.

"And this here is Bodhi," Joe said. Bodhi bowed slightly then came in for a handshake. "He's a m—"

"A monk," Bouchard interjected, finishing Joe's sentence.

"Well goddamn. Bouchard, the world traveler," Joe said.

"Spent some time at a monastery in Tibet. You could learn a lot from this one," Bouchard grinned, squinting his eyes and pointing at Bodhi.

"That's one way to put it," Joe muttered.

"Many blessings to you," Bodhi said as he shook Bouchard's hand. He was happy that someone understood him for once.

"Well sit down, sit down!" Bouchard exclaimed, motioning around the table like it was his. "We were doing a little tasting, got some of the finest spirits in the world for us to try."

Julie and the boys found their chairs. The sound of wood against wood resonated as they pulled them out and sat down. They noticed three small glasses in front of each of them.

"Now this one's from Dublin," Bouchard said, pulling out a small bottle from a leather carrying case on the table. "It's a little sweeter. You'll find notes of toasted almonds and a hint of vanilla toffee on the front." He twisted off the cap and poured a taste in each of their glasses. They grabbed them and drank.

Bodhi gagged. His mouth was prepared for something much sweeter.

"Has a dry finish, little spice on the back end, almost a nutmeg feel to it," Bouchard went on. Everyone nodded, going along with whatever he said. He placed the empty bottle to the side and reached for another from the case. "Now this one's from a small mountain town in rural Ireland," Bouchard lectured, removing the cap. He poured tasters for everyone and set the empty bottle down. "Aged fifteen years, spiced sherry notes give way to a honied yet savory mouth feel." They grabbed their glasses and took a drink. Everyone winced a little but tried to make it look like they didn't.

"So, Bodhi," Bouchard began, shuddering from the whiskey, "is that short for Bodhisattva?"

"Yes," Bodhi answered, searching the table for a glass of water that wasn't there, "I guess you could say that." The Washingtons looked on with a little confusion. Joe sat back and folded his arms across his belly.

"So you believe in reincarnation?" Bouchard asked, reaching for the next bottle.

"Definitely," Bodhi answered.

"And you believe that you've reached the top, but you leave something undone so you can teach us how to go past you?" Bouchard asked, twisting the cap off.

"More or less," Bodhi replied.

"Huh," Bouchard continued, leaning back for a second before grabbing the bottle to divvy up the next taster. "That's a lonely existence." Bodhi started to say something, then stopped. He pondered Bouchard's words as the latter poured a little liquor into everyone's cup.

"To the Bodhisattva," Bouchard said, raising his glass.

"To the Bodhisattva," they all repeated. They threw the whiskey back and shook their heads from the burn.

"Now I saved the best for last," Bouchard promised, using his hands to accentuate his words. "Pretty penny, single malt, aged eighteen years in Japanese oak."

. . . .

The sun was going down, and they were anxious to get to the park. Bouchard was out front trying to show off his new Tesla. "Gotta remote start, and look at the doors," he cried, pressing a button on his key fob. The doors opened automatically, up and out like butterflies.

"Wow," they said, feigning interest. They knew he was trying to get into the spirit of the show, and they appreciated him for it, but they came to town to see the classics.

"Alright Danny," Terry said, corralling him into the driver's seat, "you sure you're good to drive?"

"Oh yeah, sure," he replied, shutting the door and talking through the open window, "it's a straight shot back to Indy."

"Alrighty brother, take care now," Terry said. They all thanked him for the liquor and waved goodbye.

"Well shit, let's get goin'," Terry urged.

"Julie, can we put the coolers in the trunk till we get to the park?" Joe asked.

"I guess," she muttered.

Joe and Bodhi walked over to the truck and unloaded the bed. Ray took his keys and opened the trunk to the Galaxie. The men put all the food and drinks inside, and Julie cringed when she saw how low the suspension sat.

"Alright," Joe said, clapping his hands once together, "let's head out." Terry ambled toward the garage. The others made their way to the Galaxie. Ray climbed into the driver's seat and looked over his shoulder at everyone else. Julie went to the passenger seat and pressed the small metal button toward the top of it to lean it forward and let Joe and Bodhi in behind her. Joe climbed in, sitting down hard on the cushy leather seat and feeling the springs bounce against his butt before sliding over and settling down. Bodhi paused at the door frame.

"Give me a second," he said. Julie sighed. Bodhi scampered over to the truck and pulled the passenger door open, digging around on the floor for the peony cooler. He took it out and ran back to the Galaxie. "No man left behind," he joked, sliding in and sitting down with the cooler in his lap.

Julie pushed the seat back in place. "We good?" she asked, sitting down.

"Yep," Joe and Bodhi said in unison.

"None of you boys gotta get a picnic basket, or take a piss or anything?" she chastised.

"Nope, let's get to the show," Joe said, slapping the seat in front of him.

Ray turned the key and the engine roared. The smells of gas and worn leather mixed to create a musty, nostalgic sweetness that even Bodhi appreciated. He rubbed his feet against the old carpet and drummed his hands against the cooler, then looked over at Joe. The sunset hit his face and somehow made the smell even sweeter.

Ray cranked his window down. "Hey Terry, ya gettin' in?" he called.

Terry came whirling out of the garage in a cream-colored golf cart. "Kate might want me home, and you can't get a DUI in this thing," he grinned. Ray laughed and backed out of the driveway. Terry followed, but his inability to go over 12 mph soon left him behind.

The Galaxie quickly left the green space of the suburbs and pulled onto the main street of Gas City. Downtown was a quaint area with little restaurants and bars lining the street in the same way they had since the boomtown days of the 1890s. They passed Kay's Pizza, a greasy little parlor that had retained its Nixon-era charm, and turned left just before the Pour House, a legendary bar where locals and car show tourists got sloshed and played horse on the old hoop in back. The Galaxie cut through another residential area, this one closer to the park and lined with small, working-class homes with chipped paint and square green lawns. After a few stop signs they came upon a giant factory that was just a shadow of its former 1950s union-town glory; they drove past, came to the end of First Street, and turned right across the railroad tracks. Julie winced as the old car bounced over the tracks and joined a line of vehicles waiting to get inside the park.

The rumble of old engines and the smell of gasoline filled the air with possibility. There were a couple of newer cars in line too, looking for a place to park outside of the show. The locals with bigger yards had hammered makeshift wooden signs into their grass, spray-painted with *Park $7* in bad handwriting, and had enlisted their whole families to handle money and cars. People of all ages walked back and forth from the show; most stuck to the sidewalks, but some wove in and out of traffic.

"Looks like a good turnout this year," Joe observed.

They inched closer a few minutes at a time, growing impatient. Terry suddenly whizzed by them in the golf cart with his middle finger in the air. They burst into laughter and their impatience turned to anticipation.

After a while they reached the front entrance. Ray stopped and waited for the traffic guard—an old man wearing high socks and New Balance shoes, t-shirt tucked into his jean shorts—to let them through. He halted the oncoming traffic and waved them in.

They turned into the park and slowed for another man wearing the same outfit as the traffic guard. Ray pointed to the registration in the driver's corner of the windshield and received a thumbs up for his efforts.

"Here we are," Joe cried, slapping Bodhi on the shoulder.

The park was built on a pond, and at least one example of every American car made from 1945 to 1972 could be found sitting on the grass around it. To the left of the front entrance were all the food vendors—classic American diners, fried tenderloin makers, elephant ear stands, and even a small taco wagon. Near them were all the posters the city had commissioned for the event over the years—giant wooden murals with classic cars and cartoon ducks enjoying '60s surf rock parties, drinking root beer at the drive-in, or going on dates under shady oak trees. Ray eased the Galaxie past the last poster and idled by the city police, who had a 1950s squad car behind them. Even though the park was packed with alcohol, cars with flamethrowers, and a heavy dose of masculine energy, few if any fights ever broke out, giving the cops a chance to enjoy the show, too.

Ray made his way around the pond and the sound of doo-wop music reached their ears. It reminded Bodhi of the dance he'd shared with Mandy. He smiled to himself as they passed the first section of cars, filled with old Chevys.

"Dad had a '63 Biscayne, looked just like that," Ray said.

"Remember when we used to park there?" Joe asked. "Coach's kid got a bee sting on his neck. Poor sonofabitch howled like a dog."

They rolled past the first corner of the pond, straightening out by a new line of cars.

"Mom and Dad had a '59 just like that," Julie reminisced, pointing at an old Pontiac. "Packed us sideways all the way to the Ozarks."

Ray slowed as a group of teenagers ambled in front of the car. They wore trashy hoodies with ripped jeans and seemed oblivious to the line of cars behind them.

"Goddamnit," Ray muttered.

"Fuckers," Joe said, "move!" Ray got closer and they walked even slower. A woman with a stroller steered toward the car and almost ran into it before veering off at the last second.

"Goddamn two-leggers," Joe grumbled. Bodhi didn't notice. He was too busy looking at the cars—rows and rows of American steel, waxed to perfection and gleaming in the twilight.

The kids finally looked over their shoulders and made a half-assed attempt to get out of the way. Ray took advantage of the little space they made and rolled by them.

The Galaxie reached the edge of the pond and hung left, heading to the back edge of the park where old Chewey set up camp every year. He was a friend of Joe's from the old days; he'd come down on the Wednesday before the show with a tarp and some caution tape and save a space for everyone to park and drink. It was hard to say if he liked doing it or if he resented his friends for showing up so much later than him, but he was loyal as hell, and he always got it done.

Ray drifted by the pond and stopped at the last intersection before Chewey's camp. To the right was a group of rat-rodders with a few old T-Buckets and a rusty '55 Chevy that'd been through more street races than it cared to remember. Next to it was a giant sheet draped over a lump of something nefarious and a big, hand-painted sign that read *"Ask us what's under the towel."* One year, when he was very young, Coach's kid had made the mistake of asking. They rewarded his curiosity with a two-foot dildo strapped to a big block motor.

Ray waved to the rat-rodders and pushed through the intersection, forcing a 1970 Chevy Nova to pause and wait. Ray waved to the Nova as he cruised past and turned into the grassy field behind the amphitheater. They rolled by a line of old Fords and slowed as they approached Chewey's camp.

The rumble of the 390 engine caught Chewey's attention and he got out of his chair. He hobbled over to a parking spot that he'd secured with two folding chairs and a drooping line of caution tape. Ray gave him a thumbs-up as he drove past, then stopped the car to back in. Chewey dragged the chairs out of the way and started motioning for Ray to back up. One of the other campers jumped up and motioned also, not realizing how unhelpful it was. Ray finally saw Chewey hold up his hand to signify that he was set to park. He shut off the engine and the low click of metal on metal resounded as the Galaxie doors opened and everyone climbed out.

"Hey guys," Chewey said with a smile and a slight rasp to his voice. He lit a cheap cigar while waiting for them to come over.

"Thanks for savin' us a spot," Julie said with sincerity and a slight wave as she walked past.

"Oh I'm just glad everyone made it here alright," Chewey replied, putting the cigar in his mouth so he could shake hands with Ray and Joe. Julie went under the big tarp that shaded Chewey's camp. There was a modest group of people there, including the baseball coach, his kid, and some other Angola folk. They either stood around the full picnic spread atop the plastic table Chewey had brought or sat drinking beer in one of the many folding chairs that dotted the grass. Terry was already there and enmeshed in the scene, drinking vodka from a Solo cup and telling stories like he'd been there all day.

"Hey, what took you so long?" he heckled to some laughter.

"Aw you shoulda seen him," Ray hollered, walking from Chewey and under the tarp, "he hit warp speed in that golf cart, zoomed right by us." Everyone laughed and shook hands with Ray, greeting him with smiles and a cold beer.

Bodhi stood by the car with the peony cooler in his arms, a little unsure of himself.

"Hey Bodhi, c'mere. There's somebody I'd like you to meet," Joe said, motioning to Chewey. Bodhi took a few steps toward them.

"Bodhi, say your name was?" Chewey asked, putting his cigar back in his mouth to shake hands. "Nice to meet ya."

"Thank you," Bodhi said. "Many blessings to you."

"Sure, sure," Chewey said, finishing up their handshake. "Hey, might wanna wear somethin' a little warmer, gets a little cold when the sun goes down."

"Tried to tell 'im," Joe said, "but he wouldn't have it. He's a monk, that's all he wears."

"Oh," Chewey replied, interested enough to accept it but not interested enough to ask any follow-up questions. "Well, glad to have ya." He turned and went over to the picnic table to have a snack.

"Help me with these coolers," Joe told Bodhi. "Hey Ray! Throw me your keys, need to get in the trunk." Ray tossed the keys over and Joe caught them in his right hand. He turned toward the trunk and popped it open.

"Now some of these boys are a little rough," Joe murmured to Bodhi, "but you'll be alright." Bodhi knew that meant they wouldn't accept him right away. It made him nervous, but he was committed to his new outlook, and he trusted Joe. He set the peonies down and helped Joe unload the trunk.

When they finished, Bodhi realized he was in the middle of the group. He felt like everyone was gawking at him, and he froze. In reality, most everyone was smiling and he only caught one or two side-eyes. Joe recognized his struggle and came up to his shoulder.

"Grab a beer," he advised, "you'll fit right in."

Bodhi took a few paces in front of the group and opened one of the larger coolers. He brushed some ice to the side and fished out an Old Milwaukee. He cracked the tab against the mouth of the can and some vapor crawled out. He took a drink.

"How ya doin' Joe?" one of the boys said, coming up and slapping him on the back.

"Ricky," Joe cried, grabbing a beer for himself. "What's up man?"

"Oh nothin' much. Glad to get away for a little while," Ricky said.

"Yeah. How's it lookin' down here?"

Ricky surveyed the park. He was in his forties but still hadn't grown out of the frat boy lifestyle. "Gotta couple lookers, seen a young gal with some big tits. Couple old biker hags I wouldn't mind if they cleaned up a bit."

"Jesus Rick, I meant the cars," Joe choked.

"Ah shit," Ricky grinned, "you're here every year. Nothin' changes."

"Dodge is runnin' good?"

"Always."

"Well alright," Joe said, taking a drink.

Bodhi drifted over, hoping to find a place to fit in.

"Hey man," Ricky said with a squint, "what the fuck are you wearin'?" Bodhi furrowed his brow with his mouth partway open.

"This is my friend Bodhi," Joe interjected. "He's a monk."

"Ahh, Kama Sutra," Ricky grinned. Bodhi didn't know what he meant. He furrowed his brow even harder. "Read that in college," Ricky reminisced, taking a sip of beer. "Gotta lotta pussy back then."

"Let me introduce you to some other people," Joe said to Bodhi, putting his hand on Bodhi's upper back and leading him away. Ricky shrugged and lit up a cigarette.

Coach and the others were sitting in folding chairs telling stories. Coach's kid was behind him drinking from a Solo cup with gin and orange juice. He'd heard his dad's stories so many times that he quietly finished every punchline with a slight eye roll, but he was discreet enough to not ruin Coach's hold on the crowd. Every so often he'd leave and go to the drink table when no one was looking and sneak another shot into his cup, so it always looked like he was still on his first drink.

Duly was there too, a big fat man who drank beer in the sun all day, an oversized straw hat the only thing protecting him from complete dehydration. His wife Margo sat next to him. She drank Bloody Marys in the morning then switched to Bud Light sometime in the afternoon. Standing just outside of the circle were Bobby and Eddie, two affable little guys who liked good jokes and dirty rat rods. Joe was surprised to see his grumpy old friend from the factory, Don, sitting in front of them.

"There's a sore sight for eyes!" Joe exclaimed. Everybody looked up and smiled. Don gave a begrudging chuckle.

"Joe you sonofabitch," he grumbled. "Surprised they let you in here."

"Hey good to see you too man." Joe smirked. "What're the rest of you lame bastards up to?"

"You're lookin' at it," Duly replied, arms folded across his gut.

"Might go to the swap meet here in a bit," Bobby added. "Supposed to be a rear fender on a Roadrunner somewhere."

Joe nodded, acting impressed.

"Who you got there with ya Joe?" Margo asked, louder than she cared to realize. "That's quite a get-up he's got."

Joe started to defend Bodhi with the usual "he's a monk," but Bodhi cut him off. Maybe it was the beers he'd drank and the whiskey tasting at Terry's, or the fact that he'd just been through this with Ricky; maybe he was starting to feel more comfortable with his own identity.

"I'm a monk," he said. "A Bodhisattva in fact." He grinned and looked around at everyone. There were a few nods and a couple pursed lips.

"What the fuck does that mean?" Don grunted.

Bodhi normally would have been thrown off by his comment, but this time he took a drink of Old Milwaukee. He felt a rush of blood in his body and he wanted to tell them everything. He looked around and saw the pursed lips.

"What it means is, well…" His eyes settled on Joe, who wore a look that was equal parts curious and stern, as if to say, "Whatever you're about to do, don't fuck this up."

"What I mean is," Bodhi began again, taking another drink of beer and doing his best to imitate Joe, "I've reincarnated a billion times, just to end up with you lame bastards!"

Everybody laughed. Joe slapped him on the shoulder.

"Quite a character you got there Joe," Margo chuckled.

"His name is Bodhi," Joe answered.

"Bodhi! Welcome brother," Coach cried, raising his beer. Bodhi returned the gesture and took a drink.

Time passed; the campers milled around and shot the breeze. Bodhi smiled and nursed his beer.

When the sun went down, Coach's kid left his familiar spot behind his dad and came up to Bodhi. "Hey man, you smoke weed?" he muttered, keeping his voice low. About half of the people there would have smoked some if offered, but nobody wanted to be the first to ask, and it was common convention for Coach's kid to hide it from his dad.

"Usually pull them," Bodhi answered.

"Bro," Coach's kid chuckled, "come on."

Joe overheard the exchange and cut in. "He don't know what you're talkin' about," he said.

"Sure," the kid grinned, nodding his head. He tipped his cup and swayed a little. The juice had been gone for a couple hours now, and the cup was all gin. He looked around before leaning in a little closer. "I got a joint for us later," he whispered.

Bodhi shrugged.

XXXVI

Night came to the park and the air was cool and sweet. The food vendors turned their lights on, illuminating the row like a carnival.

The beer flowed at Chewey's camp. Everyone drank and told stories, only stopping to grab their hoodies from their cars and put them on. The camp was near the park amphitheater; on stage, some old guys were sound checking and tuning their guitars. There were a lot of people sitting on the bleachers waiting for the music to start, but Joe and everybody else didn't pay much attention.

Coach's kid went to the woods to smoke a joint. When he came back, smelling weird and acting goofy, Bodhi remembered the vape pen outside the bar and realized what had been offered to him a few hours before. Maybe he'd try it again later.

Meanwhile, Duly and Margo had reached their limit. "Gotta be up in time for breakfast," Duly said, "motel's got steak and eggs." They rose from their chairs, wobbling a bit, and left.

Don had been sleeping in one of the chairs, and the rumble of their engine caused him to choke on his snore and wake up. "Better call it boys," he muttered, getting up and driving away in his Mustang.

The rest of them sat or stood in a circle, contemplating whether to build a fire or tell a joke.

"I got one for ya," Coach said with a gleam in his eye. He readjusted in his chair and held his hands out for emphasis.

"This could take a while," Joe chided. He went over to the cooler and grabbed beers for everyone. Bobbie and Eddie got to work on the fire.

"You ever go to Lieutenant's back in the day?" Coach asked, setting up his story. "That old dive, way out on 20?"

"Yeah, yep, think so," Chewey said, lighting a cigar.

"Sumbitch had the hottest horseradish. I mean just melt your nose hot. So we go in, cause we wanted to try some." Bobby put an empty beer box under the logs and twigs he and Eddie had assembled and held a lighter to it. The edge of the cardboard blackened and fizzled out, but he kept trying until it caught. He moved the lighter to other parts of the box; they lit up too, and soon they had a modest fire in front of them.

"So we sit down, and The Lieutenant comes out. Everyone called him Lieu. Big, tough guy—fought in Korea. He's wearin' this apron and he's got a pad and paper. I mean, one of the baddest sonsabitches you ever saw, out there takin' orders." There was a light chuckle from the crowd. Bodhi took a step closer to the fire.

"So we order a couple beers. He just grunts and goes to the bar." Coach grabbed a Solo cup with a few shots of bourbon in it from the armrest in his chair. He took a sip and paused as the aftertaste washed over his mouth.

"So he comes back and sets 'em on the table. Says, 'You gonna eat anything?' And I said, 'You know Lieu, we wanted to try some of that horseradish.' So he grunts and goes to the kitchen." There were a few more chuckles and Bobby and Eddie poked at the fire. Ricky walked up to join them and cracked open a beer.

"Well he comes back, and he throws a cup of horseradish on the table. We look at it, then look up at him, and he's just starin' daggers. Fucker wants us to eat it right in front of 'im! So I say, 'No disrespect Lieu, but how're we supposed to eat this?' And that big ol' bastard says, he says, 'You got spoons don't ya?' and he points to the table."

"Shiiitt," Chewey said, shaking his head. The party laughed hard like it was the end of the joke. Coach's eyes lit up even more with the knowledge that a bigger punchline was coming.

"Well hell, I'm thinkin', this shit's hot, I need somethin' to eat it with. So I say, 'Lieu, ain't you got a piece of bread, or a cracker or somethin'?' He grunts louder than ever and goes back to the kitchen. Maan, that old bastard comes right back with two packets of saltines, throws 'em at me, and just as he's walkin' away, real loud he goes, 'PUSSY.'"

Coach's kid mouthed the word quietly—he'd heard the line at least a dozen times. Even so, he laughed with everybody else. It was a great story, and Coach was good at telling it.

"Never went back," Coach grinned over the laughter of his friends.

Bodhi left the warm glow of the fire to check on the peonies. He slid the top of the cooler back and looked inside. The flowers glimmered in the contrast of shadows and firelight, creating a beautiful, soft pink. He shut the lid and smiled. He walked back to the fire and Joe handed him another beer.

"What about you Bodhi?" Coach asked. "You've been quiet tonight. Got any stories for us?"

"No, I don't think so," he replied.

"Oh bullshit," Coach said with a smile. "Said earlier you've lived a billion lives, gotta have at least one, maybe two stories to tell."

Bodhi shifted his feet. He thought about his endless existence and how few memories he had from it.

"He punched Clint Toucher in the face last weekend," Joe grinned. The crowd lit up.

"You did what?"

"No fuckin' way."

"Had it comin'. God, that guy's a douche."

"No shit?"

Bodhi smiled and blushed a bit. "It was no big deal," he replied.

"You shoulda seen it," Joe cried, stepping further into the firelight and grabbing their attention. "He, well, go on Bodhi, tell it."

"Alright." Bodhi took a drink and placed the beer can in the grass by his feet. "So there I was, dancing with the most beautiful woman in the bar..." He proceeded to recount the events from the weekend before, waving his hands and acting out the scenes. He wasn't quite as good as Coach—it took years of bullshitting to get that good—but the story had enough action, and the crowd absorbed his excitement as he told it. He left out the part where he cried and had an existential crisis for five days afterwards; that didn't make good storytelling for the boys.

When he got done, the crowd looked at him with smiles and new-found respect.

"Sounds like you boys had quite a night," Coach said.

The band ended their set with a famous song from the '60s. Terry took another shot of vodka and sang along, substituting his friend's name in the lyrics: "Haaaang on Chewey, Chewey hang on!" The band finished up and the moon hit its zenith.

The fire dwindled and Ricky grew restless. "Who's comin' with me to Jonesboro?" he asked. Bobby and Eddie grinned at each other. They knew they were in for a wild night.

"We're gonna head to Terry's in a bit," Joe answered.

"Think I'll hang back, close up camp," Chewey replied.

"I'll help ya," Coach said to Chewey.

"Suit yourselves," Ricky said. He walked over to his '68 Dodge and dug the keys out of his pocket. Bobby and Eddie followed. They all climbed inside, Ricky fired up the engine, and they drove off to raise hell.

Terry snuck over to the table and poured some more vodka in his cup. When he came back, the rest were staring at the fire, watching it die.

"You about ready?" Joe asked.

"I'll drive us back," Julie yawned. Ray and Joe went with her to the Galaxie. Bodhi grabbed the peony cooler and turned to follow, but Coach's son gave him a conspicuous nod, so he stopped. The kid had another joint in his pocket.

"Dad, you mind if I hang with them for a bit?" he asked.

"Just don't stay out too late," Coach answered.

"Thanks man, love ya," he said. He came up to Bodhi. "Let's ride with Terry," he muttered.

Terry stumbled over to the golf cart and fell into the front seat. Coach's kid led Bodhi to the rear-facing seats in the back.

"You boys ready?" Terry called over his shoulder.

"Let's roll," Coach's kid answered.

"See you back at the house," Terry hollered toward the Galaxie.

The cart jostled through the grass and onto the smooth asphalt of the parking lot, passing a '64 GTO in the dim glow of the streetlights. "Damn that's pretty," Terry observed, leaving the lot and hitting the road.

They turned onto the neighborhood streets. The town was sleepy and quiet under the moonlight. Coach's kid fished the joint out of one pocket and then patted his other, looking for the lighter. He found it and put the joint in his mouth. The repeated click of the lighter echoed onto the street as the wind continued to blow out the flame. Bodhi realized what was happening and cupped his hands so Coach's kid could light the joint. A flame arose from the lighter and the end of the joint caught and turned to fire. Coach's kid drew hard then pulled it from his mouth and blew at it before leaning back. He took another hit and watched the smoke curl from the joint with satisfaction.

"Here ya go," he choked with smoke in his throat. Bodhi took the joint and looked at it, contemplating whether he should try it again. Last time it made him nervous, then happy, then open to new things. But it was hard to tell its full effects after the craziness ensued and his adrenalin kicked in.

"Don't bogart that shit," Coach's kid said.

Bodhi shrugged and put it to his mouth, taking a long, hard hit. He coughed and the high crept from his sinuses and into his head. He sat back and watched the neighborhood roll by, a sense of calm washing over him.

Terry heard the cough and caught the smell. "What the fuck are you doin' back there?" he demanded. Coach's kid lowered the joint from his mouth, holding it down by his legs. He held the smoke in as long as he could, then blew it carefully into the wind.

"You're smarter than that, smokin' in the middle of town," Terry admonished.

Coach's kid held the joint down, wondering if he could get away with a lie. "Sorry Terry," he finally muttered.

"It's alright," Terry said with some paternalism, "just pass it up here." Coach's kid grinned and reached over Terry's shoulder with the joint. Terry took a sip from his Solo cup and set it down before taking a hit.

"Alright, keep it low," he said with some smoke in his throat, passing it back over his shoulder. Bodhi grabbed it and put it down as they crossed Main Street. He took a nice, long hit when they reached the solace of the neighborhood streets on the other side. He exhaled and passed it over.

They pulled up to find Ray, Julie, and Joe waiting for them in the driveway. Coach's kid threw the roach down and leapt off the golf cart to step on it. Bodhi jumped off too, holding the cooler close.

"Be quiet when you go inside," Terry advised. He led them through the garage and into the house.

Kate was in the TV room. She sat on the couch with her back on the armrest and her legs across the cushions, watching the evening news. "You guys have fun?" she asked, turning her head to greet them.

"Yep," Terry said, leaning down and kissing her on the cheek.

"Good," she said, smiling. Terry led everyone into the kitchen. Bodhi stayed behind and tried to talk to Kate. He was incredibly high.

"What's happening?" he asked her.

"Oh, there's a big drive at the pound. Trying to get everyone to adopt a cat," she said, referencing one of the news stories.

"No, I mean with you. How are you?" Bodhi asked with a marijuana-induced earnestness.

"Me? I'm fine," Kate replied with a curious smile. "How are you?"

"I'm not sure," Bodhi pontificated.

"Bodhi, you're needed in the kitchen," Terry interjected, poking his head into the room.

"It was a pleasure meeting you," Bodhi bowed. "Many blessings."

"You too," Kate chuckled, shaking her head.

Bodhi left the room and walked into the kitchen. "What is it?" he asked.

"Have a drink with us," Terry said. Everyone was standing around the table. On it were six glasses, each with a shot or two of whiskey in them. Terry grabbed one of the glasses and handed it to Bodhi, then took one for himself.

"Cruisin' through the years," Terry said with a wry smile, lifting his glass before downing the whiskey. Everybody followed. The liquor burned Bodhi's throat and he shuddered. Coach's kid winced.

"Wooo," Terry gasped. He shook his head, then looked around. "Well, should we take a ride?"

"I'm goin' to bed," Julie muttered. She handed Ray the keys to the Galaxie. "Be careful."

"Goodnight honey," Ray said as she walked away.

"Goodnight," the boys muttered. Terry led them back toward the garage. "Goin' for a little ride," he called to Kate through the door, "be back in a bit."

"Have fun," she replied. "Be careful." Terry stepped into the garage and walked up to a fridge.

"Road beers?" Joe asked.

"You know it brother," Terry said, grabbing some Miller Lites and passing them back. Bodhi took his in his right hand, still clutching the peony cooler against his stomach.

They left the garage and piled into the Galaxie. Ray fired up the engine and backed out of the driveway. The night air mixed with the gas and leather to make that old, nostalgic smell even sweeter. They cracked open their beers and Ray turned up the radio.

"Turn here," Terry directed. They left town and headed east for the darkness of the back roads.

They reached the country and Coach's kid started digging in his pockets. It was hard to get into them while seated, but he managed to pull out a small sandwich bag and a pack of Zig-Zags. He reached into the bag and pulled out some weed, then ground it up with his fingers into an open rolling paper over his lap. The bumps, twists, and turns of the Grant County backroads didn't affect him, and he rolled up a fat joint without spilling a single flake. He licked the side of the paper and pulled out his lighter. He flicked it on and ran the flame back and forth over the joint to dry it. When he finished, he put one end in his mouth and flicked the lighter back on.

"Julie'll kill me if you smoke that in here," Ray said. "Then I'll come back from the dead and kill you."

Joe and Terry chuckled. Coach's kid grumbled and put the lighter in his pocket, then took the joint out of his mouth and put it behind his ear.

"There's a spot up here aways," Terry suggested, "we can smoke it there." They drove past moonlit cornfields while the radio played, following a few more bends in the road before he pointed ahead. "Pull over here," he advised. Ray killed the lights and eased up to a T in the road. Each way was long, straight, and dark; you could see anyone coming for miles, and it provided a good view of the highway too. Ray shut off the engine and the boys climbed out.

"Yep," Terry observed, gazing over the roads and the adjoining fields, "used to party back here in high school. You can see headlights for days. Got time to throw the weed and run." Ray and Joe chuckled, leaning back on the cold steel of the car. Coach's kid took a few steps and sparked up the joint. Bodhi stood next to him with the cooler in his arms. He looked around, breathing in the night air. The moonlight and Terry's words gave him a strong sense of déjà vu.

"Put that down and hit this," Coach's kid instructed, passing Bodhi the joint. Bodhi placed the cooler at his feet and took the offering.

"What's in there anyway?" Ray asked. Bodhi took a drag on the joint.

"Flowers," he answered with some smoke in his throat, passing the weed to Ray.

Ray took it from him and held it in his lips, taking a nice, long hit. "Flowers?" he asked, handing the joint to Joe.

"Yeah. Peonies actually," Bodhi replied.

"Why?" Ray asked.

"Well," Bodhi began, "I grow them every year. They're supposed to die in June, July at the latest. But these ones never did." The joint made it back to him and he took a pull before continuing. "Seems like they're waiting for something."

"That's trippy," Coach's kid declared.

"I know it sounds crazy, but it feels important," Bodhi said. The ember of the joint burned in the dark as they passed it around, each man silent in his thoughts. It came to Bodhi for his last drag and he looked onto the group.

"Did you guys know a girl around here?" he ventured, feeling wistful. "I met a man at the fire station. He told me his sister died." Ray, Joe, and Coach's kid gave a sympathetic shake of the head. Terry said something about seeing it in the paper.

"Well, when he told me that, I thought I remembered her. He said I looked like this guy she knew, that I lived in a farmhouse. And when he told me, I could see the dirt road that ran by it, and the old white siding, and the big tree with a tire swing in the front yard. And his eyes welled up and I could see her face. I didn't know her that well, but she was pretty." Bodhi nodded his head and lowered his eyes. "I didn't know her that well, but she was sweet." The joint died out and the boys were quiet. The wind picked up and they felt the chill on their skin.

"That's rough brother," Terry finally said.

Bodhi nodded his head and raised his eyes from the ground. "It's funny, what you said about the road. How it Ts and you can see the cars coming—I remember that too."

"Sounds like you're from around here bud," Terry said.

"Yeah," Bodhi sighed, looking up at the moon, "maybe I am." He didn't say anything else. The boys watched him for a while, respectful of his struggle but wanting to move on.

Bodhi sensed it and shook his head. "Sorry to bring the party down," he chuckled. "I don't want you worrying about me."

"We ain't," Joe chided, reaching into his pocket and pulling out his secret flask. He had filled it with Wild Turkey at the park when no one was looking. He took a big swig and wiped his mouth on his sleeve, red-eyed and a little drunk. He offered it to Ray.

"I'm good brother," Ray refused, holding his hand up.

"Here, give me some," Terry said, taking a shot.

"I'll take one," Coach's kid said with his hand out. Terry passed it to him and he threw it back. "Wooof," he sputtered, wobbling a bit. He held the flask up to Bodhi.

"Sure, why not," he replied. He drank the whiskey down. It hit his stomach fast and he felt drunk, stoned, sad, and excited all at once.

"Yo I'm fuckin' hungry," Coach's kid announced, slapping his hands together. "Let's get some Taco Bell." He closed his eyes and threw his head back to emphasize his point, stumbling a bit.

"You alright kid?" Joe asked.

"Yeah man," he hiccupped, eyes still closed, "just need to eat somethin'."

"I could go for a burrito," Terry said.

"Let's hit it," Ray declared.

They got into the Galaxie, Coach's kid flailing for a second before finding his seat in the corner.

"Quit wallerin' around back there," Joe commanded.

"My bad."

Ray turned the lights on and they peeled away from the T in the road. The car got up to speed and the cornfields rushed past.

"Ah shit! Turn it up!" Joe yelled. Ray cranked the volume on the radio and the car was filled with Tom Petty.

They sang quietly at first, but when the chorus hit, everyone but Bodhi belted the lyrics at the top of their lungs.

"You ain't from Indiana if you don't like Tom Petty!" Joe cried. Bodhi still had a lot to process from that day, but watching them laughing and singing to the music made him forget his problems. He nodded along to the boom-boom-thwack of the drums and the visceral twang of the guitar, feeling good. Ray pressed down on the gas and the boys howled at the moon.

XXXVII

Saturday is the day.

Somehow, no matter the forecast, it's the brightest day of the year. The show is packed with collectors, onlookers, and townies, and while the car guys are at first annoyed with the winding rows and hapless pedestrians, once they get settled in, they're proud to show off their beauties to an infinite number of spectators. They rise from their chairs and lecture passersby on the nuance in taillights between a '66 and '7, then they pop their hoods to show off their big block motors. The lines at the food vendors are long, but the vendors are happy with sales, and for the customer, nothing compares to finally holding that fried tenderloin or basket of cheese fries in your hands. Sock hop music blares over the park intercom and spirits are high.

Chewey got to camp early and made everyone breakfast on his flattop grill. Terry's crew dillydallied at the house but showed up in time for leftovers. Bodhi grabbed two cold hash browns and a bottle of water. Always the host, Chewey offered to throw his food back on the grill to heat it up. Bodhi insisted that it was okay, and that he appreciated Chewey for all he'd done.

Coach's kid slumped in a chair next to his dad. "One day he'll learn," Coach mused.

Margo was half-finished with her second Bloody Mary when she saw Julie and offered to make her one. Julie decided she'd loosen up a bit and let the boys worry about themselves for once.

Joe grabbed his first beer and cracked it open. "You want one?" he asked Bodhi.

"I'm good for now," Bodhi answered through a mouthful of food.

"You wanna take a lap, see some cars?" Joe asked.

"Sure," Bodhi replied, finishing his hash brown and throwing his plate in the trash. He picked up the peony cooler and followed Joe out of the tent.

They walked to an open spot of the park and into a circle of cars. The grass crunched under their feet.

"You had a lot to say last night," Joe remarked.

"Hopefully not too much," Bodhi replied.

"No, I don't think so," Joe said. He nodded at an old man sitting next to a Pontiac Catalina. "You really think you're from here?" he asked Bodhi.

"Yeah," Bodhi answered, "I do." They took a few more quiet steps. "It's weird though," Bodhi ruminated, "I—"

"Look at these," Joe interjected, walking up to two Chevys. "'63 and '4 Impalas are almost identical. But the chrome on the side of the '63 runs along the lower panel, and the logo is higher. The chrome on the '64 wraps around it, sorta like a rectangle." He inspected each car, leaning over the hoods, peering inside, bending his knees by the taillights. Bodhi followed him.

"They're nice," Bodhi remarked.

"Pretty penny nowadays," Joe said. They walked on to another row. "Lotta farmhouses in Grant County," he said, rekindling the conversation. "We can look at some later if you want."

"I don't know," Bodhi replied, "I—"

"Here we go," Joe interjected, "'64 Galaxie." Bodhi followed him toward another car. "See how the body's more round on this one? Taillights and all." Bodhi nodded as Joe went on. "'65 was square-bodied, square taillights. Started stackin' the headlights on the '5 too, where the '4 has 'em side by side. Ray's got a '67. Lot different." Joe inspected it a little longer before straightening up. "Nice car," he said to two people sitting by the bumper.

They walked along the gravel path toward the center of the park. There were thousands of beautiful cars lined around the pond, glowing in the sunlight with their own stories to tell.

"So you wanna go out later, look at some houses?" Joe asked.

"We'll see," Bodhi said. He felt anxious about it. Moreover, he'd been interrupted a few times, although he did recognize that his personal road to self-discovery wasn't the best thing to discuss at a car show. He took a deep breath and decided to forget about it. "Hey, what's that over there?" he asked, pointing to a shiny, teal car.

"'55 Buick Special," Joe observed, "pretty one too. Good eye." They walked from the gravel and into the grass to check it out.

"Looks a little like a '55 Chevy, but Buicks always had three chrome portholes on either side, up by the hood and near the door. Fins are a little softer too." Bodhi saw his reflection in the waxed teal paint. He traced the chrome trim with his eyes, noting how it made a big V by the tire. He took a step closer and peered inside, cupping his hands to reduce the glare without touching the window. The interior matched perfectly, and the dash gleamed as bright as the body.

"A'course, the Special had a 264 and the Bel Air had a 265. Sons-abitches beat 'em by an inch." Joe tried to take a sip of beer but none hit his mouth. He shook the can and looked at it, confused by its emptiness. "Out already," he grumbled.

"Beautiful car," Bodhi said to a couple sitting by the bumper.

"Thank you," they said, smiling quizzically at the sight of his robes.

"What's her story?" Bodhi asked, trying to fit in.

"Well, my daddy bought it brand new in Warsaw, gave it to me before he passed."

"Outta beer," Joe called. "Let's head back."

"Beautiful car," Bodhi said again, giving a small wave before catching up with Joe. "I was talkin' to them," he complained.

"And I was outta beer."

They walked back to the tent and found the crew as they'd left them. Joe waved and tossed the can in the trash, then went over to his cooler and dug inside. The ice rattled as he grabbed three more beers.

"You need all those?" Bodhi asked.

"Suppose you can have one," Joe answered, handing it to him.

Bodhi took it and let his hand fall to his side. "Thanks, but it's only 11:30."

"Shit, I'm behind then," Joe cried. He put one can in his pocket and cracked the other, raising it to his mouth for a long, cold drink. He wiped his lips with his sleeve and burped. "Let's check out these cars," he said.

Bodhi followed Joe past the Catalina, past the '63s and '4s, past the Buick. They saw all kinds of cars and all kinds of people—mothers pushing strollers past old trucks; high school townies admiring Ford GTs, trying to play it cool in front of their girlfriends; old men in motorized scooters rolling past Corvettes and reminiscing about faster times. They got to the end of the park and Joe stopped and gazed across the street.

"It's goin' down over there tonight, boy."

"What is?" Bodhi asked.

"The flame show," Joe replied with some mystique.

"What is that?" Bodhi asked.

"A buncha hicks bring their cars to the middle of the ballpark and shoot fire from 'em," Joe answered.

"Sounds dangerous," Bodhi said.

"Can be. Some of them flames get ten, twelve feet high."

"Damn," Bodhi replied.

"Wanna go?" Joe asked.

"I don't know," Bodhi deliberated.

"We get drunk, flames shoot out, crowd goes wild," Joe said. "It's somethin' else."

"Might be worth the experience," Bodhi said.

"Let's get back to camp," Joe suggested, shaking his empty beer can.

. . ..

Coach's kid could feel the day slipping away. He straightened up in his chair, drank some water, then got up for a beer and rallied. It was the best day of the year, and he didn't want to lose it.

Time was passing by Coach, too. He poured a few shots of whiskey in a Solo cup and told his stories with more conviction.

While the others didn't notice, or tried not to think about it, there was still a longing to make Saturday the best day it could be. Terry took shots of vodka and smoked cigars with Chewey. Ricky went to look at the motorcycles across the river while Bobby and Eddie hunted for treasure at the swap meet. Don sat around drinking beer and complaining about Liberals, wondering why every day couldn't be like the perfect little world of the car show and remembering wrongly that it was when he was younger. Duly watched Margo and Julie laugh as the sun grew weaker, offering a wry smile when they switched to Bud Light.

"And at dusk, the flame show!" the DJ cried over the loudspeaker. His voice died behind Bodhi's shoulder as he waited in line at the taco wagon, the only place that served a decent vegetarian meal within walking distance. Joe watched him from his place in line at the fried tenderloin stand. He felt a curious mix of sympathy and pride as he observed Bodhi acting normal in a crowd of everyday people.

The sun went down and excitement filled the air; it subdued the longing but did not completely overcome it. The people of Gas City were happy for the potential the night held but wistful for the past, and the night breeze on their necks reminded them of when they were kids.

The band did a sound check, and the lights from the stage joined the soft glow of streetlights to cast a dreamlike shadow on the cars. Julie wandered over to the Galaxie and put her hand on the cool steel, hearing the old doors open and shut, smelling the engine, feeling the leather on her back and the wind in her hair. Joe watched her with a grin before finishing his twelfth beer and heading to the cooler for another.

"The Way Back When Band starts in five, and the flame show starts now!" the DJ announced over the loudspeaker.

Joe heard the DJ and walked up to the liquor table to drink as much as he could before the show. Coach's kid scrambled up to him as he poured Wild Turkey into a cup with a heavy hand. "You comin'?" he asked.

"Yep," Joe replied, setting the bottle down.

"Shit, pour me some."

Joe picked up the bottle and put some more whiskey in an empty cup. He handed it to Coach's kid, who took a sip.

"You comin'?" Coach's kid asked Bodhi, who stood behind them nursing a beer.

"I guess so."

"Here, finish that," he said to Bodhi, opening the cooler and grabbing a beer, "and take this." Bodhi drained his beer and the kid put the new one in his hand. "Now let's go," he urged.

They left camp and wandered into the semi-darkness of the park. Coach's kid walked fast to get there on time; he'd gone every year since he was four years old. They followed him past the bathrooms and behind the food trucks, where he stopped, looked around, and dug a half-smoked joint from his pocket.

"You crazy man?" Joe asked. "Someone'll see us."

The click of the lighter echoed in the night as the kid lit the joint. "Not if we keep movin'," he replied. He took a hit, passed it to Bodhi, and returned to his original pace. Bodhi took a nervous drag before realizing he was being left behind and scrambled to catch up.

They reached the edge of the field and Coach's kid finished the joint, dropped it on the ground, walked over its ember in one smooth motion, and the three of them joined the crowd underneath the lights. Families, high schoolers, and hicks craned their necks to see the show as an announcer yelled into a microphone. Fire shot into the air and the crowd roared.

Bodhi, Joe, and the kid filtered through until they found a spot where they could see without obstructing anyone else's vision. Bodhi looked around, feeling high and disoriented. A chubby redneck with a ratty hoodie looked back at him, smiling through a dirty beard with crooked teeth.

"Ain't it awesome?" the redneck yelled. "Drove all the way from Lafayette to see this!" Bodhi gave an awkward grin then turned to Joe to save him. Joe took a shot from his cup and screamed like everyone else.

"Woooo!"

Bodhi looked over at Coach's kid, amazed he was still standing. He rocked back and forth with his eyes closed, took a sip of whiskey, and screamed too.

Bodhi realized he was being judgmental and turned back to the chubby redneck and gave him a thumbs up.

"Hell yeah brother!" the redneck hollered. Bodhi smiled and set his eyes on the field, making a conscious decision to enjoy the show.

The first few rounds ended and Bodhi watched as a '41 Coupe, a '56 Mercury, and a '37 Chevy Truck with a Tennessee flag rolled up to the starting line.

"These boys been savin' the real fire 'til now!" the announcer yelled. "The more you yell, the harder they're gonna push!"

The crowd worked itself into a frenzy, and everyone screamed at the top of their lungs. The man in the Mercury shifted into reverse and rolled into the spotlight.

A flash of fire lit up Bodhi's retinas and he felt its heat on his face. He watched in a trance as the driver laid on the gas and the Mercury shot its flames higher and higher into the air. Not to be outdone, the Coupe and the truck threw it in reverse and joined the line, spewing fire until there was one big supernova in the night.

Joe yelled, Coach's kid almost fell over, and the crowd went nuts. The noise fell into a soft din in Bodhi's ears as he broke from reality. He closed his eyes to the blinding light, feeling a sickness in his gut. He fought it down into the pit of his stomach and reopened his eyes slowly, a giant, fiery tree coming to form through his squint. He opened his eyes the rest of the way and beheld its awesome beauty.

It burned tall and bright with a multitude of leafy branches. He studied it in silent awe, completely unaware of his surroundings.

A tree of miracles...

Bodhi traced the lowest hanging branch to its spindly fingertips and back again. His eyes stopped on a gentle sag in the bough. He looked beneath and noticed what seemed like a tire swing hanging from it, glowing bright and spinning softly in the void.

"I can't hear you!" the announcer screamed.

Bodhi reached out and tried to grab the rope. The cars pressed on the gas. The supernova expanded to critical mass and exploded. Bodhi took a step backwards, pushing the last bit of nausea into the soles of his feet.

There was a loud, rattling boom, as if heaven and earth were moving. The flames took their last breath and receded into the tailpipes. Bodhi shook his head and the sound of the crowd returned to his ears.

"Holy shit!" Joe cried, grabbing Bodhi's shoulders and shaking him. "Holy shit!" Bodhi looked over and saw the man from Lafayette screaming at the stars.

"Hey kid, you alright?" Joe yelled, breaking from Bodhi and helping Coach's kid off the ground.

"Woooo!" he cried as Joe stood him on his feet.

"Let's get outta here," Joe urged.

The three of them left the fervor of the crowd and headed back to camp. Joe and Coach's kid stumbled ahead, laughing and singing Elton John through the carousel-like lights of the food vendors' row. Bodhi walked behind, looking at the ground, sighing, looking at the sky, sighing, gazing out over the park and considering what to do next.

They reached Chewey's and spirits were high, but there was a sense that Saturday was almost over. Everyone sat around the fire, drinking and thinking of ways to delay packing up. Joe went to the table and finished the Wild Turkey he'd brought, then grabbed a bottle of someone else's whiskey and brought it out to the fire. Coach's kid tried to reach for it, but his dad stood up.

"Better get you home," Coach said.

"Ah come on," the kid pleaded.

Coach led him away and helped him into the '66. "Swear to God you better not piss on no hotel wall," he warned.

"Aw man, I haven't done that in a while."

"Most people can say they ain't done it at all."

Coach turned and thanked Chewey, said his goodbyes, and drove off.

"R-I-P," Joe said to some laughter. He passed the bottle to Bodhi, who took a sip without thinking much. He didn't even feel the burn down his throat.

The fire dwindled. Don, Margo, and Duly were already gone. Ricky, Bobbie, and Eddie crossed the river to get drunk in Jonesboro.

Joe knew something big was going to happen, and he was getting good and drunk for it. He passed the "borrowed" whiskey bottle around. Chewey and Ray had to drive, so they only took a nip. Bodhi knew something big was going to happen, too, but he nursed a beer and turned inward.

"Welp, better pack her up," Chewey sighed after a while.

"Ah come on. It's James Dean, Saturday night!" Joe slurred.

"True, but I get here early and haul it off," Chewey answered. "You'll be sleepin' when I hit the road." He walked toward the tent.

"Shit, I'll drink to that," Joe cried, taking a shot. "Hey wait, let me help ya." Joe and Terry stumbled over to assist him, first making sure to drag out Joe's cooler. Julie nestled up to Ray's embrace, feeling drunk. Ray smiled as the wind blew through her air. Bodhi walked over and picked up the peony cooler, then came back to watch the fire die.

Chewey was more effective than the two drunks, but he appreciated their help nonetheless. When it was all finished, they each grabbed a corner of the tent and walked it in until it shrunk and closed.

"You're a goddamn legend Chewey," Joe said, shaking his hand. Chewey laughed the husky laugh of a smoker.

"Thanks boys," he said, shaking Terry's hand. "Glad everyone had fun." He headed to his car, waving at the three by the fire. They waved back, and he was gone.

Joe and Terry stumbled up to the fire. "Well shit, what do we do now?" Joe asked. Ray played with Julie's hair. She smiled, and so did he. Sometimes he forgot how loving she was.

Bodhi gazed into the fire and measured his words. "I want to find my house," he said.

Joe squinted and nodded. "Hell yeah," he said.

"Little cruise?" Terry asked.

"Whaddya say Ray?" Joe asked.

Ray tousled Julie's hair a bit more then kissed her on the head. "What do you think?" he asked softly.

The fire waned and she felt the breeze on her cheek. She didn't want Saturday to end either. "Sounds fun," she said, smiling sweetly.

"Hell yeah!" Joe cried, taking a swig of whiskey. He passed the bottle around once more as they headed to the car.

Terry, Joe, Ray, Julie, and Bodhi piled into the Galaxie, determined to hold onto the night. The slam of the doors echoed through the park and Ray fired up the engine. Bodhi clutched the peony cooler tight as they raced toward the country.

"Where to, Bodhi?" Joe asked as they left the dim lights of Gas City for the backroads.

"I don't know," Bodhi answered. He gripped the peony cooler a little harder, hoping the flowers would tell him. "Let's hit the T. Maybe I'll feel something."

"This way," Terry directed.

They pulled up to the T in the road, the party spot from the night before and perhaps from one of Bodhi's past lives. Ray cut the engine and they climbed out of the car. Bodhi felt the breeze on his face as he stood for a second, then heard the crunch of the dirt under his feet as he walked to the grass. The others hung by the Galaxie, talking and laughing as Joe passed the bottle around. Ray took a shot then went to the trunk for the beer cooler, taking it out and setting it down in front of them.

"Hey man, you want one?" Bodhi heard over his shoulder.

"I'm alright," he muttered, gazing over the fields. He took a few steps into the grass and looked up at the stars. They burned bright in the sky, and he tried to connect them to make his own constellations: the fire in the void, the tree with the tire swing, the farmhouse from his dreams. He closed his eyes, hoping to hear the voices from the house. Instead, he heard the laughter from his friends behind him, enjoying the night, and saw nothing but the back of his eyelids.

He set the cooler down and knelt in the grass. The peonies glimmered in the dark as if they had their own essence. He carefully plucked them out and held one in each hand, then stood with his hands cupped, saying nothing. He faced the sky for a few minutes, then unfolded his fingers and revealed the simple beauty of the flowers. He thought he'd be enlightened; instead, he was puzzled.

"Feelin' anything?" Joe asked, putting a gentle hand on Bodhi's shoulder.

"Not really," he muttered.

"We'll find it," Joe assured him. "Here—come on, have a drink with us."

Bodhi put the flowers away and followed Joe back to the Galaxie. He placed the cooler in the back seat and took a beer from Ray, observing the happiness in their faces and trying to forget his loneliness.

Joe was in the middle of a story—throwing his arms and stumbling around, the others laughing, Bodhi starting to smile—when a light appeared in the distance.

"Got company," Terry noted. The party looked up and clocked the headlights coming toward them.

"Better git," Joe said.

Ray downed his beer and threw it in the cooler, popped the trunk, and jumped into the driver's seat. Joe and Terry, beers in hand, used their free ones to grab the cooler and hoist it into the trunk. Joe slammed it shut and they hopped in before Bodhi and Julie scrambled to their seats with open beers of their own.

"Naw don't turn around," Joe yelled, "they'll be tailin' us!"

"The hell you suggest I do?"

"You got time," Terry advised. "Keep the lights off, start up the car, then back up a few feet. Throw it in drive and hit the lights, look like we just come around the corner."

Ray did as he was told and made it around the T. Fifteen seconds later they passed an unsuspecting cop from the sheriff's office.

"Jesus Christ," Julie muttered. Bodhi turned around and watched its taillights fade into the dark.

XXXVIII

"This ain't it either, huh?" Joe said from behind Bodhi as he stood on the edge of the gravel driveway.

"No," Bodhi said.

"C'mon buddy," Joe said, placing a hand on his friend's shoulder, "it's gettin' late."

Bodhi turned and followed Joe into the car. Ray started up the engine and drove off.

It was their fifth house and Bodhi was starting to feel hopeless. He looked around the car. Julie dozed in the front seat. Ray yawned and turned up the radio to stay awake. Terry and Joe passed the bottle back and forth, but they too felt the night slipping away.

"Where to?" Ray asked, fighting off another yawn.

"I don't know," Bodhi muttered. Everyone was silent as the radio tried to compete with the rumble of the 390.

Terry took another swig of whiskey and came up with an idea. "All this talk about farmhouses," he said, wincing from the liquor and passing the bottle back to Joe, "we should go to Jimmy Dean's old place."

"Now there's an idea!" Joe cried, throwing back some whiskey.

"Where's that?" Ray asked.

"Up here," Terry said.

Joe punched Bodhi on the arm to liven him up.

"Okay," Bodhi mumbled.

The Galaxie turned down a long narrow road, entirely dark if not for the headlights of the car and the ethereal shine of the moon. Bodhi looked out the window and saw the long grass blowing in the gentle wind of the night. He looked through the windshield and saw each inch of road appear under the headlights then disappear as time and darkness swallowed it up. It felt like a dream, and his heart raced, beating faster with each quarter mile.

Then he remembered. "This is it," he said.

Ray turned the radio down and slowed the car as they approached the farmhouse.

"Stop here," Bodhi directed.

The slam of the metal doors echoed in the night, stirring the old man awake inside the house. Bodhi walked into the gravel driveway and looked up at the faded white house. It stood on a hill like a forgotten memory: quiet and dark with its own intangible glow. The others followed him.

"I know this place," he said, clutching the peony cooler tight.

The old man relied on the backlight of the moon and stars to leave his bed and head downstairs. Outside, Joe passed the whiskey bottle around as the wind hit their hair and they waited for the monk to go on.

"I used to come here when I was younger," he said. He folded his arms and gazed at the sky, contemplating for a second. Then he turned around with his thumb and his two fingers raised by his head, as if taking a break from a cigarette.

"And some guys, and the girl that died—the one the man told me about at the fire station—they were here too." He looked over their heads and back to the night sky.

His friends watched him with a mix of sympathy and wonder.

"She was so young, so pretty." he reminisced. "Dark hair and red lipstick. Like the girl on the beer can."

The man inside the house reached the kitchen and pulled the phone from the wall.

"There's a cemetery down the road. Right over there," Bodhi continued, pointing. "Used to drive back and forth, acting like the kid in the movie. He's buried over there." He took his hand back from the darkness and ran it through his hair, then sighed and looked at the ground.

They watched him in silence, unsure of what to say.

"He was here too," he declared after a while.

The man inside took his old, fat thumb and hit the numbers slowly—*9...1...1.*

"He was here too," he cried, head up and eyes wide with epiphany.

"Who?" someone asked. Bodhi couldn't tell if it was Joe or Terry. His soul was overwhelmed with excitement and fear.

"The ghost in the dugout, the boy pushing the tire swing, the man on the couch! He was here too!"

"Jesus man!" Joe cried. The others exchanged confused frowns, but he knew Bodhi well enough to recognize a breakthrough. He ran up and grabbed his shoulders.

"This isn't it, but I know where it is!" Bodhi exclaimed.

Joe shook Bodhi as he looked up at the stars.

"This isn't it, but it's, it's—"

The siren pierced the night and destroyed his thoughts. He looked down the road at the speeding squad car, frozen in its chaos of red and blue lights.

"Run!" Terry shouted, throwing the whiskey bottle at the farmhouse.

"The car, the car!" Ray yelled, fumbling for the keys and shooting into the driver's seat. Joe grabbed Bodhi and threw him into the Galaxie. In their tussle, Bodhi dropped the cooler in the ditch. Julie jumped in after them, and Ray peeled off with the passenger door still open.

"No!" Bodhi screamed from the frame, knuckles scraping the asphalt as he reached for the fallen peonies.

"Where's Terry?" Ray yelled. Joe and Julie looked through the rear window to see Terry running in the opposite direction.

"Get in the fuckin' car!" Ray yelled through the window, slamming on the breaks. Terry saw the police lights flashing in his eyes, then spun and ran back toward the Galaxie.

"The flowers!" Joe and Bodhi cried.

Terry lumbered toward the Galaxie and scooped up the cooler like a beautiful, drunken fullback, diving into Julie's lap just before she slammed the door and her husband put the pedal to the floor. "Get offa me!" she yelled, pushing him into the back seat. Joe and Bodhi parted as Terry crashed between them by some miracle of physics.

"Here ya go," he said, casually handing the cooler to Bodhi.

Grant County's finest had just got some new Dodge Challengers, equipped with big Hemi engines, and the officer at the wheel was ready for the chase. He watched the offenders disappear, then laid on the gas.

"Ray, Ray!" Julie cried as he gunned through a tight corner. The tires squealed and the Galaxie drifted through the turn. Ray matted the pedal to pull out of it, 390 screaming toward a big bump in the road with the cop right behind.

"You better not!" Julie warned.

"Aww shit!" Ray yelled.

They hit the bump at full speed and ramped into the air. Time slowed as they gripped their seats, the door panels, whatever was available to them, eyes wide and shrieking into the silence of the void.

They hit the asphalt with a hard, sickening jolt, about twenty-five feet out, and sped off. Bodhi watched through the back windshield as the Challenger did the same.

"Woooo!" Joe howled.

"You payin' for the suspension?" Julie yelled.

The Challenger recovered from its meeting with the road and gained on them. Ray swerved back and forth without letting up in some mad attempt to confuse the pursuer. The officer in the car squinted, trying desperately to read the license plate. He could hear his wife now, nagging him to wear his glasses, but luckily for Ray and the boys, he'd been too arrogant to listen to her.

Bodhi gripped his cooler tight, gaping at the frenzied lights of the Dodge and trying not to die from fear. Ray pressed on, but as much as he hated to admit it, he knew the 390 would eventually succumb to the Hemi.

"Hold on everybody!" he ordered.

"Ray, Ray! What're you doing?" Julie screamed.

Ray cranked the wheel to the left and the Galaxie spun, burning its tires and skidding backwards at a 45-degree angle.

"Holy shit!" everyone yelled as they pressed their hands against the paneling and the car slid down the road.

"Holy shit!" the cop yelled, pulling the wheel to the right and veering into the grass.

The Galaxie righted itself, now facing the direction from which they had fled. Ray peeled out, leaving the cop in the ditch, scrambling for his radio and trying to collect himself. He dropped the CB off the hook with a "goddamnit!" then spun back on the road and opened up the Hemi.

"That bought us some time," Joe said.

"Can't run forever," Ray said, seeing the lights in the rearview.

"If you can make it a quarter mile, Potter's cornfield's up the road. Ain't harvested yet," Terry suggested.

Ray looked over at Julie with a gleam in his eye.

"Jesus Christ," she muttered, throwing up her hands.

Ray turned off the lights and shot down the road. The officer pressed on the gas.

"Here, right here," Terry directed.

Ray had to get in fast, but he couldn't make any maneuvers that would make too much noise. He pressed on the brakes but didn't slam them, coming to a stop near where Terry pointed. He cranked the wheel and slid into reverse, easing deep into the cornfield before the officer saw them. He shut off the engine and they all held their breath.

The cornstalks falling on the hood and poking through the windows created an eerie yet comforting picture, like a kid's view from a mediocre spot playing hide and seek. Ray and Julie waited with their eyes wide. Terry looked out the window with an observant gaze, ready for his fate. Joe was drunk as hell and trying not to laugh.

The lights flashed over them for one horrifying second before the Challenger flew by and the sound of the Hemi faded away.

"He gone!" Joe hollered. Julie turned around and punched his leg. Everybody chuckled in relief.

Ray paused for a few minutes, then waded through the parting corn and hit the road. They were in silent shock at first, but the mood got lighter the closer they got to Terry's.

Joe reached across the back seat and hit Bodhi on the leg. "How about that?" he grinned.

"Yeah," Bodhi muttered, giving an uneasy smile. His body was full of adrenaline, and he wanted to be happy, but everything was suppressed by the failed attempts to find his home. In the melee he never realized where it was.

They reached the light at Main Street and two squad cars flew past, undoubtedly looking for the Galaxie but deluded by a fixation on the backroads. Ray watched them go then crossed over to the sleepy suburbs of Gas City.

They got to Terry's house and the living room light was still on.

"Pull around back," Terry said, "just in case the boys come lookin'." He had a big backyard that could hide the car until morning. By then, there'd be so many classic cars leaving town that nobody would know the difference.

Ray eased the car to a stop behind the house and shut off the lights. Kate saw them pull in, a little confused as to why they parked in the backyard, and went to bed.

Ray turned the key and they stepped outside, laughing and making small talk to cover the last remnants of shock. Julie let it play for a minute before walking to the front fender of the car.

"I should be pissed," she said with a smile, "but my baby's still got it, and that feels good." She patted the cold steel then headed to bed.

"Better call it," Ray added, turning to follow her.

The door closed behind them and Joe turned to the two that remained. "Terry, go get some whiskey and bring it out here," he suggested.

"I'll have a drink with ya," Terry answered, "but then I'm goin' to bed." He snuck inside to grab the liquor.

"Some night, huh?" Joe grinned, rocking on his feet from all the alcohol he'd had.

"Yeah," Bodhi muttered.

Terry came back outside with a fifth of Blue Label.

"Don't drink all of it," Terry said, taking a sip. "Shit's expensive." He handed the bottle to Joe.

"I won't," Joe lied, taking a gulp.

"Just be quiet when you come inside," Terry advised.

"Goodnight buddy," Joe said.

The door closed, leaving the last two alone.

"You want some?" Joe asked, tilting the bottle toward Bodhi.

"I'm alright," Bodhi replied.

"Ah, come on," Joe chided as he took another gulp, wincing from the burn.

"I want to go to sleep."

"Can't go in there now, might wake up Kate," Joe said. "Come out front with me."

Joe led him to the front of the house, stopping by his truck and plopping down on the tailgate. "Have a seat," he offered.

Bodhi sat down next to him and they looked up at the sky. The moon had lowered some, allowing for other celestial bodies to shine.

"The stars are out tonight, boy," Joe said. Bodhi kept quiet, eyes turned upward.

"That's Mars overhead. Gotta little red to it," Joe said, pointing straight up. He traced his finger toward the north. "And there's Cassiopeia." Bodhi maintained his silent stare. Joe dropped his finger and looked at his friend. "You alright buddy?" he asked.

"Yeah, I'm just tired," Bodhi replied, neck tight from looking up.

"Tired tired? Or tired of somethin' in particular?" Joe asked.

"I'm tired of not knowing," Bodhi said. He sighed and shook his head, then lowered it into his hand, his gaze falling over the grass.

Joe pulled his lips against his teeth and kept his eyes on the stars. "Some things we're not meant to know," he pondered, "other things we don't wanna know."

Bodhi was taken aback. "What are you saying?" he demanded.

Joe took a long swig of whiskey and wiped his mouth on his sleeve. "I don't know." He looked over at Bodhi, his friend's face blurred from the dark of the night and the alcohol in his blood. He thought about saying something, then decided against it. He grinned instead, wobbling from the liquor.

It had been a disappointing night for Bodhi, and he sensed he was being patronized. "You know, everyone went to sleep," he scoffed, "you can stop drinking now." He got up from his perch on the tailgate and walked away.

"You're gonna wake them up," Joe cautioned.

"I'm sleeping in the truck," Bodhi replied. He opened the door and got in, then shut it behind him. Joe shrugged.

He was alone now, sitting on the tailgate with the bottle of whiskey and wondering if he'd done something wrong. He took a drink and pushed himself off the truck, drifting toward the street. He stopped at the edge of the yard and looked around. He inspected all the houses on the street. Gas City was sleeping.

He took another drink and tried to hold onto the night. The most important thing he'd ever do was happening tomorrow, and he didn't know if he had the strength to do it.

He turned his eyes to the sky and considered praying. A few rushed thoughts ran through his head but he trailed off without saying amen. He felt the cold dew forming on the grass and wetting his shoes. Morning was on its way.

Bodhi stretched out on the bench of the S10, looking at the ceiling. The last Vow of the Bodhisattva intruded upon him: *The way is inconceivable. We vow to attain it.*

He wondered if he'd ever find peace.

XXXIX

The car show ends on Sunday. It's another great day for the Hoosiers, and yet, there's a slow leak of happiness that escapes them, like the gradual loss of air from a child's balloon. Coach's kid goes back to college with a smile and a suntan, but he can't shake the feeling that the world was supposed to change and never did. Chewey doesn't think too much about it: he gets to camp at the first sign of morning, packs up, and puts Gas City in his rearview. Grandma Halsteder sits on her stoop on H street, smoking a cigarette with her coffee as Chewey and all the other enthusiasts drive by on their way out of town. "It's the last day of summer," she always says.

Terry was in his recliner waiting for the Colts game to come on and Kate was out back doing chores. The Washingtons had already left.

Tat, tat, tat.

Bodhi opened his eyes to see Joe tapping softly on the passenger window.

"Hey, he's awake," Joe said, his muffled cry reaching Bodhi through the glass.

Bodhi gave a slight grunt and exhaled through his nose, then sat up and rubbed his face with his hands. He kept his left hand on the left side of his face and reached out with his right to crank the window down. "What time is it?" he muttered.

"Time to get to the park," Joe urged, leaning into the open window and clunking the whiskey bottle against the door. Bodhi could smell the alcohol on his breath.

"You stay up all night?" Bodhi asked.

"Maybe, I don't know," Joe replied.

Bodhi shook his head and rubbed his face with his left hand some more. "Just take me home," he grumbled.

239

"You sure?" Joe asked with concern, gripping the sill.

Bodhi took a deep, existential breath. "Yeah."

Joe's heart sank but he shrugged it off. He pursed his lips and slapped the sill with his free hand. "Alright," he said. He made his way around the hood and climbed into the driver's seat. Bodhi stopped rubbing his face and tilted his head over to his right hand, propping it up with a tired fist. Joe missed the ignition with the keys and dropped them on the floor by his feet. He was too drunk to drive, but he had something important to do, so he closed one eye to straighten his vision and scrounged for the keys. He located them, then focused hard to slide the key into the ignition. Bodhi sighed again and closed his eyes.

Joe drove out to Main Street and went east toward the interstate but turned south to the backroads well before the onramp. He misjudged the turn and plowed over some off-road dirt before straightening out.

"Where are we going?" Bodhi asked, irritated but keeping his eyes closed.

"I'm takin' you home," Joe said with an incredulous tone. He cranked up the radio and rolled his window down. He hoped it would sober him up and snap Bodhi from his funk.

Joe drove on, doing his best to focus on the road. He could feel the truck swerve from time to time but righted himself with a quick excuse—"oof, just missed that roadkill," or "goddamn potholes"—then he'd talk loud and fast or tell a joke to ease the pressure. Bodhi slumped in his seat. After a while Joe took his eyes off the road and studied him. He felt pity, but also affection and a little bit of guilt.

"What's wrong man?" he asked.

"Nothing," Bodhi muttered, "I just want to go home."

Joe's eyes darted to the road for a second, then back at Bodhi. He felt the guilt again but ignored it in favor of drunkenness. "Really man? That's how you do me?" he heard himself say.

"Joe, I'm not in the mood," Bodhi replied.

"Jesus Christ," Joe cried, the truck veering as he stared at Bodhi, "are you fuckin' serious?" He understood why Bodhi was responding the way he was, and he wasn't even that mad, but the liquor was in him.

"Joe—"

"Introduce you to all my friends, pay for everything!"

"Joe—"

"Waste my fuckin' gas, drivin' you around!"

"Joe—"

"Not a thank you, not a fuck you, nothin'!"

"*Joe!*" Bodhi screamed. The truck slid off the path and toward a ditch. Joe looked up and spun the wheel, but his right tire hit the chasm at full speed and blew out. The truck lumbered for a few feet until Joe forced it toward a long country driveway, where it died.

Bodhi shook his head and put it back down against his fist with a prolonged, discontented sigh. Joe jumped out and inspected the damage.

Gabe heard the sound from inside his house and looked out the window. He hadn't received any visitors since his true love had died. He went to the porch and put on his work boots, then opened the door and headed down the dusty driveway.

Joe came to the passenger side of the truck and crouched down. He saw the blown tire and shook his head. "Jesus Christ!" he yelled, standing up and kicking it with his shoe. The air was hot and the dirt blew in the wind. He put his hands on his hips and looked out over the fields, the heat on his neck.

He shook his head then looked down through the open window. "You gonna help me?" he asked Bodhi, who didn't respond.

Joe spat on the ground then turned toward the old farmhouse. He noticed a man walking down from it, making his way toward him. He was old but fit, with silver-gray hair and a weary look in his eyes. Joe watched him carefully as his weathered face came into view. The closer he got, the more he shone like an angel.

Gabe stepped in front of the sun and the shine went away. "You boys need some help?" he asked. His voice was gentle but hard, like an Indiana sunset over an abandoned factory.

"Nah," Joe replied, playing it cool, "blown tire is all."

"I tell you what," Gabe said, surveying the truck. He squatted by the tire then stood up, seeing who was inside. "Is that you, Emmanuel?" he asked.

The monk recognized his name and looked up.

"Been waitin' for you to come back."

XL

Emmanuel looked past Gabe and saw the tree and the tire swing. His hands burned from the memory of the rope.

A tree of miracles...

He looked over at the old farmhouse, its faded white paint and tall windows, its big summer porch. His mind opened like a peony in bloom. "Where's my brother?" he asked.

Gabe motioned over his shoulder to a plot behind the house.

"And my mother?" Emmanuel asked. Gabe pointed to the same place.

Emmanuel gave a solemn nod, then took the peonies from the cooler and got out of the car. He walked past Joe and Gabe, clutching the flowers in his hands. They glowed with the shine of the universe.

He passed the old tree and tire swing, remembering the family cemetery in the back and realizing he was headed there. Joe took a drunken step toward him but Gabe stuck out his arm. "You can't help him no more," he said. Joe nodded. He walked to the truck and pulled out some tools, then went back and grabbed the whiskey bottle.

"Wanna drink?" he offered.

"Boy, you need a cuppa coffee and a lie-down," Gabe warned. Joe shrugged and twisted the cap off the bottle.

The cemetery was 100 yards behind the house on a small grassy plot. There were a few trees around, but otherwise it sat alone in the field like a morbid beacon. Emmanuel trudged toward it with a mix of resolve, anticipation, and anxiety.

He reached the first row and was suddenly overcome by a mad hope that his mother and brother were out there visiting the stones and not among the dead. He looked around but saw no one. Then he went row by row, inspecting each tombstone and finding relief when he didn't recognize the names on them.

Time passed, and the sun beat down on his neck. When he reached the last row his bowling shoes were coated with grass and dirt. He noticed two stones in the middle that seemed newer than the rest, and his soul filled with dread. Instead of walking over he looked down at the stone in front of him, didn't recognize it, and continued to check the others in order. Each step was slower than the last as he made his way toward the middle.

He reached the final stone, read the unfamiliar name, then closed his eyes as he stepped in front of the two he was afraid to read. His heart raced and he tried to remember all the quotes he'd ever learned about death and the folly of attachment. None came. The peonies glowed and he could feel their soft burn in his hands. It was time for him to know.

He opened his eyes and read the simple inscription on each tombstone:

Johnathan Slater, Forever Young

Amanda Slater, May She Never Be Forgotten

He fell to his knees and wept.

…..…..

Emmanuel never knew his father. He'd taken off right before he was born, leaving Emmanuel alone with his mother and brother. They were his constant companions.

He and his brother would play outside in the endless expanse of the yard, pushing each other on the tire swing, bouncing the basketball around, hitting baseballs for hours. Then, they'd come home covered in dirt and sweat and the warm glow of childhood, and their mom would fix them a meal. In the summers they'd sit together on the porch, reveling in twilight until the sun went down. The three of them were happy, and the boys always felt their mother's love.

When Emmanuel got older he started feeling different. He became withdrawn, determined to isolate himself from the pain of the world. He holed himself up in his room and read his books in a desperate attempt to find transcendence. He thought his family didn't understand him.

His brother graduated high school and joined the military. Emmanuel couldn't understand it. He graduated high school and joined a monastery in some far-off place.

One day during meditation, he received a letter. His mother was asking him to come home for one last dinner before his brother was deployed. He threw the letter away and went back to meditation.

Amanda and Johnathan ate alone on the porch, waiting for Emmanuel to walk up the driveway. The sun went down, the cicadas came out, but nobody came.

"He's probably busy," Johnathan reasoned. "I know what he's doing is important." He got up and went inside. Amanda nodded and fought back tears, then followed him in and went to the kitchen.

Johnathan sat on the couch in the living room. He tried not to think about his brother, but any small sound he heard had him turning toward the window. He waited all night for him to walk up the driveway and come through the door.

When morning came, Johnathan had barely slept. He went into the kitchen and kissed his mother goodbye, then left for the military. He died in the desert a few weeks later.

Amanda wrote Emmanuel another letter. He read it, threw it away, and went back to meditation.

Realizing both her boys were gone, Amanda's health started failing her. Gabe had loved her since high school and he moved in to take care of her. She didn't last long.

This time, Gabe wrote Emmanuel a letter. He read it, threw it away, and wandered off.

Now, he was back home.

He studied the graves through teary eyes and realized the mistakes he'd made. He shook his head, then looked down at the peonies in his hands and finally understood their purpose.

"I'm sorry brother. I wish we had more time," he said, placing the first flower on Johnathan's grave.

"I'm sorry mother. I should've come sooner," he said, placing the second flower on her grave. He remained on his knees, observing the simple beauty of the peonies against the gray backdrop of the tombstones.

XLI

A few hours passed before he stood up, wiped his eyes, and started the long walk back to the truck.

When he got there the tire had been changed. Joe was leaning against the truck slugging whiskey. Gabe was in front of Joe telling stories.

"Thank God for every day we spent together," he said.

"That was beautiful," Joe slurred, misty eyed, "just beautiful."

Emmanuel stepped into the sunlight next to them and they looked over to acknowledge him.

"Did you find them?" Gabe asked.

"Yeah," Emmanuel said. Gabe and Joe nodded solemnly.

"I want to thank you for looking after my mom," Emmanuel offered.

"Love of my life," Gabe said, looking into the distance. Joe and Emmanuel looked at his face and saw the pain in his eyes. After a while Gabe dug in his pocket and pulled out a set of keys.

"Welp, better getta move on," he said, placing them in Emmanuel's hand.

"What're these?" Emmanuel asked.

"Keys to the house," Gabe replied.

"What for?" Emmanuel asked.

"To open the door," Gabe said.

Emmanuel inspected the keys in his hand, noticing how they shone in the sun. He closed his fingers around them and looked up at the house. It looked just like he remembered it.

"You sure?" he asked.

"Yep," Gabe said, spitting in the dirt and kicking some dust on it, "too many memories." They stood there watching him, Emmanuel with wide, aching eyes and Joe nodding in drunken sympathy. Neither of them knew what to say.

After a while Gabe spoke over the dust like a man standing up at a funeral. "All my life...I looked for someone like her," he said softly. "And I'll find her again." He sighed and looked back at the boys. "See you around."

Gabe started down the long dirt road to nowhere in particular. They watched him until he disappeared, not sure if he'd left their sight or dissolved into the breeze.

Joe tilted his head back and finished the whiskey. He wiped his mouth with his sleeve and threw the bottle in the truck bed. "Better get goin' myself."

Emmanuel turned toward him with a look of concern. "What?"

"Yep," Joe said, stumbling toward the driver's door, "time for me to go." He climbed in and shut the door, reaching for his keys.

"You can't," Emmanuel protested, running to the passenger window.

"I know," Joe said, putting the key in the ignition, "but I gotta."

The whole truck smelled like liquor. Emmanuel looked at Joe with tears in his eyes. "But they'll stop you," he pleaded.

"Not where I'm goin'," Joe said. His voice was filled with death. Emmanuel tried to ignore it.

"Take me with you," he begged.

"You know I can't do that," Joe said.

"Why?" Emmanuel cried.

"I gotta do this alone," Joe mused, staring out the windshield. "So do you."

"Joe," Emmanuel begged, "please take me with you."

"No," Joe commanded. "You need to stay here. It's where you belong."

"But I can't do this without you," Emmanuel insisted.

Joe paused for a second. "You'll be alright," he said.

Emmanuel shook his head. "But you said it yourself. You said I was doing it all wrong."

Joe looked at his friend with compassion in his eyes. In some ways he'd been too hard on him. He felt guilty about it, even if Emmanuel had needed it. Now, he had to pick the right words to build his confidence.

"No, I said you didn't have it figured out—there's a difference."

Emmanuel squinted at him and cocked his head, surprised by his wisdom but finally beginning to understand it.

Joe started up the car and leaned toward him. "The way is inconceivable," he yelled over the engine, quoting the last Vow of the Bodhisattva. "We vow to attain it!"

Emmanuel drew back from the window in awe. Joe grinned, downplaying his sageness, then fished under his seat for a beer. His fingers clasped around an Old Milwaukee that had likely been there all summer.

"Here!" he shouted, throwing it to Emmanuel.

Emmanuel caught it without looking, then let his hand fall to his hip.

"See you on the other side!"

Joe backed out of the driveway and roared off. Emmanuel watched him as the truck disappeared through the dust of the road, then stood there listening until the last sounds of its ratty old engine faded into oblivion.

He exhaled, sad but grateful. He looked at the sky and thanked the universe for blessing him these last few months. Then he turned and walked to his house.

He sat on the porch, watching the sun fall toward the horizon and wondering what to do next. Maybe he'd visit Pleasant Lake in a few weeks and ask Mandy to come to his farmhouse. However she answered, he'd stop at the Bakers afterward, wish them well, and take Sadie back with him.

He suddenly remembered Joe's parting gift and cracked it open, taking a long drink of Old Milwaukee. It was warm and stale, but somehow tasted better than anything he'd ever had. He went to set it down, realized how good it was, then took another sip before placing it by his feet. He had a billion lives behind him but only one ahead, and that felt good to know.

There was no one around when Joe lost control somewhere in the deep recesses of Grant County. The truck faded off the dirt road and barreled straight for a tall, sturdy tree at sixty miles per hour. He closed his eyes and a sense of calm washed over him. He'd see his friend again when his work was done.

About the Author

Nicholas Hochstedler is a husband, author, and union organizer. His books center around life in Indiana, with each story having its own unique genre twist. His first book, *War in October*, is a psychological thriller about a war veteran who is convinced his medical team is part of a government conspiracy to erase his mind. Nicholas has also contributed to four successful union campaigns as a labor organizer, including the first two coffee shops to win a union election in the state of Colorado. When not writing or plotting the workers' revolution, he loves to drive classic cars, collect retro video games, drink beer, and watch Turner Classic Movies. He resides in Denver, Colorado.